MAXWELL'S MOVIE

A thrilling murder mystery with plenty of twists

M.J. TROW

A Schoolmaster Murder Mystery Book 3

JOFFE BOOKS

Revised edition 2024
Joffe Books, London
www.joffebooks.com

First published in Great Britain in 1998

This paperback edition was first published
in Great Britain in 2024

Cover art by Imogen Buchanan

ISBN: 978-1-83526-432-4

A NOTE TO THE READER

Please note these books were published in the 1990s, when social attitudes were different.

CHAPTER 1

The detective's silhouette darkened the net curtains of the front door. The lock rattled once and he was in, peering around in the gloomy recesses of the hall. The door closed behind him with a heavy click. Only the clock ticked, only the lights burned dim. He saw the peeling paint on the door on his right and the handle bright with the clawing of a thousand hands. The door to the fruit cellar.

To his left the stairs stretched up with their ornate banisters, gleaming in mahogany. That was the way he went, cautious, glancing round.

Only his own footsteps rang back, echoing through the still and empty house. He had swept off the fedora and with his other hand caught the stair-rail. He heard his foot creak on the second stair, then the third, then the fourth. All the time his eyes remained fixed on the velvet-draped light on the first landing. He didn't see the door open, above him and to his left.

There was a tightness in his chest, like the winding of a spring. His heart hammered like a drum, thundering in his chest and his ears. For a moment, he toyed with reaching for the .38 nestling in the leather by his armpit. Then he changed his mind. He'd reached the top of the stairs.

Whatever it was, came at him from the bedroom, from the door to his left. A tall, angular woman with a bad wig, her long calico dress clinging as she crossed the landing in a single stride, the gaslight shining on her silver hair. There was a breadknife in her right hand and it flashed once, twice, slicing through the dusty, summer night air to thud into his chest, slashing his braces and his shirt. Crimson leapt over his lapel, streaking his forehead and left cheek. The hat fell from his grasp. He tottered backwards, both arms raised and fingers clawing the air until his heels missed the stairs behind him and the knife was still stabbing, hacking at him as he fell, bouncing on the runners, rolling to the floor.

Whatever discordant music blared through her head, like fingernails on a blackboard, stopped. The long knife lay bloody on the carpet. She bent down. She put an arm, tenderly, lovingly, under his head and another round his waist. She hauled him upright and steadied him for a moment while the blood still pumped from his heart. Then she tilted him and took his full weight on her arms, striding for the stairs.

She walked the way he had walked, up the creaking stairway, singing softly to herself, swaying now from side to side, with that curious, angular way of hers. He felt like lead in her arms, but she couldn't stop now. One more step. One or two and she'd be there. She kicked open the door with her right foot and, careful not to hurt his head, inched him through.

The door clicked softly behind her. And there was silence. The hall lay empty where she'd left it, a hat at an impossible angle on the stair, a trail of blood down the threadbare carpet.

Then the line, beyond the door, that had chilled the hearts of millions. A young man's voice, terrified, appalled, 'No, Mother. No. Blood. Blood.'

* * *

Peter Maxwell shook himself free of its magic. The screen in front of him was poised for another snippet, this time a bearded Henry Fonda playing Wyatt Earp (fairly badly) in *My Darling Clementine*. But Maxwell was out of his plush seat by now, handling the fuzzy flock for one last time. It was all done by mirrors of course. Skinny Anthony Perkins, eight stone wringing wet, could never have lifted fifteen stone Martin Balsam, with or without his fedora. But that didn't matter. What mattered was that *Psycho* had woven its spell again. Maxwell chuckled to himself as he left the theatre, at that old fraud Hitchcock who claimed he never intended to frighten anybody with his noirest of films noirs. Not the shadow on the shower curtain; not Janet Leigh's blood flushing away through the overflow; not the creature on the landing who knifed Martin Balsam while the camera looked down from the ceiling; not the hideous corpse in the fruit cellar, with its iron grey bun lovingly styled over the hollow-eyed skull; no, not any of that was intended to frighten. You old bastard, Maxwell thought to himself.

Still, he realised as they made for the television section, they were all dead now, weren't they? Hitch, Anthony Perkins, even dear old Martin Balsam. They didn't make them that way any more, they'd broken the mould, thrown away the key; a whole cloud of clichés filled his mind.

At the exitway, he stopped, turned. In the building he'd just left lay all the dreams of his childhood. Flash Gordon, Zorro, the Scarlet Pimpernel, they were all there. And they weren't all dead. Not all of them. A new generation was wowing them now and it did it in the confines of their living rooms, with the remote and the video card Bond was still there. And Batman. And if they had to be extra careful with the lighting these days, on Moore and Connery and the rest, so what? Maxwell caught his own reflection in the glass of the door. 'We're none of us as young as we were,' he thought to himself.

'School parties?' A harassed, bespectacled thing in an anorak collided with him, forty or so screaming maniacs at his shoulder.

'That's rather a contradiction in terms, isn't it?' Maxwell asked him.

But the man was a middle school teacher and the irony was lost on him, 'No, I mean, do you know where school parties go?'

Well,' Maxwell smiled at him, 'if you had a pipe on you, I'd say "Keep playing and turn left. That way you'll reach the river and you never know your luck." As it is, I think — mind you, it's a hundred to one shot, but there you are — I think it's that gate over there; the one that says "School parties".' And he raised his shapeless hat briefly above his shapeless hair. 'Enjoy' he said, beaming at the screaming, squabbling children. 'Plenty of room in the one and nines.'

* * *

Some teachers — and all people who work in Maths departments — call school trips 'jollies'. No one quite knows why, because anything less jolly is difficult to imagine. There are those twisted, melancholy souls who have compared them with the Seventh Circle of Hell, but these are clearly sad characters with chips on their shoulders. The reason that staff in Maths departments call trips 'jollies' is that they have never been on one. After all, where does a Maths teacher go to enjoy himself?

'Jollies' start with the germ of an idea. An idea that must be communicated to kids.

Kids are difficult to define. The ones in front of Peter 'Mad Max' Maxwell at Leighford High that Monday morning were tolerably human, sitting in serried ranks in the heart of his History empire on the first floor.

'MOMI,' Maxwell said, leaning back on the hind legs of his chair, in the way he told his charges they must never do, 'the Museum of the Moving Image. It's brilliant, it's dazzling. You can fly over London, be interviewed by Barry Norman and pretend to be a Dalek. In fact, you can nearly do all three simultaneously. How about it?'

A scattering of hands went up. Eyes flickered from side to side, checking the peer group, yielding to the pressure.

'I can arrange for it to take place on the day of your chemistry test,' he said.

Bingo! Thirty-one hands shot clear in the morning air.

After the idea comes the paperwork. Forms in triplicate are not confined to Her Majesty's Armed Forces or the more cobwebbed corners of the Civil Service. They can be found in any High School in the land and many and mighty are they. Maxwell, a stranger to ware of any kind, be it hard or soft, laboriously wrote out the names of the trippers he intended to take and wrote their telephone numbers alongside each one. He checked with the file cards in the front office on their medical peculiarities — the asthmatics, the diabetics, the bed-wetters. The psychopaths he knew already. Then he made for the staffroom in search of a woman.

'Anthea!' he swept across the grubby carpet in his shambling stride and snatched her hand, 'vouchsafe, divine perfection of a woman' — he broke instantly into his Laurence Olivier doing Richard III 'grant me a boon.'

'Max!' Anthea was young enough to be Maxwell's daughter. He'd always terrified her, this grizzled eminence, and she couldn't rise to his level of repartee.

Without a flicker, the Head of Sixth Form bared his teeth in a halfway reasonable Humphrey Bogart, 'Of all the staff rooms in all the schools in all the world, you had to walk into mine.'

'What is it, Max?' the girl's neck mottled crimson in her embarrassment.

'MOMI,' Maxwell told her, perching himself on the photocopier in the corner. 'The Museum of the Moving Image. Fancy taking a coachload of ungrateful herberts on the jolly of a lifetime?'

'When?'

'Week Wednesday.'

Anthea's timetable flashed before her. Double Year 9. The weekly inter-classroom gobbing contest. That and breaktime duty. 'Love to,' she beamed.

'Excellent. Leave the details to me. Oh, could you book the coach please? Hamilton's, for my money.'

'Er . . . yes, of course.'

A cadaver in a white coat was hovering at Maxwell's elbow. 'Could I use that, Max?' it asked.

'The merest intimation from our revered Head of Chemistry and I leap to attention, Monsieur Lavoisier.' He moved his bum so that his colleague could reach the photocopier, 'Ah, so that's how you use that thing. Marvellous!' and he shook his head in admiration, his tongue firmly in his cheek. 'Oh, Ben, by the way, rather bad news, I'm afraid. The Deputy Headmaster has asked me to take a jolly to the Museum of the Moving Image and he's chosen week Wednesday That's a Science SAT day, isn't it?'

'He can't do that!' Ben Horton snapped, his finger poised over his PIN number.

'Well, that's what I told him,' Maxwell spread his arms abroad in agony and loss, 'but you know what Bernard's like. You can do it the next day, can't you?'

'Well, I don't know . . .'

'Three one eight.' Maxwell told the Head of Chemistry his photocopier PIN number.

'Er . . . yes, I know.' The Head of Chemistry didn't like the sound of that — the Head of Sixth Form being so au fait with the innermost secrets of the Science Department. It smacked of corruption.

'Well, he seemed to think it would be all right.' Maxwell beamed at him and turned to go. 'Oh, Anthea, you couldn't write the letter, could you? You know, usual thing, on History Department heading, get Paul to sign it. Oh and include a few of your set, too. It'll cut the cost per head.'

Paul Moss, Maxwell's Head of Department, was easy going and he knew the old bastard who was his Number Two only too well. Like the Queen, God bless her, Paul would sign anything initiated by Mad Max.

Bernard Ryan, the Pastoral Deputy, was a different matter. Pastoral Deputies were inevitably secondary to Curriculum Deputies in Gillian Shepherd's England. Surprisingly pompous for a man who had yet to see thirty-five, standing on ceremony was listed high on his CV.

'Does this place have any educational value, Max?' he asked the trip's instigator the next day, when Maxwell's paperwork hit his desk.

Maxwell closed to his man, grinning broadly, placing an avuncular arm around his shoulder. 'Tell me, Bernard,' he said, 'do bears shit in the woods?'

Not being a biologist, Ryan was rather stuck for an answer. 'Wait a minute,' was the best he could do, peering at the monster timetable pinned to his wall, 'week Wednesday, there's a Standard Attainment Test. Science.'

'There is, indeed.' Maxwell squeezed the man's shoulder, then let him go, 'but Ben insisted. He's happy with a week Thursday.'

'He is?' Ryan blinked.

Maxwell spread his arms, 'You know what Ben's like,' he smiled, wide-eyed.

* * *

And so it was that Maxwell's 'jolly' was sorted. In the blackboard jungle of nineties education, there were still clearings in the darkness, lights in the forest. It wasn't all Ofsted and League Tables and teacher suicides and headmasters being stabbed to death. But of course, there was still flu.

They may have put a man on the moon when Maxwell was a youngish shaver. They could play CDs in cars and thirty per cent of the nation's youth went to university. But they still couldn't cure the common cold. Not that there was anything common about the virus that hit Peter Maxwell that wet Monday morning in April. 'Hit' was the wrong word. It sidled up to him over his morning muffins, tickled his nostrils as he read out the notices in Assembly. By the time he'd covered last-minute revision of Stalin's foreign policy with Year Eleven, it had got him by the tonsils and it was singularly apt that afternoon that as he told a gobsmacked Lower Sixth cohort all about Napoleon's retreat from Moscow, he was shivering like a snowflake.

How he saddled White Surrey, his trusty bicycle, that afternoon, he couldn't remember. The slightly rusty old machine, named after the charger Richard III rode at Bosworth Field, could find the way to Maxwell's house by itself. The smokers puffing their way homeward along the boundary hedge saw him wobble across the fields and didn't give the old duffer evens on getting home alive. But this was Mad Max, who had looked life and death in the eye and lived to tell the tale. He'd once peed in an adjacent urinal to Sir John Barbirolli. *Nothing* could stop Mad Max.

He threw White Surrey against his back wall, fumbled with the Yale and staggered upstairs to bed. The coursework would have to wait. Trevor Macdonald would be talking to himself that night. The black and white cat, Metternich, watched him go with the inscrutability that has marked the feline. Maxwell had taken one look at the former bundle of fur beating hell out of its siblings in the litter and named him for Prince Klemens Lothar Wenzel, Count Metternich, the Coachman of Europe, who had similarly kicked ass for forty years of the nineteenth century in the various Chancelleries of Europe. The Count sat down at the foot of the stairs and got on with the important things in life, like cleaning his bum.

* * *

Maxwell had not had a voluntary day off in eight years. He'd forgotten the procedure, if he ever knew it. There was a number to ring, Bernard Ryan's exclusive ex-directory number, but Maxwell wouldn't have rung Bernard Ryan if he were the last man on earth. So he rang school next morning and spoke to Thingee, the girl on the switchboard.

'Maxwell here, Thingee,' he croaked. 'Bit under par this morning. Any chance of getting hold of Paul Moss for me? I haven't got my books to hand so I can't really set any work. But then, that's the beauty of the National Curriculum, isn't it? Week 24, so it must be Communist Russia the wide world o'er. I'll be back by tomorrow.'

But Maxwell wasn't back by tomorrow. Fever sat on his chest that night. He couldn't find the thermometer and anyway didn't know which end to apply it, so he reached for the Southern Comfort and curled up with a good book. Normally, he'd be assembling the latest addition to his diorama of the Charge of the Light Brigade, saddled and ready to ride through Hell in the half-light of his loft. Six hundred and seventy-eight souls of iron had thundered down the Valley of Death; lions led, as usual, by donkeys; and Peter Maxwell had set himself the task of bringing their 54 mm likenesses to life in kit-form. He lovingly assembled them, taking care not to sniff too much of the glue and painted them in the authentic colours of the Light Cavalry, October 1854 vintage. But the thought of meticulously chipping away the flash on the plastic soldier only made his headache worse and he abandoned the idea. He abandoned the book too, for the same reason, and had just settled down to catch half an hour of *The Quiet Man* when the doorbell rang.

It was Sylvia Matthews, Leighford High School's answer to Dr Quinn, Medicine Woman.

'Lordy, Miss Sylvie,' Maxwell rolled his eyes à la Steppin Fetchit until the pain forced him to stop, 'you sure are a sight for sore eyes.'

'Max,' she slapped a cool hand on his forehead, 'you're burning up, you silly man. You ought to be in bed.'

'Not just now, Nursie,' he teased her, 'I haven't been well.'

'You still aren't.' She pushed him gently upstairs.

'Is it quite seemly,' he asked her, 'for an unattached young lady to be familiar with the topography of my boudoir? That's a Galton and Simpson line, by the way. Hancock, *The Missing Page*.'

'Is it?' She slid off his dressing gown.

'Now, just a minute,' he chuckled, 'what if I were ticklish?'

'Are you?' she hauled back his duvet.

'Only about some things. Ooh!'

'Head?'

'Heads plural, I think,' he held his temple for a moment.

'You know, this never ceases to amaze me . . .' She tucked him in.

What?' He glanced down, wondering where she was looking.

'. . . That a crusty old Little Englander like you has a duvet. I would have thought you were a sheet and blankets man.'

'Ah, but that's where you're wrong,' he croaked feebly. 'It's not a duvet; it's a quilt. And blankets are for horses.'

'Are they now? Open up.'

'I beg your . . .' but the great man was silenced by the slickness of Sylvia's thermometer, jammed between his lips.

'Yes, I have done this before' — she read his mind, what was left of it — 'I've been nursing sickly infants now for more years than I care to remember. Oh, a message from Anthea Edwards.'

'What?' He took the glass tube out to make the comment.

'I'll ask the questions.' She took it from him and put it back in. 'We've got to start again now! Why did I just know you'd be a cantankerous old bugger for a patient? Ah, I remember now. Personal experience. That winter you pulled a tendon.'

'That's a barefaced lie,' the thermometer was out again, 'I damaged my quadriceps femoris and . . .' But Sylvia had rammed it back.

'The message from Anthea is "not to worry. She's got Alice Goode to go on the trip for you".'

His strangled cry let her know all was not well, but this time she was holding the thing in place and Maxwell had to behave himself. He let her take it out when she was good and ready.

'I was about to say,' he grunted, 'before that act of actual bodily harm, that I didn't lose a day over that pulled muscle — agony though it was — and I'm not losing one now, either.'

'Oh, yes you are, Max.' Sylvia could be as defiant as a Boulton-Paul when the mood took her. 'Your temperature is nearly 102. Either you stay right here in bed or I'm calling an ambulance for you.'

'Don't be daft, Sylv,' he muttered, 'we both know how stretched the NHS is. If you rang this instant, the damn thing wouldn't be here until the second Friday in Septuagesima.'

'I've still got a few oppos at Leighford General,' she assured him, 'One or two close buddies who still believe the best cure for influenza is a blanket bath and an enema, though not necessarily in that order.'

His dark eyes said it all. He looked at her like a rabbit in headlights. 'You wouldn't,' he said slowly.

She closed to him, staring him straight in the face. 'I don't think you'd want to put it to the test,' she said. 'You stay here. And that's an order.'

'Yes, Nursie,' he said.

For a moment, her heart leapt. She looked at the great, suffering thing shivering slightly under the covers. For a moment, he was a little boy, lost in the whirling wheels of his own fever. For a moment she wanted to hold him to her, kiss him, never let him go. But she was Sylvia Matthews, the school nurse. And he? Well, he was Mad Max and all that that meant. The moment was gone.

'Anyway,' she turned her back on him abruptly, putting away her bits and pieces, 'what's wrong with Alice Goode?'

'Alice?' he peered at her over the duvet. 'Nothing. Nothing at all. Except that she's a twentieth-century teacher who sounds as though she ought to be a seventeenth-century witch. That, and she looks about six.'

'She may be a bit inexperienced, Max,' Sylvia conceded, 'and they all look about six to you. Besides, Anthea's there. They're only going to London, for God's sake.'

'Ah, my dear,' he growled, 'Satan's city. "The sins of London are old, the lure of gold. The sorrow of London is this — there is no one there to kiss."'

'John Betjeman?' she asked.

'Peter Maxwell,' he told her, 'and if I was feeling stronger, I'd throw a pillow at you.'

'Got any lemons, Max?'

'Lemons?'

'Yes,' she was patience itself. 'You know, those yellow things drunks put in their G and Ts and other people sprinkle on their pancakes.'

'They'd be in the kitchen,' his lightning deductive brain told her, 'if I've got any.'

'Right. I'm making you a delicious lemon and honey drink. I'm giving you two aspirin. I'm feeding Metternich. Then I'm going home and you're going to sleep. And if you leave this bed before Thursday, I'll come back and cut your bum off!'

* * *

It rained that night. And most of the next day, the day that Ben Horton, the Head of Science, had had to cancel his Science SATs because of Peter Maxwell. That day, fifty chattering, squealing, excited children had boarded one of Hamilton's luxury fifty-three seaters and had soared North via the A3(M) to the dubious accompaniment of Blur and Take That. The driver was the long-suffering sort, with a home-rolled ciggie behind one ear and a mind like an *A to Z*.

'Moving Image, love? Yeah, no problem.'

* * *

It was still raining when Maxwell's doorbell rang. And it was late. Nearly midnight. At the witching hour, the laid-up, feeling-sorry-for-himself Head of Sixth Form shuffled down the two flights of stairs that linked the bedroom of his town house to the front door. Something in an anorak stood shivering and crying, the rain indistinguishable from her tears.

'Anthea?' Maxwell took her soaking, trembling hand. 'Anthea, what is it? What's the matter?'

'Max . . .' he helped her inside 'oh, Max. It's Alice. She's . . . disappeared.'

CHAPTER 2

Anthea Edwards was probably thirty. She'd been at Leighford High for five years, woman and girl, and she'd won her spurs on 10R3, better known to all and sundry as the dirty two dozen. But that night, as she huddled, cradling her knees in front of Maxwell's empty fireplace, she looked for all the world like a little girl again. He'd prised off her soaking coat and given her a towel for her hair, but she wouldn't take his Southern Comfort and she couldn't stop shaking. They sniffed together in the still of the morning, the cat Metternich curled up on his usual chair, watchful that his master remained a gentleman with a lady in the house.

'From the beginning, Anthea,' Maxwell said softly, 'and take your time.'

She did. It was nearly two thirty before the exhausted girl lay back on Maxwell's sofa and he draped his dressing gown over her. He turned down the dimmer switch and shuffled past the cat on his way to the stairs. He saw the ear twitch, the whisker curl and he put a warning finger to his lips. 'Not a word out of you, you sanctimonious old bastard,' he whispered. 'Miss Edwards and I are just good colleagues, that's all.'

* * *

The kids had a wonderful time at MOMI — even that sly little nerd with the spaniel haircut who constantly seemed on a different planet from everybody else. They'd been a little embarrassed by the fresh-faced young man in the fur coat who'd been telling them about the studios of Mack Sennett and the thrill of working with Chaplin. Acting out period roles was something they did very well at MOMI, but some kids couldn't handle it. By the time they got to be interviewed by Barry Norman, however, they were lost in the magic of it all. Nearly half the group had acted out a shootout in a broken-down saloon on the Paramount lot, and if 'Mother of God, is this the end of Ricco?' sounded a little flat from a thirteen-year-old girl from Sussex, well, what the hell — you should have heard Edward G. Robinson before the voice training!

Tamsin lay on the sloping surface and spread her arms. The others giggled as she appeared on the huge screen overhead, soaring and gliding like an albatross, following the line of old Father Thames with the skill of a navigator. Rory was the first to climb inside a Dalek and give the line that had thrilled his father's generation — 'Exterminate! Exterminate!'

And all their streetwise cool fell away as the spell wove itself around them too. And the generations blended and blurred as they laughed, the kids and the adults, at Stan and Ollie and Wallace and Gromit.

That wasn't how Anthea had told it, but Maxwell knew his MOMI. And he knew his kids. He could see the brightness in their eyes as she sniffed out the story to him in the lamplight of his lounge. He hauled off his dressing gown and lay back on his pillows. She had last seen Alice in the early years of the Moving Image, in the gloom of Phantasmagoric, where nameless shapes coiled and writhed to the astonishment of their plaster audiences in eighteenth-century curls and tails. The teachers had taken two sixth formers with them — Maxwell's Own as their Year Head sometimes called them. Leila Roberts, fat, ginger, helpful, had gone through at the head of the chattering column with Anthea. The foot-slogging rear had been brought up by Ronnie Parsons with Alice. It was a sane and sensible order of march. Maxwell had patted Anthea's hand and approved. That wasn't bullshit. He approved still in the silence of his room. It was what he'd have done — had he been there. And his blood ran colder, if that was possible, because he should have been there, ought to have been there. If only . . . but his deductive mind clicked in. Time enough for recriminations later. He'd have plenty of those tomorrow, because at death's door or not, he was going back tomorrow, had to go back tomorrow.

'See you at the end,' was the last thing Anthea had heard Alice say, as the Wheel of Life whirled and threw dancing shadows across her face. Anthea had turned to look for her at the Agit-prop train, where an ardent young Bolshevik told her charges how Comrade Lenin's great and glorious revolution was spreading by railway and by degrees all over Mother Russia. But Alice wasn't there. Ronnie was, that face of his as blank and expressionless as ever over his shapeless granddad shirt. Alice must have doubled back to hurry the stragglers along. Then Anthea was swept forward into the carriage as thick-necked women toiled in the soil of the Ukraine and smiled awkwardly for the Bolshevik cameramen who were telling them such lies.

By the time the kids had done the gift shop at the end of the magical movie tour, Anthea was getting annoyed. Leila was all right — in fact, for a seventeen-year-old she was quite good company, if a little over-zealous with the kids. 'Don't touch that!' she screamed at the Most Inoffensive Girl in the School, who for a horrible moment looked about to disintegrate into tears. Anthea had appeared, smiling and reassuring at their elbows and squeezed them both — as much as a teacher dare squeeze a child in the politically-correct, litigation-mad nineties. Situation defused. Problem sorted. But where was Alice? And come to think of it, where was Ronnie? Anthea checked her watch. The coach would be waiting. A few minutes' delay could make all the difference. If they didn't get across the river before five, even the kids would die of old age before they got home in nose-to-tail pollution that was Roehampton.

‘Keep them there,’ Anthea told Leila above the din of an infant school in the departure area. ‘No one goes out until I get back, OK?’

* * *

She needn’t have worried. Her single backward glance as she turned to the steel barrier gave her the sight of Gauleiter Roberts marshalling her troops. It was quite scary. What was the younger generation coming to?

But Alice wasn’t lingering in the television section. Ronnie wasn’t pretending to be a Dalek. There were none of her kids behind her at all. There were kids everywhere, laughing, chattering, pulling each other to see this, gawp at that. But not one of them came from Leighford High. And slowly, as she retraced her steps, her annoyance turned to panic. She didn’t hear the scream as Fay Wray collapsed into the huge hairy hand of King Kong in the cinema section, and she didn’t hear the calm, affable tones of Barry Norman talking to her, as she rounded every corner, checked every glass case. Alice wasn’t looking at the faded photos of the Lumiere brothers; Ronnie wasn’t drooling over the skin-flicks of Raquel Welch, old enough to be his grandmother though she was. And then, Anthea was at the entrance and the last of the school parties was being admitted, its teachers together, its numbers intact. She was aware of somebody gesturing beyond the glass doors. She focused, trying to shut out the rising fear in her heart, the dread in her head. It was their driver, from Hamilton’s, tapping the glass at her and pointing at his watch.

She nodded frantically, waving back and raising her thumbs. Then she dashed back through the museum in one last vain search before she rounded everybody up for the journey home.

* * *

The museum staff had been the model of helpfulness. Could the teacher have doubled back to find recalcitrant or confused children? Could she be in the toilets, unwell? What about the National Film Theatre next door? After all, their gift shops abutted. She'd probably be in there.

Except that she wasn't in there. And neither was Ronnie. It was time to call security. And security asked the same questions, time after time, as though they thought Anthea was imagining it, as though she'd dreamed up Alice Goode and Ronnie Parsons and was keeping fifty increasingly restless children milling around in the entrance lobby for the good of her health. She wanted to scream, except that she couldn't; to knock their stupid heads together, except that she knew they were just being reasonable and doing their job. And that made her want to scream even more. On her insistence, they called the police.

The Hamilton's driver was patience itself. He rang in, to let his people know of the delay. Anthea rang Leighford High.

'But I can't find them,' she heard herself shouting at Bernard Ryan. She might just as well have talked to the school cat, if Leighford had had a school cat. 'I don't know, Bernard. I have looked. Everywhere. No. No. Yes, I realise that. No, I can't ring all the parents to tell them we'll be late. That's why I'm ringing you. There's a copy in the staffroom. Yes. All their phone numbers, yes. Well, there are a couple not on the bloody phone, yes. What am I supposed to do about that? Yes. Yes.' She could see the end of her tether well and truly in sight. 'Of course. Yes. Right. I don't know. What time is it now?' she checked her watch. 'Oh, I don't know, about eight, I suppose. Look, I'll ring back, when we're about to leave. Oh, right. Well, I can't do more. Look, I'll have to go. Yes. Yes. All right.'

And the expressionless face of a Metropolitan bobby loomed at her through the glass of the call-box.

'Got somebody missing, then?' he asked her. It was marginally better than ''Ello, 'ello, 'ello'.

* * *

That face was still in Anthea's mind when she woke up, the silver of his helmet badge, the monotone of his voice. He'd taken everything down in long hand in his notebook and he snapped it shut again for the umpteenth time in those long, long seconds of the dream time, between sleep and waking. She focused on the face in front of her, the dark, deep eyes, the barbed-wire hair, the broad smile. And she felt like crying all over again.

* * *

'Good morning, Anthea,' Maxwell said. 'How'd you sleep?'

'Badly,' she told him, struggling out of the dressing gown cover. 'God, I must look like shit.'

'Don't do yourself down. Look, it's seven thirty. How do you feel about school today?'

'Christ, Max, I've got to be there.' She struggled upright, smoothing out the wrinkles in her skirt as best she could. 'There was no time to do anything last night. Oh, God, it's all true, isn't it? I thought perhaps . . .'

He smiled at her. 'That it wasn't real? Yes, I have mornings like that.'

'It's Bernard I can't face,' she said. 'He's such a bastard.'

'Bernard?' Maxwell frowned. 'A pussycat, that man — oh, begging your pardon, Metternich.'

But the poor emasculated animal had already taken umbrage and wandered off to the kitchen for the bits of indescribable fishy things his master referred to as breakfast.

'Breakfast?' Maxwell asked his still bedraggled guest.

Her face said it all, 'No, thanks, Max. Oh, perhaps some coffee? Oh, shit!'

'What?'

'The Parsons. I meant to ring them.'

'You told me you left a message on their answerphone.'

'Well, yes, but . . . Max, I lost their child. You don't just leave a message on an answerphone, as if you're ordering a hundredweight of bricks. You don't . . .' And she felt the hysteria welling up again, like the tightening of a spring, like a coil round her heart. She felt his hands holding her shoulders, squeezing her gently, like her father's hands. And she heard his voice, like her father's voice.

'You did all you could,' he told her. 'Ronnie Parsons is eighteen — an adult — and a big bugger with it. I'd be very surprised if this was the first time he'd stayed out all night. It's my guess he's home right now. Now, come on. The bathroom's up one floor and turn left. Make yourself even more beautiful while I roast a few arabica beans over my campfire. Then you can have the pleasure of driving me to work.'

* * *

The '60s goldfish bowl that was Leighford High looked greyer than ever that morning. It looked grey to the two hundred and thirty-eight Year Nines who were to troop into the hall to take their Science SAT. And it certainly looked grey to Anthea Edwards, fumbling with her car keys. She was still wearing yesterday's clothes, the clothes she'd slept in. And the only makeup she'd been able to muster was that rather awful lipstick Jerry had bought her for her birthday. She thought as she put it on in front of Maxwell's bathroom mirror how the lipstick was all she had left of that relationship. All that was left of nearly three years of her life. Because of that, when the bottom suddenly fell out of her world yesterday, it wasn't Jerry she'd turned to, with the recriminations and the back-biting. It was Max, mad as a March hare, but strong and solid and wise.

Together, they parted the Red Sea of children draped on the main steps.

'You're a fire hazard, Jason,' Maxwell trilled. 'If the alarm bell goes now, you'll be killed in the rush. Do move, there's a good argonaut.'

Jason didn't know what an argonaut was. He didn't know what a fire hazard was, either. He wasn't even sure about the alarm bell. But he knew Mad Max, and if he said move, even ever so politely, you moved.

Some pimply Newly Qualified Teacher was on duty in the foyer, picking up the first of the morning's chewing-gum wrappers already. He grinned inanely at Maxwell who swept past him like a galleon in full sail, doffing his shapeless hat at the 1984 Curriculum Award in the lopsided frame on the wall. 'Nice picture of Mrs Shepherd there,' he smiled at Anthea, 'brighten the place up no end to have the Secretary of State for Education watching over us all. Jenkins, you ungrateful pig, you owe me an essay'.

'Ah, yes.' The ungrateful pig had timed that badly. Three seconds more and he'd have made it to the unholy hell that passed for a sixth-form common room at Leighford High. Now he'd have to write the damn thing in his free period. 'On your desk by this afternoon, Mr Maxwell,' he promised.

'Make that twelve and we'll draw a veil over your woeful inadequacies.'

'Done!' Jenkins grinned and he knew he had been.

The office of the Second Deputy was round the corner, up the stairs to the mezzanine floor and turn right. It was actually one of the nicest offices in the school, overlooking the central quad and the lily pond where empty crisp packets and the odd sandwich floated like pastoral poetry.

Bernard Ryan was a bully. Like most of the new managerial class of teachers, he'd been promoted quickly and had come from nowhere because he knew what a CD ROM was and spoke warmly of GNVQ. He knew more buzz words than a whole hive of bees and he had the words 'Pushy Bastard' tattooed on his forehead.

'This is serious, Anthea,' were the first words he spoke to her, 'very serious.'

'Have you heard from the Parsons?' she asked him.

'They're in with Mr Diamond now. I have to say you handled this badly. Very badly.'

He watched with evident delight as her face crumpled and her shoulders shook. And he was enjoying himself so much he positively jumped when his office door slammed shut and Peter Maxwell stood there, like the Angel of Death. Anthea felt an arm around her shoulders and caught her breath. The 7th Cavalry had arrived.

'Nearly nine, Anthea,' Maxwell said softly. 'Better cut along and register 8ED or they'll demolish B Block.'

She tried to smile, but it didn't work.

'Just a minute,' Ryan frowned, 'I haven't finished . . .'

Maxwell ignored him and tapped his watch. 'It really is about that time,' he said to Anthea. She shot a glance at the Second Deputy. 'I'm sorry, Bernard,' she just about managed before she dashed through the door that Maxwell had opened for her.

'Who the hell do you think you are?' Ryan exploded, his neck crimson and his eyes watering. Maxwell had not yet closed the door and he smiled sweetly at two astonished Year Seven kids scurrying past at that moment on their way to registration.

'It's a role play exercise,' he said to them. 'You know, the sort of thing Mrs Baker gets you to do in Drama lessons.' Then he turned on Ryan and the Heavens fell. 'Second Deputy,' he growled. 'That's one up from the bloody groundsman, isn't it?'

'Now look . . .' but Ryan's heart was in his mouth and his voice had lost its fire. Maxwell was just beginning.

'Point that finger at me again, Ryan, and I'll shove it up your arse, along with the rest of your arm. Don't you suppose Anthea feels shitty enough without you behaving like some pubescent Adolf Hitler? What was she supposed to do yesterday? A member of staff goes missing along with one of my sixth form. She conducted a search, nay, several. She contacted the appropriate security forces. She contacted the police. She rang you. That's all she could have done. I'd have done exactly the same and so would you.'

'I . . .'

'Now, if you want to earn those metaphorical pips on your shoulder, you'll do what a pastoral deputy is supposed to do and that's look out for the welfare of the kids, not shit on staff who can't defend themselves.' Maxwell had snatched open the door. 'And if you want somebody to kick around, Bernard, it was my trip in the first place. So when you find some bottle from somewhere, you come and kick me around. All right?'

Ryan looked as though he'd just been hit by the school bus. And he was still looking that way when Maxwell slammed the door and was gone, shouting to no one in particular, 'Hello, cruel world!'

* * *

Maxwell should have worn his Hush Puppies, the silent moccasins he habitually wore in the exam season so as not to disturb the kids in hall or gym. True, he didn't regard SATS as exams. After all, they were only the government's attempt to reimpose the eleven-plus and to enable them to draw up League Tables. He didn't regard 'Keep Out, Hall in Use' signs as relevant to him either, so he squeaked his way across the polished floor in his lace-up brogues and didn't even wince when the Hall door crashed behind him.

An anguished Ben Horton, the Head of Science, looked up and two hundred and thirty-eight heads swivelled to see what the commotion was. Then they turned back. It was only Mad Max on his way to see the Headmaster.

James Diamond had been the Head of Leighford High for four years. In that time they'd introduced GNVQ, they'd started calling probationer teachers NQTs and the world had become a plastic set of initials. But there was nothing more plastic than Mr J. Diamond, BA, M.Ed. The man was a physicist by training — not the best start in life — and anyone who had the crassness to call him a Master of Education was indeed exposing himself to public scorn. Because he was well brought up in the traditions of the old school and not because he had any veneration whatsoever for his Headmaster, Maxwell tapped briefly on the door before gatecrashing the interview with the missing boy's parents.

'Ah, Max,' Diamond looked as grey as his suit, 'there you are.'

'Just straightening Mr Ryan out on a few points, Headmaster,' Maxwell said. 'Mrs Parsons,' he shook the woman's hand. 'Mr Parsons,' he shook the man's. 'Peter Maxwell.'

The introduction was superfluous really. Everyone the length and breadth of Leighford and Tottingleigh knew Mad Max or knew of him. He'd taught them or he'd taught their kids and many was the rising young politician or entrepreneur or professional who, in their heart of hearts, owed it all to Mad Max.

'I was just saying to Mr and Mrs Parsons,' Diamond went on as Maxwell settled into the Head's spare plastic chair, 'that I'm sure there's some simple explanation. And, of course, absolutely no cause for alarm.'

Maxwell looked at Mr and Mrs Parsons. She was a mousy woman with peroxide hair. He wasn't, but there the differences ended.

Maxwell had noticed over his four centuries in teaching how wives started to look like their husbands and vice versa. Or perhaps it was just the fusing of features in the face of their offspring that did it.

'No, I'm sure not,' Maxwell nodded, 'I'm sure the Headmaster has asked you this already, Mr and Mrs Parsons, but can you think of any reason why Ronnie should run away?'

Mr Parsons looked blank, as though the idea had never occurred to him. Besides, he left the upbringing of the kids to Mrs Parsons. This was the first time he'd set foot inside Leighford High in seven years.

'No.' Mrs Parsons bailed him out, as she always did. Ron Senior was a good provider, but he didn't know his children, deep down He was never there to know them, endlessly on the road as he was, from one building job to another. The kids were hers. She'd speak up for them. 'No, I can't,' she said.

'No trouble?' Maxwell prompted her. 'No rows at home?'

'What do you mean?' Mr Parsons stirred himself a little. He was happy to leave all this school stuff to his missus, but when there was some sort of insinuation in the offing, he thought he'd better do his bit.

'It happens, Mr Parsons,' Maxwell said. 'Family tiffs. Oh, they're nothing in themselves, but in the minds of kids, they loom out of all proportion. Things become distorted.'

'You know, do you?' Parsons snapped. 'Got kids of your own?'

'Ron . . .' Mrs Parsons reached across to pat her husband's hand.

Jim Diamond opened his mouth to say something, but whatever it was, it wasn't quick enough or relevant enough for Peter Maxwell.

'Yes,' said the Head of Sixth Form. 'Two hundred and thirty-eight of them, at the last count,' and he regretted that slightly, because now, without Ronnie, it was two hundred and thirty-seven. 'I'm father to all my sixth form, Mr Parsons; they're all my kids.'

'No.' Such a notion made no sense to Ron Parsons. Bricks, mortar; these were the things he understood. A teacher's relationship with his charges? That was beyond him. 'No, I mean kids of your own.'

For a moment, there was a silence. Jim Diamond squirmed a little. To him, Peter Maxwell was a bachelor, too wound up in whatever it was that bachelors did to have much of a life. But he didn't know Peter Maxwell. He didn't know about the little girl who had died, all those years ago, as a police car, hurtling out of control around a deadly bend on a wet road, had ploughed into her, killing her and her mother instantly. At least, Maxwell hoped it was instantly. For twenty-four years he had hoped his wife and daughter never knew what hit them. It was all that had kept him sane.

'No,' Maxwell said softly. 'No kids of my own.'

'Well, there you are.' Ron wouldn't leave it alone. 'How can you know, how can you possibly know what it's all about, then? Coming in here telling us it's our fault.'

'That's not what he said, Ron.' Mrs Parsons made a pretty decent 7th Cavalry herself when she put her mind to it, thundering to Maxwell's aid. 'Mr Maxwell is only trying to help.'

Ron Parsons sat there for a moment, on the Headmaster's plastic chair. Then he folded. His shoulders relaxed and he relented before his wife's cajoling and the steady gaze of Mad Max. 'Yeah, well . . . all right, then,' he said.

'No, Mr Maxwell, there was no row,' Mrs Parsons told him. 'We didn't see much of Ronnie the night before he went, to be honest. He went out to see his mates for a drink, but he was in by ten. You was watching the football with him, wasn't you, Ron?'

'That's right,' Ron corroborated.

'And he seemed his usual self?' Maxwell asked. 'Nothing out of the ordinary?'

Ron Parsons couldn't really say what was out of the ordinary for his eldest boy. Ronnie was clever and lots of dads would be proud, but Ron Senior didn't really understand the boy. He was doing Business Studies and History and Geography. It was all Greek to Ron. In the absence of an opinion, the boy's father shrugged.

'Have the police been in touch?' Diamond asked.

'The police?' Mrs Parsons flashed a glance at her husband. This was a nightmare from which she couldn't wake up. And she'd just entered some new and terrible depth in it. The Headmaster's pastel walls stretched up like the slabs of some dungeon. And the light at the top got smaller and smaller. 'Oh.'

'Just routine,' Maxwell said, sensing the rising tide of the woman's panic. 'They've got to ask some questions, that's all.'

'Yes,' Mrs Parsons said. 'Yes, of course.'

Maxwell was on his feet. 'Look,' he said to them both, 'please don't worry. I have to be somewhere else now, but Ronnie will turn up. I'm sure of it. We'll make some enquiries of our own. Headmaster,' and Maxwell nodded briskly to the man before shaking the Parsons' hands and making his exit.

* * *

He flicked open the file on Ronnie Parsons. Seven very average GCSEs, played soccer for the school in Years Seven and Eight. A dog-eared Incident Form bore witness to the fact that Mr Diamond, no less, had caught him smoking beyond the tennis courts in Year Ten. A copy of his Centigrade Form gave evidence that his leanings were towards business or administration. He'd had measles, all the relevant jabs and his doctor was old Edgarson, in the sea-front practice. Maxwell shook his head as he'd done countless times over the inadequacy of the system, the flimsiness of the files.

'Where are you, Ronnie,' he muttered to himself, 'you annoying little shit?'

CHAPTER 3

Peter Maxwell's feet were on the pouffe and his knees were under the table; the former literally, the latter metaphorically. Sylvia Matthews, the school nurse at Leighford High, didn't usually entertain strange men on Thursdays. And they didn't come much stranger than Peter Maxwell.

He'd grabbed a lift with Ben Horton, pretending to be vaguely interested in the man of science's verdict on the SAT paper for Year Nine. Then he'd fed Metternich the cat, soaked himself for half an hour in the bath, steeped in Radox, and saddled White Surrey for the twenty-minute ride to Sylvia's flat.

She'd welcomed him with his usual Southern Comfort and let him take off his shoes on the strict understanding that one sign of a hole in his socks and the brogues would be back on again. Odd for a nurse, to have a thing about feet. He'd partaken gratefully of her cheesecake and sat back on the sofa, his eyes closed, his hands clasped round his glass.

'This is an honour.' She brought through the cafetiere and two cups on a tray.

'What is?' He didn't open his eyes.

'A visit from you.'

He opened his eyes. 'Pressure of work,' he said. 'Oh, by the way,' he reached into his cardigan pocket, 'for you.'

She put the tray down and took the brown-wrapped box, frowning. 'Maxie,' she said, 'you remembered.'

He wagged a finger at her, laughing. 'Now, careful, Sylv,' he said, 'that Celia Johnson is frighteningly good. Any minute now, I'll just have to give you my full-blown Trevor Howard and then we're all in trouble.'

She reached across with the perfume he'd given her and pecked him on the forehead. It was as close as she dared get to Peter Maxwell, the man she loved. 'Thank you,' she smiled, 'you shouldn't have. Although I suppose you'd say that's a cliché.'

'*Au contraire*, Matron mine,' Maxwell said, 'that's a gospel fact. Have you seen the price of that stuff lately? I suppose it's because it's tested on humans. No, seriously, Sylv, it's just a little something for leading me away from death's door the other day.'

'It's nothing that any highly trained member of a caring profession wouldn't have done,' she said, suddenly afraid she'd dropped a few too many negatives in there. She was always afraid of these things with Maxie; not that he'd ever upbraided her or even commented on an infinitive more split than a raspberry.

'No, no,' Maxwell said, 'it was beyond the call.'

'Well, that's because . . .' and she stopped herself in mid-sentence. In mid-hope. 'Coffee?' One day she'd tell him. One day when she stopped being a stupid little girl in his presence. One day she'd tell him the truth, blurt it all out. But she daren't. She daren't in case he turned his back and made his excuses and left. One day would come one day. But for now, there was coffee.

'Thanks.' He took the cup from her, having drained his glass.

'Well, are you going to tell me or not?' She curled up on the chair opposite him.

'You rather pinched my line there, Nursie,' he told her.

She knew that look. The twinkling eyes. The wry smile.

'You know I rely on you for all my gossip. Where's Ronnie?'

'Ah,' she said, 'you transparent old Head of Sixth Form! And I thought it was my cheesecake you couldn't resist. Either that or my body . . .' She bit her lip, hoping he hadn't heard, hoping he'd move the conversation on, hoping the ground would open up and swallow her whole.

'You're the grapevine, Sylv.' She was in the clear. 'Countless urchins flock to your room every day with everything from period pains to paranoia. If you don't know what's happening at Leighford, nobody does.'

'Well . . .' she said, enjoying the moment, the power.

He twisted his face, indulging the pregnancy of her pause.

'What did Leila tell you?' she asked him.

'Leila Roberts? Not a lot. She seems more bewildered than upset. Anthea too, I suppose. It is bizarre.'

'They were an item, of course.'

'Who?'

'Leila and Ronnie.'

'Were they?'

She raised her eyes heavenward. 'Oh, Max,' she said. 'Do you notice nothing?'

'Well, I did catch Debbie Whatserface with her hand in the Acheson boy's trousers last year. That was quite a coup, I thought.'

'Yes, but you missed the gang bang with her and the First Fifteen, didn't you? No, no,' she laughed, 'just my idea of a joke. Leila and Ronnie were going out all last summer.'

'I wouldn't have thought he was her type,' Maxwell mused.

'Why not?'

'Well,' he rationalised, 'she's not anybody's type, really, is she, Leila? I mean, she's seventeen going on forty-eight. I've never seen a spinster school-ma'am in the sixth form before. I'd have thought she'd be fonder of her hockey stick than Ronnie Parsons.'

'That's a dreadful thing to say!' Sylvia scolded him. 'And anyway, I never noticed much difference between Ronnie and a hockey stick.'

'What, you mean bent or wooden?' Maxwell asked her. 'Or both?'

'I mean, I always had Ronnie down for a bit of a non-event.'

'Good-looking lad, though,' Maxwell ventured, 'isn't he? To women, I mean?'

'Oh, yes.' Sylvia smiled. 'Very. But I think Leila wants more than just a pretty face. Did Anthea say anything about them on the trip? I mean, was there a row or anything?'

'Anthea said not,' Maxwell told her, 'but you know how it is, Sylv, fifty screaming idiots in paroxysms of delight because we've let 'em out for the day — and the day of the Science SATs too. I blame myself.'

'Now, don't be silly, Max,' she scolded him. 'You were burning up with fever. It simply wasn't possible for you to go. How are you feeling now, by the way?'

'Well, there's nothing like a double disappearance for reducing the temperature and the size of my glands. Anyway, that Oriental Bezoar Stone you gave me was pretty powerful stuff; not to mention the old eye of newt and wool of bat. Old Maxie's pulled through again.'

'What about Dannie?' Sylvia suddenly asked.

'Dannie?' Maxwell was lost. 'Who's Dannie?'

'Dannie Roth. Don't you remember? She left two years ago.'

'Dannie Roth!' Maxwell clicked his fingers. 'Ah, how soon we forget. The siren of Year Ten, luring doomed male members of staff onto the rocks of their marriages.'

'There wasn't any truth in that, was there?' she asked him. 'Alan Tullet and Dannie?'

'Well, you know what those Drama types are like.' Maxwell sipped his coffee with all the bigotry of an historian. 'Into nymphets in a big way. Certainly he was unwise to be seen going to the theatre with her.'

'He was quite dishy, too,' Sylvia remembered with a wistful smile.

'If you like men too bone idle to shave properly, then, yes, I suppose he had a certain something. Scarcely got my blood racing, though. I shared a locker with the man for a term. He read Barbara Vine. But what's he got to do with Ronnie Parsons?'

'Not him,' Sylvia said. 'Dannie. Ronnie carried a torch for Dannie.'

'Along with half the lads and staff in the school,' Maxwell nodded.

'Where did she go?'

'Oh, Christ, now you've asked me. I'll have to check the files, of course, but I think it was Sussex. What, you think Ronnie was carrying on a seduction correspondence course with Dannie and they arranged for him to slip away from MOMI and catch a southbound train for an idyllic mid-week at Fulmer? Come on, Nursie, my garden's a better plot than that. Besides, I would have thought darling Dannie's shacked up with some ageing juvenile luvvie who'll never see forty again.'

'Oh,' Sylvia was arch when she wanted to be, 'went for the older man, did she?'

'Only when I conducted private, personal interviews with her. Oh, and every time I got some file paper from the History stock cupboard.'

'You're just an old pervert, Peter Maxwell.' She clicked her tongue.

'One of the few — the very few — perks of the job, Nursie,' he smiled at her. Then he grimaced. 'Did you put any sugar in this coffee?'

* * *

Detective Constable Jacquie Carpenter knew Peter 'Mad Max' Maxwell. A girl from Leighford had been murdered a few years back — one of Maxwell's Own, one of his sixth form. So she knew the face and she knew the style. She knew Jim Diamond too and what a waste of time it was talking to him. She flashed her warrant card and got herself conducted as soon as possible to Maxwell's office at Leighford High.

The Great Man wasn't there. He was, at that moment, attempting to guide a pretty comatose Year Ten class through the intricacies of the Schools History Project. They still, all these years on, had no real notion of primary and secondary sources or how binding bias could be. The office junior in the tight skirt had led Jacquie into the Inner Sanctum, that borne from which few sixth formers returned. And in a dither, she'd hoped she'd done the right thing by leaving her there. After all, if you couldn't trust the police not to pinch County Council property, who could you trust?

Jacquie Carpenter didn't sit down. She took in the film posters that lined the walls: Gregory Peck glaring at loony Robert Mitchum in *Cape Fear*; Charlton Heston apparently rubbing noses with Laurence Olivier in *Khartoum*; Peter O'Toole and Katherine Hepburn scratching each other's eyes out in *The Lion in Winter*.

'Of all the sixth-form offices in all the world, you had to walk into mine," Humphrey Bogart lisped behind her.

'Mr Maxwell.' She was flustered, but tried not to show it.

'Woman Policeman Carpenter,' he bowed and threw a pile of exercise books onto the coffee table.

Jacquie looked older. Her hair was scraped back into a single plait and she wore less makeup than he remembered. Was her mouth harder? Her eyes less kind? Maxwell decided that was what working with the girls in blue did for you.

'Why didn't you go into the film business?' she asked him.

He chuckled. 'You see this?' He patted the Acorn on the desk. 'Apparently, it's a computer. My colleagues tell me it's linked up to every University in the country. At a touch of a key, my sixth formers can find out what courses are on offer anywhere in this great country of ours. If they want Nuclear

Physics with Basketry, then I'm sure there's somewhere — probably Scunthorpe — that does it. Whereas in my day . . .' He waved her to a seat. 'Roughly speaking, when Julia Margaret Cameron got her first box Brownie for Christmas, my old careers master said to me, "History, eh, Maxwell?" He had this dribble problem. Shrapnel in the Great War, we thought. "History, eh?" he said. "Right, that's teaching or the Civil Service for you, my lad." Well, I vaguely knew, even at seventeen, that the Civil Service didn't give much of a service and they certainly weren't civil, so here I am. What can I do for you, Woman Policeman?'

'Ronnie Parsons,' she said, looking him straight in the eye.

'Ah, yes,' he passed her the cardboard file, 'that won't take you long to sift through. In the meantime, can I make you a coffee? Tea?'

'No, thanks.' She read the file as she spoke. 'I should explain that we are liaising with our colleagues in the Met on this one.'

'No luck their end?'

* * *

'Not yet,' she said. 'But these things take time.' 'You've talked to the parents?' Maxwell sat down in his county chair, worn after all these years to the contours of his bum.

'Yes. Have you?'

'Yes,' he smiled. 'Why do you ask?'

She thought for a moment before speaking. 'Let's say you have something of a reputation, Mr Maxwell.'

'Really?' He raised an eyebrow in a passable Dirk Bogarde, but Jacquie Carpenter was too young to appreciate it. 'Should I be flattered?'

'I don't know,' she said, still smiling. 'You seem to have a habit of . . . getting involved, shall we say?'

'I have been compared with Don Quixote in my time,' he said, 'and I suppose my old bike is the twentieth-century equivalent of Rosinante. The trouble is, the windmills. They just get bigger and bigger, don't they?'

'Tell me about Miss Goode,' she said, the file on Ronnie discarded, the notebook at the ready.

'I think you'll find that's Ms,' he confided.

'Ah.'

'And I'm afraid I can't tell you a great deal. She's an NQT . . .'

'A what?'

'Aha, quite,' he chuckled. 'My sentiments exactly. She's a Newly Qualified Teacher — a rookie in your manor, I expect. Been with us since September.'

'Good at her job?' Jacquie asked.

'You'd have to ask Deirdre Lessing.' It pained him to say it.

'Who?'

'You know,' he smiled, 'it's quite uncanny how alike we are. Sadly, I do know the answer to that question. Deirdre is Senior Mattress — er . . . Mistress here at Leighford. In charge of girls' welfare and distaff matters generally, She's also Alice Goode's mentor. Or is that mentress? I'm not sure.'

'What was Ms Goode's relationship to Ronnie Parsons?'

'Relationship?' Maxwell frowned. 'I'm not sure she knew who he was. Leighford has over a thousand kids, Woman Policeman. Ronnie wasn't taking English. Anyway, it's not policy here to unleash NQTs on the sixth form.'

'Not fair on the sixth form?'

'Not fair on NQTs.' Maxwell grinned. 'Tell me, am I following the drift of this conversation right? Do you think that Alice Goode and Ronnie Parsons have . . . what? Eloped?'

Jacquie Carpenter wasn't smiling now. She just gazed steadily with those smouldering grey eyes at the smouldering grey old man across the desk from her. 'We're keeping an open mind,' she said.

'Do you know,' he stroked his chin, 'I remember seeing a painting of your sister in the Louvre a long time ago. Enigmatic to the last.'

'How was Ronnie doing, at school, I mean?' Jacquie Carpenter could change tack with the best of 'em.

'No outstanding problems,' Maxwell said. 'Sinking a little in Bismarck's Foreign Policy, but you show me a seventeen-year-old who doesn't.'

'Friends?'

'A popular lad.' Maxwell nodded. 'Kicked a ball around with the lads at lunchtime.'

'Girls?'

'Nobody special, although . . .'

'Yes?' Jacquie Carpenter was very good at recognising the un-finished sentence, the silence that betrays.

'Well, I understand that Ronnie and Leila Roberts were something of an item a little while ago.'

'She was the other sixth former on the trip?'

'That's right.'

'Is that usual, taking sixth formers on a trip, I mean?'

'Standard enough.' Maxwell nodded. 'It's good practice for them. Leila's thinking of going into teaching, so she's clearly insane; but the practice'll do her good. I don't know who chose Ronnie — Anthea Edwards, I expect.'

'We've already talked to Miss Edwards,' Jacquie told him. 'This should have been your trip, shouldn't it?'

Maxwell paused. His conscience sat staring him straight in the face. It had slipped a little from his sleeve. 'Yes,' he said levelly, the eyes dark, the jaw set. 'Yes, it should.'

* * *

'All right, all right,' Maxwell slammed the glue down. 'You've made your point, Metternich, now leave it alone, will you?'

The cat glowered at him, sullen, resentful, but all the smugger for being right. Night had come to Leighford, all the better for being Friday night. The day's rain had given way to a fine night and the half-moon played games of pitch and toss with the faery clouds. Maxwell leaned back in his attic hideaway and looked at the stars through his skylight.

'You have the column, Mr Sulu.' He slipped inexorably into his William Shatner.

'Missing,' he said, back in Maxwell mode again and picked up the white plastic soldier before placing him astride his white plastic charger. 'Presumed killed?' He didn't like the sound of that. The presumption frightened him. 'Do you know who this is, Count?'

The cat twitched an ear. No doubt the boring old fart would tell him in the fullness of time.

'Well, when I've painted him up and stuck him all down, he'll be Captain John Augustus Oldham, 13th Light Dragoons.' He glanced across to Oldham's plastic comrades, kitted out for their unfaded glory on that October day in 1854. 'He drew the short straw did Oldham, Count. Lieutenant-Colonel Doherty was laid up with cholera at the time, so was Major Gore. Holden was the senior captain, but he was with the Depot troop back home, so that left Oldham in charge at the Charge.' His eyes narrowed on the brave features, the strong jaw, the curling moustaches. 'He was last seen, sword in one hand, pistol in the other, bleeding from his wounds.' Maxwell sat back again. 'The point is, Count, they never found his body.'

He sighed and swivelled to the cat, 'Is that how it'll be for Ronnie, do you think? That they'll never find his body?'

Metternich raised his black and white head for a moment, but it was only to find a more comfortable spot for his chin, and he returned to his snoring on the wicker basket he'd made his home in Maxwell's loft.

'One of these days,' tutted Maxwell impatiently, 'you'll give me a straight yes or no to a question. All right.' He pulled off the gold-laced forage cap, the Crimean one he wore when painting his Light Brigade, to give him empathy with the chaps, and reached for his glass of Southern Comfort. 'What do we know in the strange-but-true disappearance of Alice Goode and Ronnie Parsons? One, they both disappeared on the same day and ostensibly from the same place — the Museum of the Moving Image. Two, there was nothing to denote a problem in the demeanour of either. Three — and I hope you're taking notes, Count, 'cos I'll be asking questions later — said disappearances are either linked or they're one helluva coincidence. Four — no apparent ransom note . . . or was there? Damn, I should have asked Woman Policeman Carpenter about that. Not that she'd tell me a great deal. She was being particularly tight-lipped this morning, I thought. Five . . . buggeration, there isn't a five, Count. I actually know sweet F.A. about this business. Better stick to teaching, eh?' He glanced furtively at the beast with four paws, who lashed his tail, just the once, from side to side.

'I know,' Maxwell said, 'and of course, you're right. It was my trip — you've been colluding with Woman Policeman Carpenter, haven't you? It was my trip, so I can't just stick to teaching. Somewhere,' and he kicked himself free of the chair, 'is Deirdre Lessing's address in my Directory of the Damned.'

* * *

If you'd asked Peter Maxwell — and occasionally, when they were feeling brave or had several hours to spare, people did — what he disliked about Deirdre Lessing, he'd have said 'Everything'. And it galled him, that Saturday morning, as he pedalled across the Common on White Surrey, that he had to go, cap in hand, to the Morgana le Fay of Leighford High. He hadn't rung her in advance, because she'd know he'd half-inched her ex-directory number from the school office. It was only a short step from knowing her phone number to making disgusting, obscene calls and she was perfectly willing to concede that Peter Maxwell was clever enough to ring 141 before his perverted little fingers pattered out her digits. So he wouldn't give her the edge. He'd catch her like the law might, before breakfast, with her curlers in and her teeth in a jar by the bed.

He was all the more disappointed then when she opened the door to him in a rather fetching pink and blue jogging suit, with a sweat band where her hair line usually was.

'What a fetching glow band,' Maxwell beamed, patting White Surrey on the bell. 'Ex-kamikaze, Senior Mistress?'

Her face said it all. 'I presume this visit has a point, Max?' she bridled.

'Of course,' he assured her, 'I don't waste valuable tyre rubber on trivia. It's about Alice Goode.'

She looked up and down the road. Thank God there was no one about yet to see the freak that stood before her front door, in scarf and cycle clips, like some sort of deranged Doctor Who. 'You'd better come in.'

He did. Her hall wallpaper was indescribable, as he knew it would be, and he was sure the certificates on the stairs were tokens of gratitude from the SS and signed by Himmler himself.

'Coffee?'

'Dash'd civil,' Maxwell beamed, his Hush Puppies padding across the Flotex of her kitchen.

'You'll have to excuse the mess. It *is* the weekend.'

It was, but Maxwell couldn't see any. He felt a little guilty really. He hadn't seen all of his lounge carpet since 1986.

'Black?' She poured for them both.

'White, please. Two sugars.'

She looked at him and tutted. Green wasn't just a colour for Deirdre Lessing; it was a way of life. She offered him an excruciatingly high stool in the crisp, state-of-the-art kitchen and poured herself a grapefruit juice that Maxwell just knew she'd squeezed between her breasts.

'Lovely place, Deirdre,' he heard himself lying.

'Thank you.' She took the compliment at face value. In fact, it was the value of the place that intrigued Maxwell. Even Senior Mistresses received a pittance in John Major's England. This was an executive home, way out of Deirdre's league. Then he remembered the divorce. Deirdre had clearly taken Mr Lessing to Bolloms and back with a vengeance. If she never worked again — and Maxwell was by no means sure she ever had in the true sense of the word — it wouldn't really matter to Deirdre Lessing. To Peter Maxwell and Leighford High, however, it would be pure joy.

'How long have we known each other, Max?' she asked him, holding her coffee with both hands, as though the shock of the answer might be too much.

'Eight years, man and woman,' he told her.

'And in all that time, this is the first time you've crossed my portals.'

'Pressure of work,' Maxwell beamed.

'So it must be something important.'

So, mused Maxwell; pretty astute. Deirdre wasn't just a pretty pair of padded shoulders, then. 'I told you,' he said, 'Alice Goode.'

'Ah, yes.' She put down her cup with the air of someone who knows something — like the superior bastard across the desk from you in an interview. 'Jim said you'd be asking questions.'

'Jim? Oh, you mean Legs?'

'Why do you call him that?' she said, exasperated as always by Peter Maxwell within the first few minutes of any conversation.

'Legs Diamond,' Maxwell explained.

Nothing.

'He was a gangster. Twenties. Prohibition. You know — Eliot Ness, Al Capone. Ray Danton played him in the film.'

'I thought that was Robert de Niro.'

'No, no.' Maxwell could just about follow the woman's insanity. 'That was *The Untouchables.* De Niro played Capone in *The Untouchables*. Ray Danton played Legs Diamond in *The Rise and Fall of the Same*.' Maxwell could tell that Deirdre was none the wiser.

'But you were saying that Diamond prophesied I'd be here.'

'Well, he didn't exactly say you'd come round to my house.' It was clear that the trauma of the event had left its mark on Deirdre. 'But he certainly implied you wouldn't be able to let it lie.'

'He was right there. Tell me about Alice.'

'I don't know what I can say'. The Senior Mistress sipped her chilled juice. It probably froze further, Maxwell thought, on contact with her digestive tract. 'As you know, she joined us from college in September . . .'

'Which one?'

'The London Institute.'

'The London Institute?' Maxwell frowned.

'Yes, you know, it's a big place, where they keep the government and that sort of thing.' Sarcasm didn't sit well on Deirdre Lessing; she hadn't the wit for it.

'Go on.'

'She majored in English.'

Maxwell shuddered at the Americanism, promising himself that if Deirdre said 'Have a nice day, y'all' he'd leave. 'And her subsid?'

'French. But of course we're fully staffed there.'

Maxwell nodded. Deirdre was technically correct, but the vacuous thing who ran the Modern Languages Department could scarcely be called a full-timer and at least one of the *assistantes* was mad as a snake.

'You met her . . . what . . . twice a week as her mentor?'

'More often than that at first. Until she found her feet, you know. After Christmas she relaxed a little.'

'A little too much?'

Deirdre frowned. 'What do you mean?' she asked.

'Oh, I don't know,' he said, 'I'm just fishing, I suppose.'

'Well,' Deirdre looked at the man, her *bête noire* for eight long years, the thorn in her side, the itch she couldn't scratch, 'there were, of course, rumours.'

Of course there were. Leighford High was a melting pot of passions, a bubbling cauldron of pubescence. And as for the kids, well . . .

'What sort of rumours?'

'Max,' Deirdre was punctuating her sentences now with the firm putting down of her coffee cup, 'you know I won't deal in innuendo.'

Deirdre Lessing might have dealt in marijuana for all Maxwell knew. Two perfectly ordinary, perfectly everyday people had gone missing. There was a great deal that Peter Maxwell didn't know. 'Have the police talked to you?' he asked her.

'They have,' she nodded. 'A DC Carpenter saw me yesterday morning — shortly after she saw you, I understand.'

'And is that what you told her, Deirdre?' he asked. 'That you don't deal in innuendo.'

'Certainly not!' It wasn't difficult for Peter Maxwell to insult the Senior Mistress. He did it almost every day of his working life. 'I merely told her what I knew.'

'Which was?'

'Not a great deal. There were rumours — are rumours — that Alice was hanging around with a rather undesirable crowd. Down at the Seahorse.'

'The Seahorse?'

'Do you know it?' Nothing about Peter Maxwell would have surprised Deirdre Lessing. He probably had a collection of little girls' bicycle saddles at home.

'Of it, yes,' Maxwell told her, 'it ranks with Big Ben's as the place-teachers-wouldn't-be-seen-dead-in,' and instantly regretted his choice of words. 'Where does she live?'

'She shares a flat, with a primary school teacher in Graylands Lane. Number Thirty-one.'

Maxwell was on his feet, bicycle clips straining for the off.

'Max,' Deirdre stood up with him, 'it's none of my business, of course, but I wouldn't get involved, if I were you.'

'No, Deirdre.' He smiled broadly. 'I know you wouldn't. Thanks for the coffee.'

CHAPTER 4

'In the store today, shoppers, we have British beef down by fourteen pence a pound and there is a special offer on artichokes.'

Dorothy Parsons wouldn't have been surprised. Who knew what an artichoke was, never mind ate them? But Dorothy Parsons wasn't listening. She'd manned the till at Tesco's now since her Ronnie was in junior school. She was just part of the furniture. But that wasn't why she wasn't listening to the announcements over the tannoy. It was because she was listening out for her Ronnie's voice. Every time she looked up at her next customer, dumping down the six packs or wrestling with the carrier bags, she thought it might be him — 'Hello, Mum.'

But it never was 'Hello, Mum.' It was always, 'Got any carriers? Where's your boxes? You put them Smarties back, Shane, or I'll bleeding kill ya!'

Dorothy Parsons rang up the totals and slid the credit cards through the reader. Life at Tesco's had to go on. And it was still early days, that nice police lady had told her. Still early days yet.

* * *

The Victorians had come to Leighford, as they had come to all the resorts of the south coast, as their fathers in turn had come to Brighthelmstone in the wake of mad King George and his son, the indescribable Prince Regent. They'd built their villas for their month in the sun and the chance to see the Queen, God bless her, sailing on the steam packet across to the distant Isle of Wight. Now, the Victorians had gone and their great houses were subdivided into flats, with the telltale six bells on the front door.

Sad, Maxwell thought, as he always did when he saw such vandalism. He parked White Surrey against the wall and pushed the grubby bell of Flat 4, No. 31, Graylands Lane.

'Yes?' a distorted female voice answered.

'Mrs Hagger?'

'Who's that?'

'Peter Maxwell. I'm a colleague of Alice's.' There was a pause. Maxwell looked up to the blank windows where Flat 4 might be — he couldn't tell from that angle.

'She isn't here,' the voice said.

'I know,' Maxwell talked to the cobwebbed slats of the intercom. 'That's why I'm here.'

Another pause. 'You'd better come in.'

There was a whirr and a click. Maxwell pushed the heavy front door with the pebbled glass window. The hall was anonymous, with a set of pigeon holes to his right and the door of Flat 1 to his left. An arrow told him that Flats 3-6 were upstairs. He felt a little like Martin Balsam as he heard his feet creak on the risers, his hands slide up the smooth banister. He glanced back. No fruit cellar at least. But who knew about Jean Hagger, Alice Goode's flatmate? Who was to say she wasn't tall and flat-chested with silver hair and a breadknife? He'd better be on his guard, just in case.

If anything, Jean Hagger was worse than mad old Anthony Perkins. She was a typical junior school teacher, complete with fag and neurosis. It's a bit like the big wing and little wing of the RAF in World War Two — Bomber Command and Fighter Command. Their job was the same

— to trounce the Hun — but they loathed each other and had no mutual respect. So it was with senior and junior school teachers. Jean Haggr regarded the likes of Peter Maxwell as privileged, over-paid and pompous. He in turn regarded her sort as under-qualified botty-wipers and nappy-changers.

'Mrs Hagger,' he smiled and doffed his cap, extending a hand.

She put the fag in her mouth and took his hand in that awkward way that women do, with weak wrists and stiff fingers.

'You'd better have a seat,' she said, moving a fairly awful piece of knitting.

'Thank you. I'm sorry to arrive unannounced.'

'That's all right.' She flicked her thick hair away from her face, 'Er. . . ciggie?'

'No, thanks,' he smiled.

'Coffee?'

'No, really. Look, I'll come straight to the point. I'm looking for Alice.'

'You are?' Jean Hagger sat down on the chair opposite.

'Maxwell, PI,' he threw her, casually, as though without trying, his best Tom Selleck.

'Private Investigator?' she giggled nervously. 'I thought you said you were Alice's colleague.'

'I am,' he laughed. 'And no, in my case, "PI" means politically incorrect. I'm Head of Sixth Form at Leighford High.'

'Oh, yes. I remember now. You were in the paper the other week, weren't you?'

'Er . . . Young Enterprise, yes. Bit of a con, really. I just posed with the team — the kids did the work. I wouldn't know a business if it fell on me, still less how to study it.'

'Alice has talked about you,' Jean nodded.

'Doesn't see me as a knight errant, then?' Maxwell asked.

'What?'

'I got the impression a minute ago that you find it a little odd that I'm looking for Alice.'

'Er . . . no,' Jean flustered, 'it's just that . . . well, I thought . . . the police?'

'Have they been here?'

She blew smoke down her nose, 'Have they fuck!'

'Ah.' Maxwell smiled. It was nice to know our children were in such genteel hands. But then, with five-year-olds wielding knives these days, it was probably the woman's only salvation. 'What about Alice's parents?'

'Her dad's dead. She hasn't spoken to her mother since she was a student.'

'Does the mother know? About her disappearance, I mean?'

Jean Hagger blew smoke to the ceiling. 'Don't know,' she shrugged. 'Not from me, she doesn't. I've no idea where the woman lives.'

'So nobody's been through her things, then?'

'Things?' Jean frowned.

'Yes,' explained Maxwell, 'you know, her room . . .'

'Look,' the junior school teacher laughed that uneasy laugh that people do when they feel uncomfortable, 'I'm not going to let you rummage through my flatmate's underwear. Are you some sort of pervert?' For the first time, Jean felt genuine alarm. Peter Maxwell was just the age when weirdnesses start. *Cosmopolitan* had told her so. He was also a thickset bugger. The phone, in the entrance lobby, suddenly seemed a long way away.

'I just want to know what's happened to her,' Maxwell said. 'Where she's gone.'

'Well,' Jean blinked defiantly, determined that the smoke wouldn't defeat her, 'that's Alice's business, isn't it?'

Maxwell's smile vanished. 'I'm not sure it is, Mrs Hagger,' he said.

'What does that mean?'

'What's the first thing that goes through your mind when a girl goes missing?' he asked her. 'You hear it on the news all the time. On *Crimewatch*, on those sad little posters outside police stations. What do you think?'

'That she's been abducted . . . or . . .'

'Or . . .' nodded Maxwell. 'I can't believe the police haven't been here.'

'A student went missing too, didn't he?' Jean asked.

'Ronnie Parsons in my sixth form, yes.'

'Well, there you are.' Her face was bitter, hard.

'Am I?' Maxwell smiled.

'Look,' her cigarette had gone out. Irritated, she relit it with a plastic lighter. 'It happens, doesn't it? It doesn't always make the *Sun* or the *Daily Sport.*'

'"Sexy Siren Seduces Schoolboy"?' Maxwell said. 'Yes, I suppose it does. Was she the type, your Alice?'

Peter Maxwell had never seen a woman change so fast. It wasn't just her face, the vicious stubbing out of her cigarette, her body was like a toasting fork, rigid, hard, standing over him.

'I think you'd better go.' She sounded like Mercedes McCambridge dubbing for little Linda Blair in The Exorcist — all dark, all demon.

'Er . . . I was hoping for a look at her room,' he ventured.

'Well, hope on, you fucking creep. Alice wouldn't want an old pervert like you handling her personal things. Go on, get out! Or do I have to call the police?'

Maxwell stood up, towering over her. 'No,' he said softly, 'no, I don't think you'll have to do that.'

And he didn't hear Jean Hagger collapse into hysterical sobs as he saddled White Surrey in the street below.

* * *

He pedalled past Leighford High late that night, the tower block square and dark against the pinkish purple of the April sky. Through the trees he saw the low silhouette of the Technology Block and Smokers' Corner beyond it. Then he put his head down and cycled like a thing possessed along Wellington Street, across the park, following the signs to 'Town Centre' and 'The Sea'.

The police station at Leighford, by contrast with the school, was lit like a Christmas tree. He pushed the recalcitrant door, where posters reminded him that there was a thief about. Even here, he tutted to himself. Who could you trust nowadays, uh?

A silver-haired sergeant appeared before he could ring the bell. He had the years, but not the heart of George Dixon and there was a sneer in his voice which dear old Jack Warner wouldn't have contemplated.

'Can I help you, sir?'

'Yes, I was wondering if Detective Constable Carpenter is on duty.' The sergeant looked Maxwell up and down as though he was something caught on the sergeant's shoe.

'What's it about?'

'Personal,' chirped Maxwell.

'Then I suggest you come back in the morning.' The desk man was helpfulness itself.

'It's about the missing teacher,' Maxwell said, 'Alice Goode.'

He expected the third degree, if not the Spanish Inquisition, but instead the sergeant picked up a phone and muttered a few words into it, 'Jacquie? Yes. Tom. There's a . . . may I have your name, sir?'

'Maxwell.'

'A Mr Maxwell to see you. Says it's about Alice Goode. Right. Right you are.' And he put the phone down.

'DC Carpenter won't be a moment, sir,' he said.

'Thanks.' Maxwell took a seat. No sooner had his bum touched the vinyl, however, than a door swung wide and Jacquie Carpenter stood there. She looked tired. Worse, she looked worn out.

'Mr Maxwell,' she said.

The Head of Sixth Form clambered to his feet. He'd gone to a good school. 'I hope I haven't called at a bad time.'

'I should have gone off duty nearly three hours ago,' she told him, checking her watch, 'But apart from that . . . Thanks, Tom.' She took Maxwell up the flight of cheerless concrete steps that led to the CID offices on the first floor. He knew this building well. He'd helped the police with their enquiries three years ago when Jenny Hyde had been found murdered. She was one of his sixth form. Leighford High had never been the same since. They walked past VDUs and office doors without glass. Then she swung out a chair at her end of the corridor and sat her visitor down.

'I'd offer you some coffee,' she said, 'but the machine's switched off. What is it you want, Mr Maxwell?'

'To know where Alice Goode is,' he told her.

She sighed. 'If it weren't confidential, I'd bring up on the screen the hundreds of people currently missing in this county alone. Multiply that throughout the forty-three police forces of England and Wales and you've got a pretty big problem.'

'So we shouldn't bother?'

She looked at the floor, trying to control what she felt inside. 'Mr Maxwell,' she said, 'it's been a long day. And believe it or not, there are only so many hours in it. Now, at the moment I'm doing all I can to concentrate on Ronnie Parsons. We're all of us short of resources and manpower and time. We have to prioritise. Ronnie Parsons is my priority.'

'Good for you,' Maxwell winked.

She flashed fire at him. 'Are you saying he shouldn't be?'

'I'm saying he shouldn't be alone, no.'

'So you think wherever they are, they're together?' He didn't like the enthusiasm in DC Carpenter's eyes.

'I don't know,' he said.

'Precisely!' Her voice was louder than she'd intended. Why did she let this man get to her? 'Precisely,' calmer now. 'You think that because we've got links with other forces, computers, Interpol, Christ knows what, we know any more than you do? Ronnie Parsons, Alice Goode, they're just two needles in a bloody haystack, Mr Maxwell. And if those needles don't want to be found, well, frankly, there's not a lot we can do about it.'

Maxwell looked at the girl of the mixed metaphors. Her hair, a chestnut gold in the late lamps of the office, was still scraped back into the single thick plait. Her lipstick had all but gone — much of it, Maxwell noticed, was on the rim of a canteen coffee cup on her desk. Why did canteens the world over use that pale green stuff? But it was her eyes that gave away her exhaustion. Her eyes and the confession she'd just made, that the police didn't have the first bloody clue.

'I can understand that you're concerned,' she said, 'we all are, but please,' and she tried to save what face she could, to retain some vestige of professionalism, 'leave it to the experts.' She was on professional ground here at the nick, aware that the plywood and plaster walls had ears.

'Do you think they've eloped?' he asked her, ignoring the plea to keep his nose out. 'Gone north to Gretna Green?'

She shrugged. 'Bit old-fashioned that, isn't it?'

'Perhaps,' he agreed, 'but romantic.'

'You think they were having an affair, then?'

'It happens.' He remembered Jean Hagger's sudden hysteria that morning. 'Have you searched her flat?'

'Mr Maxwell, Ms Goode has been missing now for four days. She is an adult, and as far as we are aware, in full possession of her faculties. Despite what you may read in the papers, it is a free country. At the moment, we're more concerned for Ronnie Parsons. For the time being, Alice Goode will have to fend for herself. You've got people to cover her, haven't you? At the school, I mean?'

Maxwell turned pale and held his fingers in front of him in the shape of a cross. 'Supply teachers,' he said. Alien beings from another planet.' He was growling in his best William Conrad, 'They're here. At a school near you.'

She ignored him. Levity wasn't on her list of priorities tonight. 'Well, then,' she said, 'you can cope. Now, unless you have some more information on Ronnie . . .'

He stood up, knowing a lost battle when he saw one. 'No,' he said, and turned to go, 'but I'll have a little bet with you, Woman Policeman Carpenter. I'll lay you . . . oh, a fiver . . . that Ronnie Parsons comes home any day now, bringing his tail behind him. But Alice . . . well, I'm very much afraid

Alice doesn't live here any more.' He held up his hand. 'I'll see myself out,' he said.

* * *

Hamilton's Coaches weren't open on Sundays. Their drivers, by the end of April, were scattered to the corners of the country, driving little old ladies and gentlemen around southern country lanes, leafy already in the early spring. But Maxwell had struck lucky. He knew where they parked the coaches, on the old brewery site, and not only was there a vehicle parked there, in its distinctive red and white, but a driver had his head buried in the engine.

'Morning.' Maxwell tilted White Surrey's front wheel so that the machine stayed upright, with him straddling the crossbar, both feet on the ground.

'Hello.' The driver peered at him from under the bonnet.

'I'm looking for Dave,' Maxwell said.

'Well, now,' the driver wiped his grimy hands with a cloth, 'is that Dave Warwick or Dave Freeman?'

'Ah.' Maxwell grinned. Just his luck to have a choice. 'Fell at the first there, I'm afraid.'

'Well, who are you?' the driver asked.

'Peter Maxwell.' The Head of Sixth Form extended a hand. The driver wiped his on his grubby overalls and shook it. 'I'm from Leighford High.'

'Christ, mate,' the driver tutted, 'you have my condolences. Have a look at this.' He climbed into the coach, Maxwell parking White Surrey and clambering aboard too. The tenth seat back was punctured with the telltale brown-edged holes made by cigarettes. 'One of your little bastards did that,' the driver told him.

'What, on the London trip?' Maxwell asked.

'That's right; MOMI. I've been on to your Headmaster about it. Gave me the usual soft soap. He'd leave no stone unturned. Couldn't believe it was one of his kids. Usual crap.'

'You took the trip then?' Maxwell couldn't believe his luck.

'Yeah. Oh, I'm the second Dave, by the way: Dave Freeman.'

'Excellent. I rang your boss on Friday.'

'Yeah. Why?'

'Well, you know we've lost one of the staff and a sixth former?'

'Yeah,' Freeman sat down on the nearest seat, across the aisle from Maxwell who did likewise, 'that was very peculiar.'

'Was it?'

'Well, I don't know about your day, mate, but in mine we didn't have any women teachers. To be honest, I was astonished at the way he was talking to her.'

'Really? Why?'

'Well, taking liberties, you know. They were sitting behind me, over there. That other teacher and the sixth-form girl sat there, across the aisle. Course, you can't hear complete conversations, but I picked up the odd snippet here and there. Sounded to me like he was chatting her up. And the thing was, she was loving every minute of it. Wouldn't have done in my day.'

'Nor mine,' agreed Maxwell. 'Is that what you meant by peculiar?'

'Well, yes, that and the disappearing act. Mean, that other teacher lost them both in the museum, didn't she? By the time I come to get them, she was running around in circles. Damn near disappearing herself, up her own backside.'

Maxwell thought it best for the moment to laugh with the idiot. He might remember more in congenial company.

'It's like that film, isn't it?' Freeman went on. '*Picnic at Hanging Rock*. Did you ever see that?'

'Yes, I did.' Maxwell beamed. Could this be a kindred spirit, working for Hamilton's? 'One of my favourite films, in fact.'

'No, really?' Freeman laughed. 'Mine too. There's something mystic about it, isn't there? Something indefinable. Do you know, when I went to see that in the cinema, I just sat there at the end, riveted. I hadn't noticed everybody else filing out.'

'That's extraordinary,' Maxwell said. 'That's exactly what I did. Started getting funny looks from the usherette in the end. Where did you see it?'

'Er . . . Brighton. You?'

'Here in Leighford. Well, well, well.'

'Sort of fitting, really, isn't it?' Freeman said.

'What?'

'Well, a film like that, where people disappear on a school outing. And here we have people disappearing on an outing to a museum of film.'

'Know the museum well?' Maxwell asked.

Freeman shrugged, reaching into his overalls for a cigarette. 'Not really. Oh, I've been in once or twice; you know, with kids. Great place. I'm not too ashamed to admit I climbed inside the Dalek and made "Exterminate" noises.'

Maxwell extended his hand again, 'A chip off the old block,' he said, delightedly, 'I did exactly the same thing.'

'Bloody marvellous. Look, what's your favourite film; ever, I mean?'

'Er . . . oh, God.' Maxwell gnawed his lip. 'Difficult one, that. *Charge of the Light Brigade*, I think — the Tony Richardson version.'

'Yeah, brilliant,' Freeman enthused. 'One or two dodgy bits of direction though.'

'Charles Woods's dialogue made it for me.'

'Shame about the red trousers for the whole Brigade.'

'Mr Freeman,' Maxwell asked after a pause, 'you're not a wind-up, are you?'

'You what?' the driver looked confused.

'It's just that we've got an Ofsted Inspection coming up soon and I wondered if you were some sort of advanced guard sent ahead to catch me out.'

'No,' Freeman chuckled.

'Well, it's not many people know that only the 11th Hussars wore crimson overalls. Presumably, Richardson had them all dressed that way for reasons of cost.'

'Blimey!' Freeman stubbed his ciggie out on the floor. 'Overalls. I've got to get these hydraulics sorted this morning or I'll be an usherette by tomorrow' He stood up, 'Look, Mr Maxwell, I'm sorry I can't help with your little problem. If anything occurs, can I reach you?'

'You certainly can,' Maxwell said, 'I'm in the book. Oh, and by the way, I've got a better video collection than John Paul Getty, so if you ever want to come and share the one-and-nines with me . . .'

Freeman shook his hand again, 'You may have made me an offer there I am powerless to refuse,' he said.

* * *

As a kid, which essentially he still was, Peter Maxwell had always hated Sundays. It was the day his mother had done the washing, and he never popped his head out of the covers on a Sunday morning without smelling that starchy, ironing smell and hearing the thrub of thumbs on skiffle board. Those are the memories you have when your mother was Lonnie Donegan.

He heard the bells of St Olave's clanging somewhere beyond the neat lawns of the estate where the proverbial English were resolutely ignoring the call to prayer and starting on the important things like tinkering with their cars and watering their flowerbeds before Southern Water got serious with a hosepipe ban. Driest April since records began, they claimed. But they claimed this sort of thing like some people claimed benefits.

He spent the morning ploughing through the timed essays that the A-level historians had offered him rather as ancient man had given sacrifices to his gods. But there was no appeasing Mad Max, no dodging his thunderbolts. Just the deadly aim of his pen, circling bad grammar, unsplitting split infinitives, ridding the land of the ever-present apostrophe. And from these things there was no escape.

Lunch was a cheddar ploughman's at The Green Man, washed down with a pint of his host's best. Then back to Columbine Avenue, where most men of his age would doze over the Sunday papers or snore their way through the Sunday match. Peter Maxwell put on his video of *Picnic at Hanging Rock* and watched with growing fascination as the Pan pipes and sunlight played on those weird stones and the lovely, frothy girls who vanished among them. Ronnie Parsons had gone that way, drawn into the magic of MOMI, and Alice Goode had followed him. Or was it the other way round? They had vanished into the whirring spools, become invisible in the subliminal scenes.

He was just staring at the dead face of Rachel Roberts, lying in the shattered glass of the school conservatory, when the doorbell rang. He checked the clock. Half past four. Not likely to be a Jehovah's Witness. The last one had run away screaming after half an hour's diatribe from Mad Max. He put his slippers on and flopped downstairs from the living room. Through the distortion of his front door glass, he could make out a woman's shape.

'Woman Policeman Carpenter.' He bowed low as he held the door open to her.

'I wish you wouldn't call me that,' she said, glancing nervously from side to side, 'Jacquie. Call me Jacquie.'

All right . . . Jacquie,' said Maxwell. 'Is this a social call?' The girl was wearing jeans and a dark blouse, utterly unlike the office efficiency uniform she'd worn last night. Her hair reached her shoulders and there was a holdall in her hand. 'Should I get my piggy bank down for your collection for the police benevolent fund?'

Her eyes smouldered at him. 'Do you ever drop that irritating front of yours?' she asked.

'All right,' he said, the smile gone. 'Consider it dropped. What do you want, Jacquie? What are you doing here?'

'What am I doing here?' She found the second question easier to answer than the first. 'I'm putting my career on the line, that's what I'm doing here.'

Maxwell's smile was back, and broader and bigger than before. 'Well,' he said, 'in that case you'd better come in.'

CHAPTER 5

'From the beginning, then,' Jacquie Carpenter said, rummaging in the holdall that served as her handbag off duty. 'I shouldn't show you these. I shouldn't even tell you about them.'

'Would you like some tea?' Maxwell asked. It looked as though the girl needed something to steady her, some reassurance.

Jacquie looked at him. 'You haven't got anything stronger?' she asked.

'Well,' he smiled, 'I'm a Southern Comfort man, myself.'

'Fine,' she said and he clattered about in his drinks cabinet. 'You realise that what I'm about to tell you is absolutely confidential?'

Maxwell looked at her. 'Of course,' he said, 'inscrutability is my middle name. By the way, you'd better call me Max if we're going to be working together.'

'Who said anything about working together?' Jacquie sat upright.

'Nobody,' Maxwell beamed, swiftly, 'nobody at all.'

She snapped shut her file and stuffed it back into her bag. 'I can't do this,' she said and she stood up to go.

'Wait,' Maxwell was standing with her, 'if this was a movie, I'd stop you with a kiss now, wouldn't I? Cut to steamy sex scene.'

Jacquie Carpenter looked at him in an old-fashioned way. 'As this isn't a movie, try anything like that and you'll have an extra pair of tonsils, followed by a charge of assaulting a police officer.'

'Well, fine,' Maxwell smiled, 'I just like to know my parameters, you know — just in case.'

She stood there for a moment, facing him. Then she collapsed into giggles and sat down. 'All right.' She took the glass from him as he sat beside her. 'But you breathe a word about this to anyone and I'm finished.' Her smile had gone. 'Now let's get on with it before I change my mind again.'

'I'm sitting comfortably.' He sat back and raised his glass to her. 'You may begin.'

'Carly Drinkwater,' she said, 'a twenty-year-old student,' she placed a black and white photograph on Maxwell's coffee table, 'from the London School of Economics.'

Maxwell crossed himself. 'God save us,' he muttered. 'By the way, are these the things you shouldn't be showing me?'

She looked at him, out of touch with the depth of his academic snobbery, 'Yes. And He didn't save her. She was found dead on waste ground in Raines Park two years ago. She'd been raped and strangled.'

Maxwell looked at the dead girl, the clear eyes, the warm smile, the everything-to-live-for in her face.

'Unsolved,' Jacquie said. 'Incident Room closed down.'

'You mean, you've just given up?'

'I mean,' she told him, 'you can only do so much. The Met is the most public institution in the world. It's also one of the busiest forces in the world. Do you remember this case?'

'No.' Maxwell shrugged.

'Well, there you are. She was somebody's daughter, Max. She could have been yours.'

He looked at the photograph again and for a moment a little girl sat smiling back at him. His own little girl, Jenny, two and a half. Then there was a roar of screaming tyres and he wrenched himself back to the safety of the here and now.

'I expect you read about it in the papers,' Jacquie was saying, 'You saw it on the news. *Crimewatch* did a piece on it. But it was just another statistic, wasn't it? To you, to Joe Public. But to the blokes — and the women — who worked on this, it was more than that. Far more. You had to be there. To pick up the pieces of somebody's life. I've been to murder scenes like the one they found her in. It's not something I'd wish on my worst enemy. She'd have looked like a broken doll. Naked. Sodden with rain. The rats had already taken bits of her. And people ask why the police want the death penalty brought back.'

There was a silence. 'How do I feel?' Maxwell said at last.

'The investigating officers tried all the usual angles. There was a boyfriend, um . . .' she rummaged through her notes, 'a Kenneth Cassidy. They'd had a row.'

'Ah . . .'

'Apparently not.' She saw the way his mind was working and shook her head, 'He was eliminated. Watertight alibi. He was distraught, the report says. Either he was genuine or a bloody marvellous actor. The irony was, she'd gone off in a huff to the cinema immediately after their row. That was the last time he'd seen her.'

'He identified the body?'

'No. That's done by next of kin wherever possible. Her father did that. Didn't want to put his wife through it.'

'I don't really see . . .'

'That was March two years ago.' Jacquie produced a second photograph, 'This is June of last year. Georgianna Morris, twenty-three. What do you notice?'

Maxwell placed the girls' photographs side by side. 'My God,' he murmured, 'they could be sisters.'

'They could. And who do you suppose their third sister is?'

He blinked at her. Jacquie would have to help him. 'OK, so they've both got chestnut hair and their eyes are grey. You can't tell that from these photos. Fuller lips, perhaps . . .'

'Alice Goode,' he said, the penny dropping with a jarring clang.

'Alice Goode,' she nodded.

He grabbed her arm. 'Jacquie, that's brilliant. Absolutely brilliant. What a detective!'

'Yeah,' she grinned, 'tell me about it.'

'So,' his mind was racing now, 'what have we got? Three women what?' and he found himself dangling in mid-hypothesis, already twirling over an abyss that threw his unanswered questions back, like echoes in the night.

'Slow down,' she said, 'you're running before you can walk. Georgianna Morris was abducted from a cinema in Notting Hill. She's alive.'

'Alive?'

'But traumatised.'

'Oh.'

'She was found running in her underwear in a local park. She'd been slashed across the face and forearms, probably with a breadknife.'

'Sexual assault?'

'Attempted. We think the bastard was disturbed.'

'In all sorts of ways,' Maxwell agreed.

'Georgianna couldn't help apparently. The Met tried everything. We've got special officers trained in rape cases, shrinks who aren't associated with the police directly. They even tried the girl's priest — she was Catholic. Nothing. She couldn't remember anything. Not even the film she'd been to see.'

'Unsolved,' Maxwell said, gazing at Georgianna Morris through the ambered distortion of his glass.

'Unsolved.' She sat back.

'Even so,' Maxwell wasn't one to be defeated so easily, 'you're saying there's a pattern here. Two girls, presumably abducted from cinemas. A third — Alice Goode — from the Museum of the Moving Image. It all fits.'

'Nothing fits!' she slammed her file shut. 'Not in the eyes of my lords and masters, anyway.'

'Oh?'

'When you'd gone the other night, I did a bit of thinking. You were talking about Alice Goode and I was wrapped up in Ronnie Parsons. So I stood back from it all, saw it from another point of view. I did a bit of digging in the computer. Routine stuff, but I accessed these cases. I thought, what if Alice's disappearance wasn't the first one? Well, there was nothing else from the Museum, but I found these two from cinemas.'

'Look . . . er . . . this isn't some elaborate ploy, is it? I mean, I'm not in the frame, am I?'

'You were off sick on the day in question,' she told him. 'Flu. You had a temperature of 102.'

'Yes,' he said, slightly alarmed, 'yes, I was. How . . . ?'

'How did we know?' she smiled. 'It's our business to know. We talked to Deirdre Lessing who'd talked to Sylvia Matthews. And please don't think any the less of them. Casual conversations have taken men to the gallows before now. How do you know which university a kid should apply to? Or why the Russian Revolution started?'

'Sheer bloody brilliance, I suppose,' he beamed modestly. 'When I gave all this to the Chief Inspector, however, he wasn't impressed.

'Henry Hall?' Maxwell knew the man. 'Well, no, he wouldn't be.' Hall was a copper of the new school, University educated, bookish, careful. He and Peter Maxwell instinctively gave each other a wide berth.

'Why, he asked, has our man changed his MO? Carly was strangled. If Georgianna hadn't got lucky, she'd probably have been stabbed to death. And why switch to the Museum? Cinemas are so much easier. Dark, secret places with almost no security.' She sighed. 'Hall didn't buy it.'

'Well, I'm going to,' Maxwell said.

She looked at him. 'Good,' she said.

'Good?' he repeated. 'Woman Policeman Carpenter, do I detect a little trappette here?'

'Max,' she leaned towards him, 'I don't know if Alice Goode is alive or dead, but I didn't sleep last night. I don't know what it is about you. You have a way of . . . I don't know . . . You make people do the out-of-the-ordinary, the unexpected. But I can't get involved. Not officially. I can do some snooping around, some digging into the files. But that's all I can do. If my guv'nor says there's nothing in it, then there's nothing in it. Nobody likes a maverick in the police. It's by the book or not at all.'

'Why, Ma'am,' Maxwell delivered a devastating James Garner, 'Maverick's ma middle name. Now, if we're not going to have that steamy sex scene, let's go over all this again.'

* * *

Benny Pallister hadn't had the job long. He'd drifted from one waste of time to another, achieving nothing in particular, except a dedicated sense of aversion to hard work. His idea of a perfect life was lying on his bed at home watching endless videos, the nastier the better. But eventually, his mum had snapped and told him to get off his backside and down the Jobcentre. So here he was that morning as May broke, gazing out over the wild sweep of forest that was the Devil's Punchbowl. He saw the sun flash on the metal and glass of the traffic, already building up for the morning's helter-skelter along the A3. For all it was nearly summer, on his slope of the hill the sun had not yet reached and it was still chilly. He pulled his jacket closer round him and hauled the rubbish for the last trek across the car park. The ground fell away sharply to his left. He was just glad he wasn't still working for Sainsburys and having to wrestle with twenty trolleys at an angle like this. The green Mercedes was already there, parked under the patio where the braver diners downed their prawn cocktails and poire Helene of an evening. What a total shit Piers was, he thought again, as he did every time he saw the man or his car. Piers! What a poncy bloody name. And the bugger was mean. He toyed with slashing the bastard's tyres, except that the windows of the Ladle looked out over the car park and you never knew who was watching.

He stuffed the fag back in his mouth and whistled to himself as he reached the bins. Mechanically, he slid back the lid and emptied the black plastic bag.

'Oh, fuckin' hell,' he muttered to nobody in particular. Some bastard had dumped a roll of lino under the hedge. That was the problem with having a transport cafe next door. At least it wasn't used condoms or sanitary towels. Benny had had the lot in his three weeks working there. He glanced back at the French windows of the restaurant behind him.

'Bollocks!' he inhaled savagely. There he was, Piers the Bastard, staring out at him. Probably taking a break from counting his money. Piers didn't smile. He never smiled at anybody who didn't have a Range Rover or wasn't a member of Rotary. He just glared at Benny and nodded.

So it was that Benny Pallister stooped to manhandle the roll of lino. Then he stepped back. From the window, Piers Stewart saw the good-for-nothing reeling backwards as though he'd been shot. Worse, he saw him turn towards the green Mercedes and vomit explosively all over his tarmac. 'Jesus Christ,' the restaurateur muttered and stubbed his cigar out quickly in the nearest ashtray. That's what came of letting Wendy hire the casual labour. Say one thing for his wife, she was a fool for anything in a T-shirt. But a man's biceps did virtually nothing for Piers Stewart. This useless little shit Pallister would have to go. Chucking up all over the car park was just the last straw. He batted aside the French windows, dashed down the steps and crossed to the still-heaving labourer, leaning, pale and sweating against the oak step at the edge of the car park.

'What the bloody hell is going on?' Piers demanded to know.

'I'm sorry, Mr Stewart,' Benny gasped, 'It's . . . it's a woman.'

'What?' Piers looked at the shivering wreck in front of him. 'What is? What are you talking about?'

'There,' Benny wheezed, unable to trust his voice for long, 'in the lino.'

Piers took a step forward, gingerly kicking the lino with his Gucci toe. It fell back and a face was looking up at him, the colour of an old napkin, the eyes staring sightlessly into his. The tongue was protruding through teeth that were brown with blood and there was a deep purple line around the throat. Unable to look away, Piers let his eyes trail down the naked body. A pale slender arm lay modestly across the girl's small breasts, and as he looked it slid away to flop noiselessly on the tarmac.

'Jesus Christ,' Piers whispered. For a moment he was lost, confused. He didn't know where he was or what to do. Then the panic subsided and he was a restaurateur again. 'Get a grip on yourself,' he ordered. 'Cover her up for Christ's sake. We can be seen from the road. I'm going for the police.'

* * *

Piers Stewart had no reason to thank whoever it was who left a woman's body wrapped in lino on his restaurant car park. By mid-morning the whole area was cordoned off by fluttering tape — the thin blue line — and knots of policemen in and out of uniform stood chatting together. Benny Pallister was disappointed. He's just about got the sight of the dead girl out of his tiny mind and was starting to realise he'd be famous. There'd be press conferences, news programmes; he'd be on *Crimewatch* for sure and then of course, the Sunday papers would be after his life story as The Man Who Found The Body. In the meantime, though, there were no flashing blue lights, no car chases, no SWAT teams bristling with sidearms and riot gear. Just a single ambulance and two dull-looking blokes wandering in and out of the makeshift tent they'd put over the body.

The one dull-looking bloke was Detective Chief Inspector Henry Hall, of Leighford CID, thirty-something having given way to forty-something while his back was turned. His oppo was George Cainer, of the same rank, Surrey Constabulary.

‘Thanks for getting me in on this one, George,’ Hall said, ‘just what I need on a Monday morning.’

‘Sergeant of mine recognised the face,’ Cainer said. ‘That in itself is going to cost me. He already thinks he’s bloody Sherlock Holmes by way of Columbo. You know the sort.’

Hall did. He’d come up the soft way, people said, via university, but you didn’t get to be a DCI these days by hiding in the office. He knew the sort.

‘Right, Alan, give Mr Hall the benefit of your years of wisdom as Scene of Crime Officer.’

Alan was one of those people that look and sound terminally bored with life — a sort of depressed John Peel, though without the added trauma of being Liverpudlian. His white overalls made him look even pastier than he was. ‘I understand you know the young lady, sir?’ he said to Hall.

‘She’s Alice Goode,’ the Chief Inspector said. ‘She’s a teacher at a comprehensive in my manor.’

‘Well, I’d say she’s been dead for two or three days. The lab’ll confirm that, of course. I’d also say the cause of death was strangulation by ligature, although there are some superficial cuts to the forearms.’

‘She didn’t die here?’ Hall asked.

‘No, no. She was dumped in the lino several hours after death. I can’t find any blood on the lino at all. There’s no sign of any clothing.’

‘We know approximately what she was wearing when she went missing.’ Hall looked at the body-bag they’d put her in. ‘Looking for that lot won’t be easy. What are we looking at here? Sex as a motive?’

‘I’d say so,’ Alan nodded, checking his notes. ‘Again, the lab will confirm.’

‘George, do you mind if I have my man look at this one? Seeing that she’s from my turf.’

‘Be my guest,’ Cainer shrugged. ‘Frankly, Henry, I’d be delighted. My man’s up to his neck in it at the moment. He won’t shed any tears at losing this one. Who is your man, by the way?’

'Jim Astley,' Hall told him, 'a cantankerous bastard, but he knows his job.'

'Well,' winked Cainer, 'there's a rarity in the medical profession.'

* * *

There was a sign in Dr James Astley's laboratory that read 'You Don't Have To Be Morbid To Work Here But It Helps'. Every time he saw it, Henry Hall was convinced it was true. What genuinely sane person wanted to be rummaging about inside dead people all day? Still, it was a nasty job and somebody had to do it. That somebody in the Leighford/ Tottingleigh area was Jim Astley, the police surgeon.

'Strangulation by ligature.' He confirmed the initial findings of Cainer's Scene of Crimes man. 'Something unusual. Something with a straight edge.'

'A straight edge?' Hall didn't like to stand too close at moments like this.

'I tell you what it reminds me of,' — the doctor was quietly going about his business over the corpse of Alice Goode — 'those things kids use to draw graphs with, those bits of grey plastic; something like that. She put up a fight, though. Classic debris under the fingernails.'

'Can DNA help us there?'

Astley looked up under the green cap. 'Leave it out, Henry,' he chuckled, 'you've been reading Joseph Wambaugh again, haven't you? We can only check DNA if we get a match. You boys haven't got your compulsory genetic fingerprinting facility set up yet, have you? What with tapping phones like other people tap their fingers.'

'I'll get straight on to the Home Secretary about it,' Hall said. It was unusually flippant for him.

'We've got some semen that might be more useful, however. Per vagina, as we Latin scholars say.'

'Was that consensual intercourse, would you say?'

'I would not,' Astley peered closer with his magnifying lens, 'but we're also talking about several times. Probably after, as well as before, death.'

'Are we now? What about time of death?'

Astley stood up. His back was in half. 'Now, you're rushing me, Henry. You know I refuse to be drawn on these matters. When was the body found?'

'Yesterday. About seven a.m.'

'Monday. Hmm. I'd say she died on Wednesday, possibly early Thursday.'

'So her body had been kept somewhere, perhaps for a day' Hall was talking to himself. 'I'd give a substantial part of your salary to know where. Nothing out of the ordinary there, I suppose?'

'What, you mean telltale signs like an abattoir or paint spraying shop? No, I'm afraid not. How did the parents take it?'

'How do you think? The father's dead, the mother took some finding. The last she knew was that her daughter was at university; the next she's lying on a slab.'

'Ah,' said Astley ruefully, 'life's a bitch like that. A little bird told me she was on a school trip when she went missing.'

'That's right,' Hall confirmed. 'What I want to know is who she met there.'

'Ah well,' Astley smiled, 'the miracles of modern science can provide some of your answers, Chief Inspector. The rest of it's down to you coppers. Do you mind?' He was twisting the dead girl's neck to one side. 'You're in my light.'

* * *

'So, Geraldine,' Peter Maxwell's hypnotic gaze was searing through the recalcitrant little tart with attitude, 'let's see if I've got this right. Michael here called you a fat slag. Correct so far?'

'Yeah,' Geraldine scowled, glowering under her purple eyelids at her nemesis.

'Would you agree with that, Michael? Have I conveyed the sense of your remarks?'

'What?' You could see the strain in Michael's eyes.

'Is that what you said?' Maxwell made the boy's life easier for him.

'Yeah.'

'Good — if a little heartless, Michael, me ol' mucker. Geraldine doesn't have an ounce of fat on her from where I'm standing.' Where Maxwell was standing was at the front of his class, the indescribable 10D, they who had contributed to the early retirement of at least three members of staff at Leighford High and the incipient nervous breakdown of a fourth.

'So.' The class were rapt by the Great Man's delivery. Moments like these were pure joy. Not so much fun for Geraldine and Michael, however. 'At that point, Geraldine, suitably disquieted by Michael's momentary lapse of good manners, you did what any other genteel young lady would do — you fetched him a powerful kick to the bollocks . . .'

10D convulsed in hysterics.

'. . . from which he may never fully recover. What do you have to say for yourself?'

'He asked for it.'

'Of course he did,' Maxwell nodded sympathetically. 'He said, "Geraldine, please place your rather ugly, but probably fashionable, platform heeled boots into my genital area, as is your right in today's egalitarian society." And how could you, loyal colleague that you are, let him down?'

He took a careful hold on the girl's shoulder and placed her directly in front of him. For that alone, at this pinko-liberal end of the century, Peter Maxwell knew he could be done for assault. Geraldine knew it too, because all children born since 1979, the Year of the Child, had it ingrained in them by their parents that life was all about rights. Responsibilities? Nah, they used to have them in the olden times; not now.

'Now, Geraldine, in the good old days, I would have put you over my knee and spanked you soundly.'

'You can't do that!' the sullen girl blurted out.

'Indeed not,' Maxwell smiled. 'Thanks to the Court of Idiot Rights. I would then have taken you, Michael,' and he placed the boy in front of him too, 'out behind the bicycle shed and given you the thrashing you both deserve, probably with a rattan cane of fearsome dimensions.'

'You wouldn't . . .' Lads were less sure of themselves with male teachers than were girls.

'No, I wouldn't,' Maxwell reassured him, smiling broadly. 'No cane. So, instead, I'll just pop you both in detention, giving you of course the statutory twenty-four hours' notice. And that nice Mr Garrett, the Deputy Headmaster from hell, will give you a jolly good letting off.'

There was a knock at the door and Thingee, the office junior who was on the switchboard, stood there.

'Now, sit down,' Maxwell barked, Mr Nice Guy having disappeared, 'at opposite ends of the room. And any more of this nonsense and I'll put my career on the line and knock you two into the middle of next week.' He leaned and bellowed into the lad's ear. 'Got it, Einstein?'

The boy winced and made a dash for his chair. As she saw the Maxwellian lip poise to assault her eardrums too, the girl did the same.

'Now, Thingee,' Maxwell turned with a satisfied sigh, 'while the class continues to practise their GNVQ in joined-up writing for the remaining two minutes, to what do I owe the pleasure?'

'Oh, Mr Maxwell, I'm sorry to interrupt your lesson.'

'Not at all,' the Head of Sixth Form bowed, 'I am honoured that you should give it the title of lesson. I'd say it was closer to a saloon brawl.'

'It's just that there's an urgent 'phone call, from a Miss Carpenter. She sounded anxious. I didn't just want to pop it in your pigeonhole.'

'Quite right, my dear.' Maxwell took the slip of paper from the slip of a girl. 'Remind me to see the Headmaster about promoting you.'

* * *

'Jacquie?' Maxwell could be as conspiratorial as Cassius when he had a mind. And today was only Tuesday. He still had a mind left in the early part of the week. 'I'm sorry I couldn't get back to you straight away. Thirty little swine eager to catch my pearls. What's up?'

'It's Alice,' he heard the voice say on a bad line, breaking up, 'it's Alice Goode. They've found her. Can we meet?'

* * *

Theirs was the only car parked on the edge of the park known as The Dam that May night. Other couples hadn't arrived yet, except for the pair whose respective parents had said they had to be in by ten. They'd been and gone.

Peter Maxwell wasn't there for adolescent fumblings. He'd been there and done that. In different cars, different times. And for more years than he cared to remember he'd been fumbling at the chalk face with adolescents ever since. Only in the strictly professional sense, of course.

'I'm only telling you this because it's going to hit the fan tomorrow anyway. Christ, why do I feel so guilty?' Jacquie Carpenter looked softer in the moonlight, younger, less harrowed by her world.

'Where was she?'

'They found her dumped in the car park of a restaurant — The Devil's Ladle at the Devil's Punchbowl, near Hindhead. Do you know it?'

'I know the Punchbowl,' he nodded. 'Not the restaurant.'

'It's likely she was dumped in the early hours of Monday morning. Nobody seems to have seen the bundle there before that.'

'Bundle?'

'She was wrapped in lino.'

'Wow!' Maxwell's eyes widened.

'What?'

'Well, that establishes quite a bit.'

'Does it? Why?' She looked at the inscrutable old History Man through narrowed eyes.

'Well, I thought lino had disappeared along with bags of blue for washing and planes going bang through the sound barrier. It at least proves chummie is an elderly gentleman.'

'They still make lino,' Jacquie told him, 'and anyway, this wasn't new stuff. It could have come from anywhere.'

Maxwell had been saving the next question up, but he couldn't save it any longer. 'How did she die?' He was looking at the dashboard. When you asked one young girl how another young girl was murdered, you didn't look her in the face. Not happily. Not if you were Mad Max.

Jacquie Carpenter's professional life flashed before her. The Pinko-Liberal Brigade never saw it, but there were ethics in her job. The lads knew. The lads who stood by you when you told a mother her son was dead, smashed to pulp by a joyriders' car; or when you told a weeping father that his little girl had overdosed on E. But Peter Maxwell wasn't one of them. 'She was strangled, Max,' she heard herself saying nevertheless, as though in a nightmare of betrayal. What was she doing here? Why was she telling him all this? 'Doc Astley seems to think it's one of those things kids draw graphs with.'

'A flexicurve. Bit short, isn't it?' Maxwell frowned.

'Not if he pressed down on both sides. That would do it.'

'Had she been assaulted?'

'Yes.'

She couldn't say any more. Wouldn't say any more. He didn't ask her.

They sat for a moment, both of them staring ahead. 'Max,' she spoke first, watching the moon dapple on the line of silver birches that ringed the car park, 'it'll be a circus at Leighford tomorrow. Mr Hall will be on to your Head first thing in the morning, but you know what the media are like.'

'I do.' Maxwell nodded. 'We've been this way before, Jacquie, when Jenny Hyde was found.'

'Yes, I know.'

'Is there news of Ronnie?' he asked, 'Any hint?'

Her eyes flickered away from his, 'No,' she said, 'nothing concrete.'

'Concrete is grey stuff,' he told her, 'that they make buildings from. Oops, pardon my preposition. You're being evasive, Woman Policeman Carpenter.'

She sighed. 'You know,' she said, looking at him for the first time, 'the Gestapo missed a real gem when they didn't hire you.'

'Ha ha,' he chuckled, 'so Heinrich told me. What is it you're not telling me?'

Her fingers rapped a furious tattoo on the steering wheel. She was in a corner again. A corner of her own making. And there was no way out. 'What . . . what I am telling you is that the boys went round to the Parsons again last night. They specifically asked Ronnie's mum about his flexicurve. She said he had one, but she didn't know where it was.'

'That's it?' Maxwell had waited the regulation five seconds for an explanation, 'I'm not sure I could tell you where my Pink Panther boxer shorts are, either, if you pressed me. But that doesn't mean I've left them draped round the neck of a woman I've just strangled.'

'It's not just that,' Jacquie started up the engine which roared into life. 'I've told you this bloody much. I may as well tell you the rest. It's a letter. They found a bloody letter.'

* * *

A letter, Count,' Maxwell sat with his feet on the pouffe. Metternich raised his aristocratic head, scenting the air, scenting danger. 'To be exact "a bloody letter". What bloody letter is that, I hear you ask, cleverly parodying the Bard? I haven't the faintest idea, since Woman Policeman Carpenter got a fit of the consciences at that point and clammed up. Must be difficult for her, though, involving me like she is. I wonder why she's doing that? I tried every trick in and out of the Maxwell Book of How To Charm Slightly Unprofessional

Policewomen, but she wasn't having any. Perhaps it's just as well. I wouldn't want her to be landed in it. So that means . . . no, don't interrupt . . . Daddy's thinking. That means that after that bloody interminable staff meeting tomorrow pip emma, White Surrey and I will be nipping round to the Parsonage. After all, they can only slam the door in my face.'

CHAPTER 6

'The Parsonage' as Maxwell called it, was actually a semi-called 'Rondo'. It wasn't named after a piece of music, but after Ronald and Dorothy Parsons, who with their offspring, had lived in the dull-looking stuccoed semi for nearly ten years. You'd think a builder would have a bit more imagination.

Maxwell had dozed for at least half of the staff meeting. It was the bi-annual financial report and the silly old fart who in a public school would be called a bursar, had droned on about this balance and that deficit until the Lethe had rolled over Mad Max and he'd fallen fast asleep.

Nothing else had happened. There was no line of obnoxious newshounds at Leighford's front gate, anxious to interview the Headmaster, to harass some unprepared and unsuspecting kid into a reaction to the news that their favourite teacher had been murdered. And Legs Diamond seemed the same boring, plodding ineffective he always was. If he'd received a call from DCI Hall that one of his staff had been found dead, he was being pretty cool about it. Maxwell wasn't. All day, the face of Alice Goode, strangled, cold, dead, swam in his vision. In the lunch queue, he thought he saw her and again crossing the quad. Like the ghostly wife of William Wallace in Mel Gibson's Braveheart, she probably glided past him a dozen times that day. But the key still dangled in her locker where she'd left it and her name had not been removed from her pigeonhole in the staffroom. Of the thousand souls who thronged through the corridors of Leighford High, each on his way to the stars, only Mad Max knew the girl was dead. It was the loneliest feeling in the world.

A little girl answered the door marked 'Rondo'. This was Sonya Parsons and her mum weren't in. Where was she? Up Tesco's. When would she be back? Dunno. Sonya was of the generation told never to talk to strange men — and they didn't come much stranger than Mad Max. Only her left eye peered round the door jamb, only her left hand clutched it nervously. Her big brother had gone. Her mum spent her nights crying. Only her dad didn't seem to care.

So, up Tesco's it was. Out of town shopping had come a long way since Stanley Cohen had trundled his barrow in the Old Kent Road of a Sunday. Maxwell parked White Surrey near the sliding doors and lashed the machine to the frame that held the trolleys, just in case. Well, a funny lot shopped in Tesco's these days — you couldn't be too careful. Dorothy Parsons wasn't on any of the checkouts. Perhaps she'd been demoted? Perhaps she was packing shelves, along it seemed, with half of Leighford High. How different they looked, Maxwell observed for the umpteenth time, in their white hats on the fish counter and their polythened fingers hacking and probing through the delicious array of cheeses. Kids who last year had been flicking paper pellets and vying with each other to see who could gob furthest down the school stairwell, were now model members of corporate Britain, where the customer was always right. Only the pieces of bright blue tape on their ear lobes bore faint testimony to the fact that they wore earrings. Half the girls probably had bright blue tape on their navels too.

He fought his way past the queue of hopefuls and compulsive gamblers who waited patiently in the lottery line for the winning-ticket-that-would-change-their-lives-for-ever, and sat himself down in the cafe over a hot chocolate and

Danish. From here, he could see the tills in both directions. So he sipped and supped and waited.

Dorothy Parsons came back from her tea break around six. Maxwell helped himself to a bottle of Southern Comfort and something indescribable of the Vindaloo variety and headed for the till.

'It's quicker down the end, sir.' A helpful supervisor motioned the two-item customer in the direction of those with nine items or less.

'Thank you.' Maxwell beamed at her, but made absolutely no effort to move.

'Do you have a Clubcard?' Dorothy Parsons had not looked up. After all her years chained to the till, all customers looked alike.

'I'm afraid not,' Maxwell said, then he leaned over the plastic screen. 'Mrs Parsons, I need to talk to you.'

It was then that she looked up. She seemed years older than Maxwell remembered her from only days ago. Her eyes flickered for a moment. 'Mr Maxwell,' she said.

'Do you have any news?'

An elderly woman behind him was already unloading her tins of doggie-goo on the checkout.

'About Ronnie,' he urged the till operator, 'any news?'

She shook her head. Two toddlers from the next checkout had spilt over into Maxwell's and they decided to wrestle with each other inches from his kneecaps, shrieking and laughing.

'No,' he heard her say flatly over the noise. 'No, nothing.'

"The police,' he moved as far as he could to get out of the toddlers' way, 'they've been to see you.' It was a statement, not a question.

'Yes,' she nodded, sliding his purchases down the conveyor belt. He struggled with the carrier bag, he, who had no life skills at all when it came to separating pieces of polythene.

'What . . .' he carefully edged his way past the squabbling, hysterical children, 'what did they say?'

She glanced at the stone-faced woman, who seemed to have amassed enough dog-food to survive the millennium. 'That'll be eighteen pounds thirty-four, please,' Dorothy said.

Maxwell fumbled for his wallet. 'What time do you get off duty?' he asked. 'I must talk to you.'

'Look here' — the dog-food woman had had enough — 'I don't expect to have to wait while you two arrange some clandestine liaison.'

Maxwell turned. 'Tell me,' he asked sweetly, surveying the old crone's purchases, 'do you have that on toast?' He turned back to Dorothy Parsons, 'What time?'

'Nine,' she said, 'when the store closes. But . . .'

'What?'

She gave him his change and the receipt, 'Well, Ron, my husband . . . comes to pick me up.'

'Disgusting,' the dog-lady hissed.

'I'll be waiting.' Maxwell took up his shopping. 'Madam,' he turned to the daffy thing at the next checkout, wrestling with her carrier bags and talking hairstyles to her till operator, 'are these delightful children yours?'

The daffy thing frowned at him. Some old pervert wearing a bow tie and asking about her kids? Something unnatural here, 'Jason,' she bawled at one, 'Shane.' They ignored her completely, so Maxwell batted them aside with his carrier bag.

'Yes,' he smiled, 'what charming names. How did I guess that's what they'd be called? How old are they?'

'Jase is four and Shane's two and a half. Why?' The daffy thing was even more suspicious now. Well, you heard such things, didn't you? About them paedophile rings and so on.

'Oh good,' Maxwell smiled, 'by the time they're eleven, I'll have taken early retirement.' He raised his hat. 'Good afternoon.' And he was gone.

* * *

The car park had thinned out by nine. Only one or two vehicles still waited under the twilight sky. This was as downtown as Leighford got, scruffy Victorian buildings with peeling paint and boarded-up windows. The kiddies' playground was locked and deserted and only the odd, stray gull winged its way overhead, crying into the distant darkness far out to sea. The season had not bitten at Leighford yet. The great British public were waiting to see which way the weather jumped before they made their final holiday choice — Leighford or Lanzarote; what a facer!

'Evening, Dee for Douglas.' A sandy-haired man with a freckled face got out of his Mondeo.

Douglas was older, waistline widening, hairline retreating. 'Jonathan,' he nodded.

'What is it tonight?' Jonathan asked. 'Cynthia was getting a little inquisitive. I had to burn my programme.'

'I've got it billed as *Desert Death*,'' Douglas told him. 'It'll have to go some to beat last month's.'

'Little corker, wasn't she?' Jonathan smirked. 'What an arse.'

And they made their way through the back streets to that green door marked 'film club'.

* * *

A battered black Capri, on its way to becoming a classic car, crunched its way onto the Tesco forecourt. Maxwell had parked himself on a trolley rail for the last quarter of an hour. It was chilly now as the lights went out all over Tesco's and night came to Leighford. He pulled his jacket round him and kept faithful watch on the staff entrance, all feeling gone from his bum.

A jolly woman with scraped-back hair came clattering out and with her was Dorothy Parsons. Maxwell hopped off his perch and swooped on his prey.

'Mrs Parsons,' he lifted the shapeless tweed hat.

'Oh, Mr Maxwell . . . See you tomorrow, Ellen.'

'Yeah, tara!' Ellen, the jolly woman called, looking Maxwell up and down so that she could commit him to memory for tomorrow's gossip in the staff canteen.

'The police . . .' Maxwell said.

Ellen lingered a little longer, taking her time to get away. The gossip would be juicier than she hoped. But the horn on the Capri was insistent and she had to go.

'All right!' she bellowed as the security manager rattled his locks behind her. 'Keep your bloody hair on!'

Dorothy scanned the car park. No beige van. She'd have to wait. 'Look, Mr Maxwell,' she looked up at her son's teacher, 'I told the police I can't help. I just don't know nothing. Ronald and me, we're worried sick, that's all.'

'The police found something,' Maxwell said. 'A letter. What was all that about?'

Dorothy Parsons looked away again. Where was he? When would her Ronald come? He was already ten minutes late.

'Some letter,' she flustered, 'some stupid thing. I don't know what it was. He'd written that teacher a letter. There wasn't nothing in it, Mr Maxwell. You know Ronnie. He wouldn't hurt a fly.'

Not a fly, no. But Alice Goode was dead and Dorothy Parsons didn't know that. 'Did you see the letter, Mrs Parsons?' Maxwell asked. 'Do you know what was in it?'

'Dot.' She jumped at the sound of her own name. Ronald Parsons stood behind her, the van keys in his hand, his dark eyes narrowed in Maxwell's direction.

'Oh, Ron,' she whined, 'where were you?'

'I parked round the back,' he said. 'What's up, Dorothy? What's the matter?'

'Nothing, Ron,' she said quietly, taking her husband by his thickset arm. 'I thought you'd be here early tonight.'

Ron hadn't taken his eyes off Maxwell. 'Mr Maxwell.'

'Mr Parsons,' Maxwell nodded back at him. If this was downtown Chicago, Ronald Parsons would have passed for a Goodfella, with his slim moustache and his wardrobe-sized shoulders.

'Thanks for waiting with my wife,' Parsons said, 'There's some funny people about these days, isn't there? It's good to know she's in safe hands.' And he hustled Dorothy around the corner to the beige van tucked away out of sight.

* * *

'How did you get this number?' Jacquie Carpenter snapped angrily.

'I keep my nose to the wheel and my flies open,' Maxwell said. 'What — if you'll excuse the vernacular — the shit is going on?'

'What do you mean?'

Maxwell sat down heavily on his bottom stair. 'Woman Policeman Carpenter, did you or did you not tell me only yesterday that your Metropolitan colleagues had found Alice Goode's body?'

'That's right,' she confirmed.

'And did you not say that your boss was due to speak unto my boss on that very same revelation?'

'Well, yes, I . . .'

'Well, why hasn't he? I know Legs Diamond. He couldn't keep a secret if his life depended on it. There was no such call.'

'I know!' she shouted.

He held the receiver away from his eardrum.

'Look,' she'd regained whatever composure she had left and was back on track again, 'I can't be held responsible. I shouldn't have told you anything in the first place. For whatever reason, the DCI had held the story back.'

'I know,' he said, 'I've just seen the non-item on the local news. Chap called Cainer posing outside a nick I've never seen, saying, in effect, "Mind your own business".'

'They have their reasons,' Jacquie told him.

'Oh, great!'

'Max!' she bellowed. It wasn't like Jacquie Carpenter, but she'd compromised herself. Her job was on the line and all the time she felt the train was getting closer. It frightened her. She'd never done anything like this before. Never broken rules or her word. And now, here she was, in over her head, with panic at her elbow.

It was his turn to calm down. 'Tell me about the letter.'

There was a pause. 'I can't.'

'Ronnie is in trouble,' Max reminded the detective.

'Exactly,' her voice was cold, different, official. 'In more trouble than you know. Now, Max, please, for my sake, for Ronnie's sake, for yours, I'm asking you to stay out of this. Please don't call this number again.'

And the line went dead.

Maxwell looked at his cat. 'First she's in,' he said to the animal, 'then she's out. Now she's shaking it all about. It looked suspiciously to me, Count, as if Woman Policeman Carpenter's losing it.'

Metternich yawned ostentatiously. He could have told his master, had man-animal communications improved over the last seven million years, that that was women for you. Maxwell would have to try another tack.

* * *

Exactly how long Sylvia Matthews had loved Peter Maxwell, she couldn't say. It wasn't something she'd scrawled in graffiti paint across the bike sheds or carved with her Girl Guide penknife into the bark of the sweetheart tree. It was just a feeling she had, every time she saw him in the corridor, heard his voice booming through the hall, caught the wind as he rattled past her on White Surrey, pedalling north. Every time, she felt her stomach tighten and her heart loop. Then she'd mentally shake herself free of it, of him. How stupid, Sylvia, she'd say to herself; you're old enough to know better, dammit. You'll never see forty again. Nor come to think of it, forty-five. Now, pull yourself together and get back on that shelf, where you belong.

So when his barbed-wire hair appeared around her office door that Wednesday afternoon, a little after lunch, followed almost immediately by his smiling face, she felt it all happening all over again. As if she wanted to run home and say 'Mummy, Mummy, he did it. He smiled at me. He talked to me.'

But Emma Dollery was having her period pains again and sat sullenly against Sylvia's office wall, blaming the world in general and 'that horrible Mr Ryan' in particular. As Sylvia had pointed out to the girl, the Second Deputy may have his faults, but gynaecological irritations were not among them. Emma had just fled from a particularly bad lesson with Mr Ryan. She was unconvinced.

'Ah, Matron mine,' Maxwell beamed. 'Care to go for a drive this afternoon?'

Emma Dollery's eyes widened. Wait till the girls back in 9S heard this.

'Er. . .' Matron flashed an old-fashioned look in her direction.

'The History Department are taking a drive up to that archaeological dig on the Rimble. Care to come along? Apparently the pot-sherds are exquisitely interesting. Samian ware to die for.'

'Of course.' Sylvia was quicker on the uptake, hopefully, than was Emma. 'What time?'

'Well,' Maxwell checked his watch, 'we were hoping for four-thirtyish. I've just some sixth-form heads to crack together first. Car park?'

'Er . . . yes,' Sylvia said. 'Car park it is.'

And Maxwell beamed at Emma. She scowled at him. That bloke was barmy. He'd never taught her, but that didn't matter. Why let a thing like personal experience stand in the way of a pupil's misconception of a teacher?

* * *

'It was actually Mrs B's idea,' Maxwell said to Sylvia as she rattled her way up through the gears.

'Oh?' Sylvia wasn't buying it. Mrs B. 'did' for Maxwell as well as cleaning at the school. Salt of the earth was Mrs B., but ideas were not exactly her stock in trade.

'Well . . . now, Sylv, don't look at me like that.'

'Like what?' she chuckled, checking the main road as she pulled out of the school gates.

'As if I've done a murder. Somebody has and it isn't me.'

'Max — look, I don't mind in the slightest driving you a few miles, but where are we going?'

'Did you see the news last night; local?'

'Er . . . yes, I think so,' she said.

'What was the first item? It got a small mention on the national too, sandwiched between All-Party talks for Northern Ireland and the Rhode Island Red in Garboldisham that can dance the rhumba.'

'Oh, God,' she covered her mouth, 'I'm sorry, I can't remember.'

'Quite,' Maxwell clasped his hands across his seat belt, 'which is precisely why the media revolution has failed. The bastards bring us so much news into our own living rooms, every half-hour, on the half-hour, that we don't remember a word of it. They've found the body of a woman.'

'Oh, yes,' Sylvia remembered now.

'Alice Goode. Left here.'

The Subaru left the road for a moment and careered along the verge, until Sylvia wrestled the wheel back and slammed on the brakes.

'What?' She sat looking at him, wide-eyed and open-mouthed.

'Oh, Sylv.' He put his arm around her, steadying her, lifting her chin as it dropped. 'What kind of fool am I?' It wasn't the best Norman Wisdom she'd ever heard. 'I'm sorry,' he said. 'I've known for nearly forty-eight hours now. Familiarity breeds contempt.'

'Alice?' she repeated.

'Yes. Look, I'm so sorry, that was dreadful. I shouldn't have blurted it out like that. The news didn't give the name, did it? I wanted to choose my time. I . . . oh, shit!' and he thumped the dashboard.

'No,' she said, her knuckles still white on the wheel, the engine idling. 'No, it's all right. It's just . . . well, I didn't know.'

'I know' He took her in his arms, seat-belt allowing, and kissed her forehead. For a moment her face came up to his and their eyes locked. Then there was a blast from a passing motorist and a car screamed past, yobboes hanging out, thrusting fingers skywards.

'That'll be the Scholarship Sixth,' mused Maxwell, 'on their way to debating society. Sylv, I'm a complete arsehole. I've got you here under false pretences.'

The beginnings of a smile played around her lips. 'I don't think even Emma believed your archaeological dig story, Max.'

'No,' he sighed. 'Not one of my most inspired. However, here we are.'

'We're going there, aren't we?' she asked him. 'Where they found her?'

'No, Sylv,' he said softly. 'Not if you don't want to.'

She slammed the car into gear, straightening her rear-view mirror.

'You know,' she said, sniffing back what might have been hay fever, might have been tears, 'you're right, you are an arsehole,' and she drove off the kerb and went north.

'What do you mean, by the way,' she said, after a while. 'Mrs B.'s idea?'

'Well, you know Tuesday is the night she does for me?'

Sylvia nodded. Mrs B., full name unknown, a tall, angular woman, who may have been ITMA's original Mrs Mopp were she not too old, may have had a heart of gold, but her mouth was pure sewer.

'Well, she'd seen the item at six. "What abaht that woman, then, Mr Maxwell?" she said to me, "The one they found in that lino? Me and Mr B.'s got some just like it. *And* I've eaten at that restaurant too, that Devil's Label. They do a bleedin' beautiful plaice and chips there, they do. Fancy, having been to the scene of a murder." Well,' Maxwell was himself again, 'perhaps "fancy" is the wrong word, but I had a feeling, a sense I ought to be there.'

'But how do you know, Max?' Sylvia asked him. 'There was no mention of a name on the telly last night. How do you know it's Alice?'

'I can't tell you that, Sylv,' he said. 'Let's just let it be our little secret for a while, hmm?'

* * *

Maxwell was buying. It wasn't quite the weather for eating on the patio and Sylvia was grateful for that. She wasn't sure she could eat much anyway, knowing what she now knew; but to eat at all overlooking the spot where the dead woman had been found would require all her sangfroid. Piers Stewart, all DJ and prosperity, had put them in Nookie Corner, as he pleased to call it, irrespective of any embarrassment he might cause his customers by seating them there.

'Mr Stewart.' Maxwell hailed him as he tackled his coffee. The place was fairly empty as yet and the restaurateur seemed to be free enough.

'Sir?' The word stuck in Piers Stewart's throat every time he heard himself saying it. He had yet to meet any one of his customers who was on the same intellectual and social level as he himself.

'I'm making enquiries into the death of Alice Goode. Can we talk?'

The restaurateur looked about him, then he leaned over Maxwell's table. 'Are you the police?' he asked.

'No, I was a colleague of the dead woman.'

'A colleague?' Stewart's face had contempt written all over it. 'You mean you're a pimp?'

Sylvia looked as startled as Maxwell. 'I beg your pardon?'

Stewart looked around him before scraping a chair back and sitting down with them. 'Look, I've had the law swarming over this place for the last three days. This Alice Goode was some sort of tart. God knows what riff-raff she knew. Now I'd be very grateful if you'd finish up your meal and go.'

'She was an English teacher,' Maxwell said steadily, 'with a subsidiary in French. I think you've been misinformed, Mr . . . er . . . Stewart.' Maxwell had read the sign over the door.

The restaurateur looked at the couple before him. Clients, he guessed, of Alice Goode. Middle-aged swingers still trying to pull the birds. He could just imagine the ads they placed in the Contact mags — 'She, forty-something, good body. Likes adventure. He, hung like a mule. Travel anywhere'. Stewart stood up. 'I have a choice who I serve,' he said loudly and, as if from nowhere, two heavies stood at his elbow. 'This gentleman and his wife were just leaving,' he said.

Maxwell didn't like the look of either of the waiters, so he lifted Sylvia gently by the arm. 'You'll forgive me,' he said, 'if under the circumstances I don't leave a tip.' And he led her to the door. 'Just as well he doesn't recognise me, isn't it, Mrs Ronay?' he said loudly as dining couples turned to stare. They saw themselves out.

* * *

Maxwell broke into the Headmaster's study the next day. Well, no, that phrase needs qualification. Legs Diamond wasn't a headmaster; he was a headteacher and there was a world of difference. And he didn't have a study; he had an office. And breaking in? Well, not really. Maxwell merely waited until the man had gone to some out-of-school management meeting, then he'd knocked boldly and gone in. The key was in the Head's top drawer, unlike the Head himself. Maxwell lifted it with the ease of the Artful Dodger and rummaged in the filing cabinet that he knew contained the confidential staff files.

Jacquie Carpenter had had an attack of professionals or the consciences — he couldn't be sure which. So he was on his own now, Maxwell PI, a gumshoe down on his luck, a dick in several senses of the word. He found her file, the one marked Alice Goode. First post, bla, bla. Goldsmith's. Oh dear. Second-class degree. Specialised in Philip Larkin. Jesus! It just got worse. PGCE from the London Institute. Glowing references from a school in Essex, another in Kent.

They farmed them far and wide did the London Institute. No home address. No next of kin.

'Who mourns for Adonais?' Maxwell murmured to himself. Then he heard the door click. But the Head of Sixth Form was faster. Years of turning tight corners to catch smokers had given him the edge. The file was away, the cabinet locked and the key returned before Margaret, Legs' secretary, stood there staring at him.

'Maggie, thank God!' Maxwell rushed to her side, gripping her shoulders warmly. 'A beacon in the darkness as always. You haven't seen the Head's copy of the Deering report, have you? I seem to have misplaced mine.'

* * *

It was on Thursday that DCI Henry Hall decided to unburden himself to the world. A quick phone call to Jim Diamond and a press conference hard on the heels of that did the job effectively. The body in the lino on the car park had a name at last. The paparazzi gathered at the gates of Leighford High and laid siege to Alice Goode's flat where a distraught Jean Hagger came home from junior school to be hit with the news right between the eyes.

At Leighford High, there was a whole school assembly. Only the Sports Hall was big enough to hold the huddled masses of a big comprehensive and Peter Maxwell stood at the back while Bernard Ryan attempted to assert what authority he felt he had to bring the multitude to order. They paid about as much attention to him as to a woodlouse and in the end, Maxwell took pity on him and took up Ryan's position at the front of the Hall where the PA system had been hastily set up by the Drama Department.

'Allrighteethen.' He gave the entire school his best Jim Carrey as Ace Ventura and the chattering stopped. 'Ladies and gentlemen' — the Head of Sixth Form was giving them his best Peter Maxwell now — 'we have some rather sad and some rather serious news. Mr Diamond?'

Maxwell had never seen Diamond perform better. He told the school that Miss Goode was dead. He told them the police were treating her death as suspicious. He told them all to talk to no one except the police. And if the police asked to talk to them, they must have their parents present at the interview. There was silence in that Hall where the trampolines bounced and the shuttlecocks flew. Diamond saw the odd lips quiver on the faces of some Year Seven girls sitting cross-legged in front of him.

'Mr Ryan, please dismiss the school row by row. The buses will be waiting. Duty staff to accompany them, please. Mr Maxwell,' he turned to his Head of Sixth Form and waited until they'd both slipped out of the side door. 'Is it me or is the Leighford grapevine working extra well today?'

'Headmaster?' Maxwell was a genius at the evasive line, the hurt look. It wasn't like Diamond to be so on the ball.

'"Some rather sad and some rather serious news" I think you said. You knew, Max. You knew about Alice before I told you. Only Roger and Bernard knew. How did you know?'

Maxwell folded his arms languidly. The day he'd be fazed by anything Legs Diamond did, hell would freeze over. 'I have a degree, Headmaster,' he said. 'First Class Honours from Cambridge University. That gives me an MA which is, in effect, a licence to think. One of my colleagues, a pretty young girl, goes missing on a school trip and no one hears from her for nearly a week. Then the police find a body not many miles to the north. The body of a young girl. You call a whole school assembly at the wrong end of a routine day. Now pardon me all to hell if I make the odd deduction.'

Diamond looked a little shamefaced. 'I see.' He shifted a little, clearing his throat under Maxwell's steady barrage and Maxwell's steady gaze. 'Right. Well, thanks, Max.'

'What did the police say?' the Head of Sixth Form asked.

Diamond shrugged. 'Not a lot,' he said. 'They're coming over shortly. Chief Inspector Hall.'

He nodded at Maxwell as the clatter of doors announced that the kids had gone. Why my school? he thought to himself. Why me? Maxwell went back into the Sports Hall where knots of his colleagues still stood in stunned tableaux around the room. He picked up a stray piece of chewing-gum wrapper on his way out.

CHAPTER 7

That Friday, Peter Maxwell played hookey for the first time in his life. He rather enjoyed it, in fact, pedalling past the science labs where rows of children were dying of terminal boredom, wrestling with the complexities of the latent heat of fusion of ice or grappling with the various coefficients of linear expansion. God, what a waste of precious time when there was so much they didn't know about that magic land, the past.

At home, he swapped his cycle clips for a pair of corduroys, threw a few things together and popped a note through old Mrs Troubridge's door next to his, asking the old trout to feed Metternich for the weekend as he'd been called away. By just after four, he was standing in the rather tatty foyer of the London Institute, looking for someone, anyone, who might be able to help. Knots of education students, some shell-shocked and shaking after a week's teaching practice, hurried past him to the nearest pub. A whistling cleaner directed him to the Students' Union on the first floor.

Grubby posters about Saving the Unborn Gay Whale flapped in the breeze of an open window. Above the hum of a photocopier, Maxwell called to its operator, a black girl who must have spent days braiding her hair into tight little curls.

'Miss . . . er . . . ?' Maxwell raised his hat.

'Ms,' she told him dispassionately.

'Of course,' Maxwell beamed. 'I wonder if you can help me. I'm trying to trace a former student of yours. A Miss Alice Goode.'

'You a relative?'

'Uncle,' Maxwell lied.

'Name?'

'Peter Maxwell,' he didn't intend to compound the felony.

'How long ago did she leave?'

'Last year. Last July.'

The girl had crossed to a computer and was fiddling with that plastic thing that IT people for some reason best known to themselves call a mouse and slid back her swivel chair. She crossed to a filing cabinet. 'Is that G-o-o-d?'

'E,' said Maxwell. 'There's an 'e' on the end.'

'Right. What did you say? Alice?'

'Yes.'

She flicked her way through the index cards. 'No. Oh, hang on. Yeah. Here we go. Alice Goode. Date of birth 6.8.73.' Maxwell's heart sank. He was on his third plastic hip by the time this girl was born. 'Got a job at Leighford High School, West Sussex.'

'That's right,' Maxwell said.

'There's no address,' the girl told him.

'No, I don't want a current address,' he explained. 'I want to find out where she lived when she was here.'

'I thought you said you wanted to find her.'

'Find her?' Maxwell grinned. 'No, no, you misunderstand. I'm trying to locate her former landlady. They were very close and Alice has lost touch with her.'

'Landlady?' The girl frowned. 'Christ, mate, she lived at Twenty-seven Napier Road, Balham. If she had a landlady there, it was bloody Lizzie Borden.'

'That's it,' Maxwell clicked his fingers. 'Miss Borden. Alice speaks so warmly of her. Good afternoon.'

The girl watched the silly old fart trundle out through the doors. Obviously a poof, she assumed. Just as well he hadn't committed the cardinal sin of middle-aged honky poofs everywhere and called her 'my dear' or she'd have been forced to fell him.

* * *

It wasn't Lizzie Borden who opened the front door at Twenty-seven Napier Road an hour later, but a thin West Indian who might have been Huggy Bear from *Starsky and Hutch*, except that he was about twenty years too young to remember *Starsky and Hutch*. 'Miss Borden?' Maxwell raised his hat.

'You what?' for all his Dreadlocks and Rasta shirt, the man was pure Balham.

'I was looking for the owner,' Maxwell said.

'Oh yeah? Why's that then?'

'Alice Goode,' Maxwell said and watched the Rasta's face fall.

'You filth?' He scanned the road, looking for the dubious unmarked car.

'Teacher,' Maxwell smiled.

'Yeah,' the Rasta grinned, 'that's what I said. Alice don't live here any more.'

'Yes,' said Maxwell, 'I know that line. What I want to know is something about when she did. You knew her?'

'Look, man,' Huggy Bear leaned menacingly on the doorframe, 'what's your angle?'

'Obtuse, as always,' beamed Maxwell. 'You know Alice is dead?'

The Rasta nodded. 'I watch the fuckin' telly,' he said.

'Good,' said Maxwell, 'so do I.' And he pushed past his man into the scruffy hall.

''Ere.'

'If the "filth" haven't been yet, Mr . . . er . . . ?'

'William Shakespeare.'

Maxwell looked oddly at him. 'Mr Shakespeare, then rest assured they will. If I can find Alice's old address, it's only a matter of time before they do.'

The Rasta hesitated. 'They've been 'ere, all right,' he said. 'You'd better come in.'

'In' was a dingy room strewn with old copies of *Viz* and *Time Out*. Here and there, the odd empty beer bottle lay among the dust.

'It's the cleanin' lady's day off,' Shakespeare told him. 'If you can find the sofa, you're welcome to park your arse.'

Maxwell could and did. It was the big, grey piece of furniture under the remains of the KFC wrappers.

'Difficult to beat a good Zinger, isn't it?' He tweezered the crushed carton from under his bum.

'What's your thing with Alice?' Shakespeare leaned back against the door, his arms folded, his jaw flexed.

'I am . . . was . . . a colleague of hers.'

'Oh yeah?'

'Want to see my NUT card? My piece of chalk?'

'How'd you find this place?'

'Same way the police did I imagine. Student records at the London Institute. Most places keep files for two years at least, five in some cases. Her Majesty's Government keep them for up to a hundred years and then snigger "No, you can't see them, you nosy piece of shit".'

The Rasta's lips broke into an uneasy smile. 'Yeah,' he said. 'Right on.'

'What did the police want to know?' Maxwell asked.

'Dunno. I wasn't 'ere. My oppo gave 'em the brush-off. When "Tight-Lips" Henderson don't want to talk to you, man, you stay not talked to.'

Maxwell took off his hat and plopped it down beside him, careful it didn't land in anything too gruesome. He looked at Shakespeare. 'Somebody strangled Alice Goode and dumped her body in a car park,' he said. 'Now, I don't think that's a very nice thing to do, do you, Mr Shakespeare?'

'No,' The Rasta shook his head. 'No, I don't, man.'

'And I intend to find out who did that. And to put the bastard away. With or without your help.'

'You sure you ain't the filth?'

'Positive.'

For a moment, Shakespeare tried to weigh his man in the balance. He'd heard nothing of Alice Goode for nearly a year and now, four times in two days. First, he'd seen the car park where they'd found her, then a photo of the girl herself. Then the filth come calling. And now this old honky was sniffing around.

'Teachers!' Shakespeare spat into the corner. 'I spent the best years of my life getting shat on by fuckin' teachers.'

Maxwell sighed. 'All right,' he said, 'I suppose I owe you the truth.'

'Yeah,' said Shakespeare, nodding slowly, 'right.'

'MI5,' Maxwell said.

'You what, Grandad?' Shakespeare sniggered. 'You're winding me up.'

'What do you think we look like, Mr Shakespeare? Pierce Brosnan by way of Sean Connery? I'm a civil servant, concerned with the defence of the realm. I can give you my Whitehall office number, if you like.'

'Yeah,' Shakespeare's smile had gone, 'right.'

'We have reason to believe that Alice had got in with the wrong crowd.'

'You can say that again.'

'We know from her time at Goldsmith's College that she had . . . shall we say, Leftist tendencies?'

'Come off it, man' — Shakespeare spread his arms — 'that cold war guff's all over now. All that George Smiley bollocks.'

Maxwell chuckled. 'George Smiley, yes. George Blake, no.'

'Who?'

Maxwell's face straightened. 'No, I've said too much.'

'No.' Shakespeare sat down opposite him. 'No. Who's this George Blake, man?'

Maxwell leaned towards him. 'Burgess? Maclean?' He might just as well have said Burgess Meredith.

'Er . . .'

'Spymasters,' Maxwell whispered. 'Recruited at Cambridge.'

'And Alice . . .'

'Working for them.'

'Never.' The Rasta pulled a flat ciggie out of his shirt pocket.

'That's what they said about the Krogers.' Maxwell leaned back as bravely as he dared.

'Who?'

'I'm sorry, Mr Shakespeare,' Maxwell said. 'I thought you watched the news. The Krogers were your average, everyday couple. Folks next door types. Except that they were selling secrets to the other side.'

'Yeah, but . . .' Shakespeare was beginning to wish he hadn't spent the best years of his life being shat on by teachers now. 'What other side? I mean it's all gone, innit? The Evil Empire.'

'Oh, Lord, yes' — Maxwell smiled, crossing his legs and cradling his knee — 'the USSR has gone, Mr Shakespeare, but there's still the CIS. And of course, China.'

'Oh, yeah.'

'Tiananmen Square.'

'Right.'

'I was there.'

'Get away.'

Maxwell wished he could. The arch storyteller, the spinner of dreams, was getting in over his head. 'Alice,' he said, 'tell me about Alice. You knew her.'

'Oh, yeah,' Shakespeare said, 'Yeah, she lived here for . . . oh, four, maybe five months. Had the room upstairs.'

'She posed as a trainee teacher?'

'Yeah. English.'

'Are you the landlord here?'

'Nah, I collect the rent, that's all. The owner is Mr Villiers.'

'Was she regular with the rent — Alice?'

'Oh, yeah.' Shakespeare nodded. 'Look, man, I need to see some sort of ID.'

Maxwell sighed again and rummaged in his inside pocket. 'Here,' he said.

Shakespeare looked at it. 'Countdown,' he read. 'This is a credit card.'

'I told you,' Maxwell shrugged. 'I'm a teacher.'

'But . . .'

Maxwell leaned forward again. 'Mr Shakespeare, I have to have a cover, don't I?'

The light of realisation dawned in the Rasta's eyes. 'Oh, yeah. Right.'

'Alice was on a grant.' Maxwell got his man back to the point.

'A grant?' Shakespeare sniggered. 'Look, man, this is John Major's fuckin' England, know what I mean? A grant don't buy shit.'

'Indeed,' Maxwell nodded. 'So how did she pay her rent?'

Shakespeare winked. 'Porn,' he said.

'Porn,' Maxwell repeated.

'And for that, you'll need to see Mr Villiers. Frith Street. But look, man, 'mean — you're not goin' to mention my name, right? 'Cos it's my fuckin' kneecaps, know what I mean?'

'A name like William Shakespeare?' Maxwell frowned. 'I'd find a name like that very difficult to remember.'

* * *

Soho is a circus within four circuses — Oxford, Piccadilly, Cambridge and St Giles. Its name, they say, comes from the hunting cries of the 18th century when bucks and blades raced each other over the watercourses that criss-crossed the edge of the parish of St-Martin-in-the-Fields. The film world had descended on Wardour Street in the wake of three centuries of arty-farty types who wrote poetry and music. But there were other elements in Soho, who catered for the London of the Night.

Maxwell left the tube in the twilight at Tottenham Court Road and turned right into Soho Square where the curious tower was all that was left of the Church of St Anne to remind the world of the lost gentility that had left for healthier places. Soho of a Friday evening was crawling with people who were of the superficial stamp of Peter Maxwell — middle-aged men wandering the lanes of love, the siren streets. The neon lights flashed before him — revue bars, girls, peep shows — jostling with the clash and clamour of China Town with its huge ornamental gate and the sleek, black cars of theatregoers. Maxwell was in the forbidden city.

He lingered a little longer than he should have looking for Gregory Villiers' emporium and a gum-chewing piece of totty flagged him down. She lounged against the doorframe of a strip club that was all flashing light bulbs and floating plastic streamers.

''Ello, love,' she winked at him, shifting her weight so that her hips swung provocatively and one powerful thigh showed even longer below the leather skirt.

'Hello,' Maxwell smiled.

'What you looking for, then?' she asked.

'Gregory Villiers,' he said.

The girl straightened, her hands on her belted hips. 'You filth?'

That was twice in one day that Maxwell had been asked that. 'No,' he said, wiping his fingers on his jacket, 'just mildly grubby. I need to talk to Mr Villiers about one of his girls.'

'Oh, yeah?' the girl chewed. 'Who's that, then? I might know her.'

Maxwell peered at the keeper of the gate. What was she under that purple eyeshadow, those blushered cheeks? Fifteen? Sixteen? 'Have you finished your coursework?' he asked.

She stopped chewing. 'You what?' Then a broad smile crossed her hard, insolent face. 'Oh, I get it, Grandad. You're into schoolgirls.'

Maxwell couldn't resist a snigger. 'Oh, yes,' he said. 'Everyday.'

'Well,' the girl took his arm, 'come on in, then. Third booth on the right.' She placed her small hand with its glittering rings and purple nails against his chest below the bow. Her smile had gone.

'That'll be five quid. Up front.'

Maxwell ferreted in his pocket and produced a crumpled note.

'I'll give you ten if you tell Mr Villiers that Mr Maxwell would like to see him.'

The girl hesitated, then snatched the note. 'All right,' she said, 'third on the right.' And she was gone, leaving Maxwell alone in the semi-darkness.

From nowhere a large coloured man in a white T-shirt was standing in front of him. 'Get your change here, squire,' he said, all teeth and attitude.

'Change?' Maxwell frowned.

'Look, man, you're not telling me you ain't done this before. It's a quid a peep, all right. You feed the machine. Now, how many d'you want? Ten? Twenty?'

'What do I get for my quid?' Maxwell asked.

The coloured man blinked at him, looked him quickly up and down. 'Bleedin' 'ell, you ain't done this before, have you?' He jammed his fingers down on the till and the drawer slid open with a clash. 'Let's say five, shall we? We don't want nobody havin' a heart-attack on the premises.' And he held out his hand for the note.

'I just want to see Mr Villiers,' Maxwell persisted.

'Nah,' the coloured man was pulling out five pound coins. 'Take it from me, man, he's not your type. You have a little shufty in number three, now. That'll get your pecker up.'

'Mr Villiers.' Stubborn was Maxwell's middle name.

'All right.' The coloured man raised both hands, 'Felicity has gone to get him, but while you're waiting, you might as well have some pleasure before business. Besides,' he closed to his man, 'if you're looking for a particular girl, it might be that number three's the one.'

'No,' Maxwell smiled sadly, 'that's not likely.'

'A fiver,' the coloured man insisted, towering over Maxwell in the eerie blue light.

'All right,' Maxwell decided to buy some time, 'a fiver.' And he exchanged his note for the coins.

There was a small door ahead of him with a scratched star on the front and the number three below it. He pushed gently and found himself standing in a narrow booth, lit by a single red bulb in the top corner. Raucous music blared through the wall facing him and a disembodied voice said, 'You put your money in the slot, Granddad. To your right.'

Maxwell peered into the gloom and found it. As his first coin hit the mark, a grille flew open at eye level and he found himself staring into a small, well-lit room with mirrors on all its surfaces. An Asian girl in a blonde wig and plaits stood in a far corner, sucking an enormous lollipop. 'Worst Shirley Temple I ever saw,' Maxwell muttered to himself. The girl was all of thirty, but she wore white ankle socks, a short pleated skirt and a school blouse and tie. After a few seconds, she undulated around the room and Maxwell became aware of other slots in other doors giving other men the same view he had. What grabbed him most though was the face of the coloured man directly across the room from him, cheek by cheek with the girl at the doorway. They both stared intently at Maxwell.

The thirty-year-old Year Ten girl was peeling off her tie and ripping off her blouse as the grille slammed shut. Damn! Maxwell wanted to watch those two across the room as much as they clearly wanted to watch him. He fumbled with his second coin and the grille flew open again. The pair were still there, talking silently under the shrill blast of the taped jazz while the girl cavorted in the centre, swinging her large breasts to the music and rolling her tongue around the lolly. Then in the grille across the room, the girl's face was replaced by a man's: dark, swarthy, watchful. There was something about those eyes that Maxwell didn't like. And he couldn't look away.

The schoolgirl was in front of him now, in his way, jutting her nipples out at him, inviting him to suck her lolly. He waved her aside, but the grille snapped shut again and he found himself feeding the machine for all he was worth. The coloured man had gone from the far grille now and only the dark, hypnotic eyes stared at him, like Svengali to his Trilby, a cobra to its prey.

The girl had hauled herself up onto a frame Maxwell hadn't noticed was there, bending her knees and lifting her skirt to reveal her skimpy white knickers. She leaned towards his grille. 'Would you like me to do something sexy?' she asked.

'What?' He was trying to see past her.

'Anything you like,' she purred, misunderstanding the tone of his question. 'Have you got yourself out?' She tried to peer into his cubicle, her hand stroking across the knicker elastic, sliding between her legs. Under her tense thighs he saw the dark eyes blink, close and vanish and the grille came down again.

He spun to the door, wrenching it open and collided with a fat man with a shiny bald head. 'Here,' Maxwell stuffed his remaining two pounds into the punter's sweaty hand, 'have one on me, but I wouldn't accept her lolly if I were you. I'm not sure where it's been.' And he was out in the foyer, making for the stairs.

He found them faster than he intended, because the coloured man in the white T-shirt had grabbed his arm and had pushed him against the wall. Maxwell felt the world spin and the most indescribable nausea swept over him as he felt a boot in his kidneys. Then he was dragged down a corridor, his right cheek scraping on the flock wallpaper and he was thrown into a back room.

As he steadied himself in a desperate attempt to keep his feet, he was aware of a desk and, sitting beyond it his feet crossed over at the ankles on a level with Maxwell's waist, was the man with the eyes.

'I hear you're looking for Gregory Villiers,' the man said. He was the wrong side of fifty and even further the wrong side of sixteen stone.

'That's right.' Maxwell tried to stand up, but the pain in his back wouldn't let him. He was aware of the coloured man at his elbow.

'And who might you be?' the man with the eyes asked.

'I might be the bloke who reports you to the police for GBH,' Maxwell winced. He felt iron fingers yank back his hair and his neck all but snapped. With what little strength he still possessed, Maxwell clenched his fist together and swung sideways, catching his man in the ribs and knocking him off balance. The coloured man crashed against the wall, but bounced off it and came forward with eyes blazing.

'Prince!' the man with the eyes barked and the coloured man stopped like a frozen frame from a film, his jaw flexing, his fists still in the air. 'Leave us now, will you?' The accent was thick, but unplaceable. 'Mr Maxwell and I want to have a little chat.'

'We do?' Maxwell's eyes narrowed.

'I'm Gregory Villiers' — the man leaned forward over the desk — 'won't you have a seat, Mr Maxwell?' Villiers tilted his head imperceptibly and Maxwell heard Prince leave. The Head of Sixth lowered himself gingerly to the padded plush.

'Cigar?' Villiers was doing his best to live up to the reputation of sleaze. Surely he wasn't going to offer to make Maxwell a star?

'No, thanks. If it isn't a cliché, I'd like some answers.'

Villiers leaned back and lit a Havana for himself. 'What do you think of Amrit's act?' he asked.

'Who?'

'The Lolita in booth three.'

'Rather long in the tooth, I thought.' Maxwell believed in calling a spade a spade.

'Quite,' he said. 'It's the law, of course. Vice. Not like the old days, Mr Maxwell. Half of C Division'd get in here of a night. Now they're all squeaky-clean, wet-behind-the-ears kids. Now, look, I'm sorry Prince was a little . . . what shall we say, martial? . . . earlier. He's got a heart of gold and was just obeying orders.'

'Bit like Himmler,' Maxwell beamed.

The impresario was fazed for a moment. 'Yes,' he grinned, coughing a little over his cigar and pointing it at Maxwell, 'yes, that's right. Very similar. Now, what can I do for you? Er . . . something special? Golden showers, perhaps? Trip to the farmyard?'

'Alice Goode.'

Villiers blinked, the dark eyes for a moment lost, confused. 'What's that?' he asked.

It was Maxwell's turn to lean forward. 'Not what, Mr Villiers,' he said levelly. 'Who. Alice Goode was a young lady. She's dead now.'

'I don't think I follow . . .'

'She worked for you year before last, last year, whenever. Whether it was this dive stripping for weirdoes in French maid's outfits or whatever, I don't know.'

'How did you get on to me?'

'The same way the police did,' Maxwell told him.

'The police?' Villiers repeated. 'No, you've lost me.'

'I was told that Alice worked in Soho . . .'

'It's a big manor,' Villiers shrugged.

'. . . for Gregory Villiers,' Maxwell finished his sentence. 'Or are you going to tell me the phone book's full of them?'

'All right.' Villiers could fence with the best of them. He'd been closed down three times by the Vice Squad. He employed the Met's Obscene Publications as letter-openers for him. 'Alice worked for me. But that was then. What are you talking about, dead?'

'She was murdered,' Maxwell told him.

'Christ!'

There was something in the man's tone that Maxwell hadn't expected, hadn't bargained for. 'You didn't know?'

'So help me God.' Villiers shook his head.

'You don't read the papers? Watch the news?'

'Too depressing.' Villiers blew smoke rings to the brown ceiling. 'Violence and viciousness everywhere you look. And the economy! I mean, I like a laugh.'

'They found her body four days ago. She'd been strangled.'

'Jesus!'

'When did you see her last?'

'Alice? Christ knows. Where are we now? May? It must have been last spring — yeah, over a year ago.'

'What did she do for you?'

'For me?' Villiers had suddenly tired of his cigar and stubbed it out on his silver ashtray. 'Not a lot, personally. Too lanky. I like them more solid. She was desperate, she said, needed the money.'

'You put her in the booths?'

'Nah, she hadn't got the temperament for that. No, Alice had a certain something. Don't know what you'd call it. Charisma, I suppose. Couldn't waste her talents on such a small turnover. She did some shoots.'

'Shoots? You mean films?'

'Yeah. With the late, great Pryce Garrison.'

'Late? Great? Pryce Garrison?' It wasn't often Maxwell needed confirmation of nearly every word in a sentence.

'All right,' Villiers grinned, 'so maybe he wasn't so great. Still, ten inches isn't bad, is it?' He winked. 'And his name wasn't Pryce Garrison, either. It was Kenneth Winkler. But,' he raised a triumphant finger, 'he is late. That I do know. Died five months ago. Drove his car into a brick wall, the stupid shit.' He shook his head.

'People die in your business, Mr Villiers,' Maxwell found himself observing.

The impresario scraped his swivel chair back slowly, 'Which bring us to another point, Mr Maxwell,' he said. 'Business. For the last half-hour you've been in mine. Now, I've been generous. I've given you my precious time and some honest answers. Now it's your turn to tell me, what's your business? Private dick?'

That in itself was a rarity in Villiers' business, 'I'm a teacher,' Maxwell admitted.

'A teacher?' Villiers started to snigger. 'Well, then,' he said, 'you've got your own resources. Don't know why you needed booth three.'

'I didn't,' Maxwell told him. 'I needed you.'

'Sweet,' Villiers said, but he wasn't smiling. 'But I don't think I can help you any further, Mr Maxwell.'

'The films,' the Head of Sixth Form said, 'what films was she in? Were they distributed? If so, where?'

But the interview was at an end. Villiers had nudged a button under his desk and Prince and a friend, equally black, equally massive, stood in the shadows by the door.

'Would you show Mr Maxwell out?' Villiers asked. 'The side door, I think.'

Maxwell knew a brick wall when he saw one and he stood up, collecting his battered hat. 'I hope, for Alice's sake,' he said, 'you were more forthcoming with the police.'

'I haven't had a visit from the police in a month of Sundays,' Villiers said. 'They're so squeaky clean these days, I think even crossing the threshold offends them. Goodbye, Mr Maxwell. Do call again if you change your mind about Amrit. She can do things with bananas that would make your eyes water.'

Maxwell didn't doubt it. He didn't doubt it either when he felt a fist in the small of his back and heard his own skull crack on brickwork. And so he wasn't at all surprised when the lights went out.

* * *

Gregory Villiers tapped his phone numbers with his plump glittering fingers. He let it ring four times.

'Dee?' He recognised the voice on the other end of the line. 'It's Gregory. What do you know about an old geezer called Maxwell? Fiftyish, bow tie; smartarse type. Says he's a teacher. He's sniffing round about Alice Goode. Right. Yeah. Your patch, I should think. Make a few enquiries, will you? I've given him a bit of a smacking, but he might be the persistent type. Can't have that, can we? Keep an eye.'

CHAPTER 8

'Contusions,' the freckle-faced kid was saying, 'suspected concussion. Severe bruising.'

Maxwell groaned.

'Painful, sir, I expect,' the lad said, poised by the bed with his notepad. Maxwell was vaguely surprised they didn't give the coppers lap-top computers these days. Or at least a course in shorthand. The lad wrote down everything laboriously. That he could write at all, Maxwell silently thanked a teacher.

'It's my bum.' Maxwell steeled himself to adjust whatever of his tackle remained intact. 'You've seen *The Eiger Sanction*, *The Hudsucker Proxy*? Well, this feels like *The Maxwell Prolapse*.'

'Just bruising.' A crisp, Irish nurse swept in through the screens. 'Are you going to be long, officer?' she asked, hands on hips. 'Only some of us have a hospital to run.'

'Nearly finished,' the lad said and waited for her to tut at him, look at Maxwell, tut at him and go. 'I don't suppose,' the boy-detective said, leaning a little closer to his victim, 'you'd care to tell me what you were *really* doing in Soho?'

Maxwell toyed with chuckling, but discretion was the better part of valour and he abandoned the idea in a blur of pain. 'I told you,' he said, 'just taking in the sights. That little card on the door frame offering French lessons on the third floor didn't sound very kosher, but when another read "Quantum Physics Explained", well, I obviously jumped at the chance. Wouldn't you?'

The lad's cold blue eyes just got colder. He closed his notebook with a sigh and stood up. 'No, sir,' he said. 'I wouldn't leap at anything in Soho, especially after dark. We'll do what we can, of course, but . . . "I was hit from behind, officer. It all happened so quickly", isn't a lot to go on, is it?'

'Your life must be full of clichés, I suppose.' Maxwell looked up at his man. As he feared, the lad didn't know what a cliché was and he nodded vaguely before disappearing behind the green screen.

No sooner had the material stopped shaking than the Irish nurse was back, all flaming red hair and starch and belt. 'Bath time,' she announced. Maxwell was about to protest, when it suddenly crossed his mind that that belt might not be a nursing credential at all. What if Judy O'Grady here was seventh Dan of a seventh Dan? He'd taken one beating this weekend already; he really wasn't up to another. So his sole effort of protest was to try to hide under the covers.

* * *

'Jesus!' Sylvia Matthews hauled open the front door of her flat and helped the walking wounded inside. She ran her fingers lightly over the purple ridge above Maxwell's right eye, the blue swelling across his left jaw. Both his eyes were black and there was a plaster across the bridge of his nose — clearly a bridge too far. 'Max, Max,' and she cradled his head, 'what happened to you?'

'This is what you get,' he slurred, 'for trying to ride first class on British Rail without a first-class ticket.'

She helped him limp over to the settee and eased him down. 'Where've you been?' She fussed around him, the nurse in her taking over from the lover. The man she'd loved now for more years than she cared to remember lay broken in her living room, his body stiff and hurt, his eyes wild with pain.

'Soho,' he told he. 'You should see the other guy.'

'Should I?' she wondered aloud.

'Not a mark on him. Actually, there were two of them.'

'Soho, Max?'

He caught the whiff of disapproval in her voice. 'Now, don't come the Victorian matron with me, Matron. I got a lead on Alice Goode.'

'A lead? Max, what are you getting into?'

'Why, Nursie,' he shook his head, 'are you or are you not the one who got me embroiled when Jenny Hyde was killed?'

'That was different,' Sylvia flustered. 'Jenny was one of your girls.'

'And Alice was one of my colleagues,' Maxwell nodded. 'It's the same thing.'

'No, it isn't.' She plumped up the cushions for him. 'If you were in Soho, Max, you were out of your league. And if Alice was there, so was she.'

'Yes,' Maxwell admitted, 'Now, there, I think you're right. I got onto a decidedly shady character who goes by the name of Gregory Villiers. Nice and aristocratic that — family name of the Dukes of Buckingham and so on. In fact, our Mr Villiers comes from downtown Athens unless I miss my guess — Greg the Greek — though he's quite good at accents.'

'Can I get you anything, Max?' She was still appalled by the state of his face. 'A drink?'

'Southern Comfort would be dandy, Sylv,' he said. 'And one of those bendy straws.'

She crossed to the cupboard that passed for her drinks cabinet. 'What's Villiers' link with Alice?'

'He employed her last year, making porn movies.'

Sylvia stood up, bottle in her hand. 'Really?' Her eyes widened.

'The girl needed money, apparently.'

'Rubbish. Nobody needs money that badly.' She poured him a drink.

'Now, Nursie,' he smiled as well as he could, 'there's nothing like a bit of salaciousness to reveal peoples' prejudices.'

'Well, I'm sorry, Max,' she gave him the glass, 'but this isn't the Dark Ages: girls driven onto the streets by abject poverty. It's like something out of *Gaslight*.'

Maxwell was too polite to point out how woefully off Sylvia was in her periodisation. Still, it was probably meant as a figure of speech. 'So maybe she enjoyed it,' he suggested. Her look said it all. 'I know,' he stepped in as quickly as his swollen tongue would allow, 'you're the sort of person who goes around the London Underground sticking "This degrades women" all over the bra adverts, but you've got to accept that not everyone subscribes to that view.'

'That's not fair, Max,' she scolded him. 'Anyway, they stopped doing those years ago. I just can't believe it of Alice.'

'Well, that's the point, isn't it?' He rested his head back and closed his eyes. 'We didn't know Alice; any of us. She was a colleague, an NQT. I expected her to crawl along walls and avert her gaze as the great Maxwell swept past. Her role was to laugh at my jokes, be in awe of my dazzling brilliance — oh, and maybe learn how to be a teacher somewhere along the way. I don't suppose I addressed more than a dozen words to her since she joined us.'

'And now she's dead!'

That was one of the things Maxwell hated about Sylvia Matthews. She had a habit of being right so bloody often. Actually, he didn't hate it in Sylvia Matthews. It was exactly how he felt and he hated it in himself.

'Are we saying,' Sylvia sat at his feet, resting her head on his good knee, 'that Alice was killed because of her porn activities?'

'I don't know' He wanted to shrug, but that gesture was beyond him at that moment and he let it go. 'But I'd probably place odds on it.'

'Why now?' she asked him. 'I mean, was Alice still involved in all that?'

Again, I don't know.'

'Max, who did this to you?' She was looking at his wounds again.

'One of them was a black man the size of an outside lavatory. His name was Prince. The other one I only saw fleetingly. First they knocked me along the corridor and then down some steps, I think. I'd show you my bruises except it would embarrass you.'

'I'm a nurse, remember.' She looked at him knowingly, 'But why did they do it?'

'Orders from Villiers would be my guess. Perhaps he doesn't like snoopers, or perhaps . . .'

'Max,' she looked at his dark-circled eyes, 'you've got that old inscrutable look in your eyes. What is it?'

Maxwell gave her his Christopher Lee Fu Manchu. 'Perhaps I got too close.'

'You can say that again. Max, you must tell the police.'

'I have, or rather they've already talked to me. Some fresh-faced kid still wet behind the ears interviewed me in hospital. It was a patrol car that picked me up — I think; it was all something of a blur. But how did he know?'

'The fresh-faced kid?'

Maxwell was propping himself up on his one good elbow. 'No, sorry, I'm getting ahead of myself. Where did we hear about Alice?'

'Er . . .'

'At the Devil's Ladle,' he reminded her. 'Stewart, that officious prig of a proprietor, said she was some sort of tart.'

'Was she?'

'No. He was a bit off there. Although God knows how else she eked out her grant. The point is where did Stewart get his information?'

'The papers?'

'Nothing there.' Maxwell shook his head as vigorously as he dared. 'All the stories I read carried the same thing.

Teacher at Leighford High. Most of them also carried Diamond's official "No comment". Looked really caring, that, didn't it?'

'Perhaps Stewart had heard some gossip,' Sylvia offered.

'Ah yes, Nursie, but the source. We historians always consider the source. Is it reliable? Does it show any signs of bias — and the other codswallop they invented when they dreamed up GCSE courses . . . how long ago was it now?'

'We could always ask him,' Sylvia said.

'Mr and Mrs Ronay? No, I think we've blown our cover there, old girl. He wouldn't give us the time of day. But . . .' and he propped himself up still further, '. . . I know a woman who could.'

* * *

Monday mornings at Leighford High were something else. The foyer was full of Year Nine girls gossiping about what they had or had not done at the weekend and with whom and how — the graphic and feeble fumblings of adolescence. It all stopped, however, as Maxwell shuffled past them, his bandages contrasting nicely with his swarthy face. They stared at him in disbelief.

'Good God, Max,' Roger Garrett, the First Deputy, stepped aside in the main corridor as though Maxwell were a leper.

'Thank you for your concern, Roger,' the Head of Sixth Form mumbled. 'Got caught in a revolving door at Allders. Bitch, isn't it?'

'Bloody 'ell, sir,' was the next compassionate rejoinder.

'Joseph.' Maxwell nodded at the brick shithouse in Year Ten who blocked the stairway.

'Me and Eric'll sort him, sir, whoever it was panned your head,' Joseph promised solemnly.

'I'm sure you would.' Maxwell couldn't have put a sheet of paper between the boys' biceps, standing as the lads were, shoulder to shoulder. 'And if I had the bugger's address, I'd send you round there, believe me. Now, off the stairs, 'cos you're a fire hazard, know what I mean?'

The shoulders broke. Mad Max had asked. That was enough.

'I should take more water with it next time, Max,' was the cold comfort of the Ice Maiden, Deirdre Lessing, as she swept past him on the upper corridor.

'You'd know, dear lady,' he beamed, raising his hat with what bonhomie he could muster and he half fell into his office, careful to reach the soft chair before the floor reached him.

'Max!' Helen Maitland was the Deputy Head of Sixth Form; a French teacher who'd discovered that perennial pregnancy could get you away from the chalk face for months at a time. In common with most men, Maxwell thought there ought to be a law against it, but he was too much of a public schoolboy to say so. 'What on earth happened?'

'Not so much earth, my dear,' Maxwell plonked his hat on the desk beside him, 'more carpet, followed by stone steps, followed by narrow passageway. Helen, can you handle the UCAS Assembly today? The thought of explaining the university entrance process to the hundred herberts of Year Twelve is a little daunting for me this morning.'

'Max,' Helen sat next to him, 'you ought to be home in bed.'

'Aha,' Maxwell beamed, 'I bet you say that to all the boys.'

Helen's face said it all. She lived for her own kids these days, not somebody else's. Gareth had walked out on her, on them. There'd be no more pregnancies, no more maternity leave, no more going home to the strong arms and the discarded socks. But what did Maxwell know? The cantankerous old bastard was a bachelor. He'd probably never had a relationship in his life. 'Of course,' she said, 'I'll do the Assembly. You go home. Roger will cover you.'

'Now, there's a prospect I don't relish,' Maxwell grimaced, 'being covered by Roger Rabbit.'

'Oh, Max.' She'd crossed to the door, an armful of paper clutched across her chest. 'I almost forgot. There was a phone call for you. About ten minutes ago.'

'Oh, who?'

'Don't know. Ask Pamela.'

'Who?'

'The girl on the switchboard.'

'Oh, Thingee. I do wish you'd be more accurate, Helen.'

'Max.' His Number Two had stopped in the doorway. 'What happened to Alice? Really, I mean?'

'Really?' Maxwell hobbled across to his phone. 'Someone killed her, Helen. That's all I know.'

'No, Max,' Helen shook her head. 'I know you. You're Mad Max. That's not all you know' And she exited with the heavy tread he'd learned to recognise in her year at the school, her great white blouse and oatmeal skirt reminding him again why the sixth form called her The Fridge.

* * *

'Young, Count,' Maxwell was dabbing the bruise on the ridge of his eyebrow with the stuff they'd given him when he discharged himself from hospital. 'That's all Thingee could remember.' He paused and looked in the mirror to where his black and white Tom who-wasn't-quite-a-Tom-any-more sat on the linen basket, flicking his tail in an irritated sort of way. Had he passed up a good night's hunting for this? Who the Hell was Thingee?

'You know,' Maxwell read the beast's mind again, 'the girl on the switchboard. Apparently her name's Pamela. There, now, I knew it was worth going in on a Monday, the things you find out.' And he found himself singing through a thick lip the words of the old Wayne Fontana song '"Pamela, Pamela, remember the days, of inkwells and apples and books and school plays." Anyway, ow,' his fingers had probed too far against his sensitive cheekbone, 'the phone call came from a young male, Thingee didn't know how old. She's only a slip of a thingee herself, of course. Still it was odd.'

Maxwell turned to his pet, 'Why, I don't hear you ask? Because the caller said he had to talk to Mr Maxwell and that he was afraid no one else would do. That's what Thingee's note said. Unfortunately, punctuation isn't her strong suit. Remember *The List of Adrian Messenger*, Count? Of course you do. Kirk Douglas is the baddie but half the cast are in disguise. Well, that bit where the Frenchman is remembering, for George C. Scott's benefit, his conversation after the plane crash with the dying Messenger? It's all to do with punctuation, really, the stresses on various words and so on. Insert the odd full stop, Count, and what do we have? "I have to talk to Mr Maxwell and I'm afraid no one else will do" — that could be my bank manager, my dentist or the man from the Forestry Commission telling me I can sponsor that sapling after all. But with that full stop, that little black spot that killed old Billy Bones, what do we have now? "I have to talk to Mr Maxwell and I'm afraid. No one else will do." That makes it one person only, Count. That makes it Ronnie Parsons.'

* * *

'Mr Maxwell?'

The Head of Sixth Form didn't know the voice at all, the one at the other end of the phone. 'Hello?'

'It's Dave, Mr Maxwell. Dave Freeman, Hamilton's Coaches.'

'Mr Freeman,' Maxwell's mind was focusing now. He vaguely remembered the man wiping his fingers on his overalls.

'Look,' the voice faltered on the other end of the line, 'I've been thinking about this business.'

'You have?' Maxwell was grateful to put his red pen down. He hadn't read a bigger load of tosh on the causes of World War One since he'd been forced to read A. J. P. Taylor a long, long time ago.

'Well, I mean, this Alice Goode business. It's terrible, isn't it? I mean, I've got girls myself'.

'Yes,' Maxwell was still in moving gently mode, 'yes, it's terrible.'

'I hope you don't mind me ringing you, at home, like.'

'No,' Maxwell assured him, reaching for a top-up to his Southern Comfort — it was all that made Year Ten marking bearable. 'No, not at all.'

'Well, the truth is,' Freeman went on, 'I feel responsible.'

'No, no,' Maxwell said, 'how can that be?'

'Well, it was my coach,' the driver said. 'When you're behind the wheel of a ten-tonner like that, the passengers are your responsibility. Especially when they're kids.'

'Alice wasn't a kid, Mr Freeman.' Maxwell was looking for let-out clauses for the man.

'She wasn't much more,' Freeman said. 'Don't you feel it too?'

Damn, thought Maxwell. Another Sylvia Matthews. His own conscience was talking to him on the other end of the receiver, reverberating around his brain. It was like that robot cop in the *Phantom Tollbooth*, the one that came from nowhere, belching exhaust and muttering 'Guilty, guilty, guilty.'

'Yes,' he said, 'we teachers have a saying, Mr Freeman — in loco parentis — in place of parents. That's what we are. And you're right. Alice Goode wasn't much more than a kid. You know I should have been there?'

'Yeah,' Freeman said, 'you told me.'

'Perhaps they'd have found me wrapped up in lino if I had been.'

'I don't think so, Mr Maxwell,' the driver told him. 'Look . . . er . . . do you know the old Labour Club in Henshaw Street, back of the bus station?'

'Yes,' Maxwell did.

'It's a film club, now. Newly opened.'

'Really? Are you a member?'

There was a pause. 'Me?'

'Didn't you say you were into films? *Picnic at Hanging Rock*, wasn't it?'

'Yes, I am,' Freeman said, 'but not films like that.'

'Like what?'

'Mr Maxwell, you go along. You have a look for yourself. Have a good look, know what I mean?'

'Mr Freeman?' But the line had gone dead, like Alice Goode.

* * *

He had planned to call on her, but in the event she called on him. It was a little before midnight, the witching hour, and Peter Maxwell had nodded off over Sir Ron Dealing's 16-19 Recommendations. The doorbell made him drop the thing with a jolt.

'Sorry, Sir Ron,' he bent as best he could to pick it up, 'nothing personal,' and he padded off down the open-plan stairs, promising himself for the umpteenth time that he must get an intercom gadget like Jean Hagger had.

'You haven't seen a black and white cat, have you?' he asked the girl on his doorstep. 'Sort of slow, sort of easy-go, smell under his nose?'

'Christ, it's true, then?' Jacquie Carpenter was staring at the battered apparition in front of her.

'This?' Maxwell's crooked smile was straightening all the time, 'Self-inflicted. I'd just got so tired of being ignored in the staffroom. Now, I'm the centre of conversation.'

'Mr Maxwell, I have to talk to you.'

'Miss Carpenter, I'm really very happy about that,' and he held the door open for her. 'But what happened to "Max"?'

'I've just read the Met reports passed to us at Leighford nick.' She took in his face properly now that she could see it in the full light of his hall. 'Could we?' She flicked a glance at the front door.

'Oh, sorry,' and he closed it. 'I didn't think we were speaking any more.'

'Look,' she was in his hall now, searching for the words, the way, 'I'm . . . I'm out of my depth with all this. I told you things I shouldn't have. You,' she jabbed a gentle finger into his chest, 'are a difficult man to stop talking. I was wrong. And you were right. Could I sit down, please?'

'Dear lady' and he swept his arm up the stairs, 'after you. And I promise not to look up your skirt. Tell me, is this visit an official one?'

At the top she turned to him. 'No,' she said. 'Unless you'd care to become a Special?'

He frowned and sucked in his breath. On his list of priorities it was below joining the Methodists — way below.

'As I thought.' She plonked herself down on his disorganised settee and the rough pile of books slid everywhere, 'Oh, God, sorry.'

'How did you know?' he asked her, shuffling through into his kitchen.

'Know what?'

'My marking technique. That's what I do. I knock the books over and the ones at the bottom get four out of ten, the ones on the top get eight.'

She couldn't see his face to know if he was joking or not. 'Don't you ever give more than eight?' she asked.

He was back in a trice with two steaming cups of cocoa. 'Never,' he shuddered, the very idea appalling him. 'Gets the little bastards excited, then blasé. History is too sophisticated a discipline to get full marks -1 leave that to a Mickey Mouse subject like Maths.' He pointed to the mug in her hand, 'That's got two sugars with full cream milk — the most politically incorrect cocoa in the world. Get it down your neck. You look dreadful.'

'*I* look dreadful?' she laughed.

'That's better' — he sat opposite her, cradling the mug in his hands — 'you should do that more often. Laugh, I mean.'

'In my job?' she asked.

'Aha,' he managed a reasonably normal chuckle, 'so it's going to be the Who's-Got-The-Worst-Job contest, is it? Ready? Fingers on buzzers. No conferring,' he was already well into his Jeremy Paxman.

'No.' She was serious again. 'What happened to you in Soho, Max?'

Max? Were his ears playing tricks? Had the beating dulled his brain?

'I had an altercation,' he told her.

'I read the report,' she reminded him. 'You weren't being terribly helpful. You'll get a follow-up visit tomorrow, probably from Dick Hennessey. Needless to say, you haven't seen me.'

'Absolutely' he nodded. He looked at her again, this pale, thin girl with the tired eyes. And he sighed. 'All right,' he said, 'The truth. But,' and he raised a grazed finger, 'just as your visit is unofficial, so is this conversation. I went to the Devil's Ladle.'

'Where they found Alice's body? Why?'

He shrugged as well as could be expected. 'Because I'm a ghoul. Remember the crowds outside 25 Cromwell Street?'

She did. Night after night as solemn, shell-shocked policeman carried away the last mortal remains of the victims of Fred and Rose West, the television had shown lines of weirdoes, hoping for the worst, the nastiest.

'No, you're not.' She dismissed it.

All right, then. I'm a sucker. Sylvia Matthews has me down as some latter-day knight errant, the Don Quixote of Leighford High. So have you. The trouble is, I'm not sure who my Sancho Panza is. Is it you, Jacquie? Are you my right hand man?'

Jacquie Carpenter hadn't read the book but she'd seen the musical. She shook her head. 'I can't get involved,' she said.

'Jacquie,' he put his cocoa down, 'you came to me in the first place, remember? And now you've come to me again. I need some help, for God's sake; I don't know which way you'll jump. The bottom line is that I'm not very good at sleuthing. Sylvia thinks I'm in over my head. And Sylvia might be right. What has the Met got on Villiers, can you tell me?'

'Who?'

'Gregory Villiers,' Maxwell repeated, as though for the record. 'The charmer whom I suspect is largely responsible for my condition.'

She looked exasperated. 'Max, you didn't tell the Met this. You didn't give them a name. They may be good, but they're not psychic.'

He'd lost the thread of all this. 'Do you know how far they've got in the Alice Goode case?' he asked her.

'Nowhere, as far as I know. Cold trails. Brick walls.'

'Yes,' he felt his cheek, just to make sure it was still there, 'I've met a few of those recently. But surely they've traced her old digs by now? Napier Road? William Shakespeare?'

'I'm sorry, Max,' Jacquie frowned, 'If they have, they're holding out on us. Who, if you avoid the obvious, is William Shakespeare?'

Maxwell tried to clear his head. Had he dreamed the London Institute where he posed as Alice Goode's uncle? Of Napier Road, where he played the spy? He certainly hadn't imagined Gregory Villiers or the meatballs who'd worked him over in a Soho alley.

'Do your powers of arrest extend as far north as the Devil's Punchbowl?' he asked.

'If they have to,' she said. 'Why?'

'Because there's a particularly shifty restaurateur whose collar I'd like you to feel at the earliest opportunity, that's why.'

CHAPTER 9

Junior and Infant Schools aren't the same as High Schools. The chairs are smaller and there's less revolting graffiti in the loos. There's not much to choose between the standards of spelling. It's not just that the kids are less surly, more bubbly, omnipresent, but the teachers are different too. Like Maxwell's colleagues, those of Jean Hagger had an air of resignation, world-weariness. But theirs was born of bum-wiping, pencil-sharpening, sticking bits of screwed-up tissue paper onto walls full of spring lambs, each one of them looking like a Chernobyl fallout in terms of deformity.

Easter had already gone, but the 'Easter Story' still dominated the headlines in Jean Hagger's classroom as Peter Maxwell sat gingerly on her desk, waiting for the woman to arrive at the end of her day. In the corner, a cluster of malevolent looking locusts crawled over each other to get nearest to the scorching heat of the light bulb in their sweaty glass case. Around the room, he was pleased to note a historical time chart from the Stone Age to the assassination of J.F.K., the day the music died. You could tell a school that had recently been Ofsteded.

You could tell a school after Dunblane too. And no school would be the same again. Not since a lone gunman had wandered into a gym in Scotland and emptied a pistol magazine into a class and its teacher. Peter Maxwell had had to sign the visitors' book and fill in the time. He was given a sticky Visitors' label in bright yellow, like Southwark tart in Good King Henry's golden days, and he was taken to Room Six by Bishop Billington's answer to Thingee, the girl on the switchboard.

Thingee had told Jean Hagger that a Mr Maxwell was waiting.

'What do you want?' She swept past him with the air of someone who had been trapped between a double-glazing salesman and a Jehovah's Witness.

'To offer my condolences about Alice,' he said. Mad Max had a way of disarming most people.

'Thank you.' She put what Maxwell would have called a Gladstone bag on a side table and rummaged about in it. 'Do you?'

He declined the cigarette. 'I'd rather go of something historical, thanks,' he said. 'The plague of Justinian, perhaps. Or off to Prague for a spot of defenestration.'

She lit up for herself. 'I do have marking,' she told him, waiting, flicking the noxious weed nervously from side to side of her brown fingers.

'Of course.' He eased himself back onto her desk. 'I just wanted to talk about Alice.'

'And I don't,' she told him, slamming a pile of books down on the table, 'Ever since they found her, I've had the media on my doorstep, here at school, ringing me up. I've gone ex-directory now,' she exhaled savagely. 'Those bastards.'

'I'm not a journalist,' he reminded her.

'No' — she sat down, flicking open the first exercise book, looking at him hard — 'I'm not just talking about journalists. Those scum from . . .' and she stopped, checking herself, flicking glances at the door. 'And you, I don't know what your game is.'

'Mrs Hagger,' Maxwell closed to her, his black and swollen face inches from hers, 'Jean, how can I persuade you we're on the same side?'

She leaned back, searching that battered face, those sad eyes. 'Are we?' she asked him. 'What makes you think that?'

'Miss Hagger,' a child's voice broke the moment, and a ragged blond kid stood at the classroom door. 'Can I get my ball now? Cor, what happened to you?'

'Keith!' she screamed at him. 'How about a few manners?'

'No, it's all right.' Maxwell raised his hand, smiling at the boy. 'It's a perfectly fair question. Keith, is it?' The boy nodded.

'Well, Keith, I was rather rude to Mrs Hagger the other day'. He watched the boy's eyes widen. Then the kid turned to his teacher, 'Tell you what, Miss,' he said. 'You keep the ball, yeah? I don't want it no more.' And he looked at Maxwell once more before making for the door. 'You want me to feed the locusts tomorrow, Miss?'

'Thank you, Keith,' she said, 'I'd like that.' And he was gone. She looked at Peter Maxwell.

'It's all right,' he said, 'Keith knows you didn't really do this.'

'Oh?' She decided to humour him. 'How do you know?'

'How old is he?'

'Nine,' she told him.

'In these days of Enlightened Video Watching and Abandonment of Parental Responsibility, he'll have seen *Dirty Harry*, where good old nutcase Andy Robinson claims Clint Eastwood beat him up. Eastwood denies it, saying that Robinson's clobbered face looks too damned good.'

For a moment, Peter Maxwell thought that Jean Hagger would throw him out. Instead, he saw a sight he'd never seen before and perhaps wouldn't again — Jean Hagger laughing. 'What did happen?' she asked.

'I was beaten up,' he told her. 'Asking too many questions about Alice Goode.'

He watched her smile fade. And she gazed again into his face. 'You look like I feel,' she said. And he sat back, waiting for her to go on. She got up and wandered to the window. 'They're not a bad bunch, this lot,' she said, 'my current Year

Six. You'll have to watch out for Fiona Grayson, bed-wetter, tea leaf. Jamie McFee's quite a handful for us, but you'll cope better at the High School. Then there's Keith you just met . . .'

'Alice Goode,' Maxwell said softly, 'How will we cope with her?'

And Jean Hagger's back was still turned to him as he heard her say, 'Alice Goode I loved. She was like . . .' and he saw her shoulders square, '. . . well, how would you know?'

It surprised them both when Mad Max put a gentle hand on the woman's arm. He felt her stiffen. She hadn't felt a man's hand in so long, she'd forgotten how to react. 'Try me,' he said. And he turned her round.

For a moment she couldn't face him, couldn't look him in the eye, then she took a deep breath. 'We were lovers,' she said, 'Alice and I, not just flatmates. There was something . . . small about her, tiny and vulnerable. She was like . . . like an eggshell.' He saw a single tear splash her cheek. 'That sounds silly, doesn't it?'

'She returned your love?' Maxwell asked, a little out of his depth if he was honest.

'Oh, yes.' Jean closed her eyes, choking back the urge to cry, to scream.

'Was there — this is difficult for you, Jean — was there anybody else?'

The junior school teacher blinked, confused, lost. 'No,' she said, 'no, of course not. Why do you ask?'

'Men, I mean.'

She shook herself free of his spell, the old Maxwell charm offensive. 'There were no men in Alice's life,' she said. 'Only those sad bastards . . . I'd have known. I mean, she wasn't a virgin or anything like that. It's just that she preferred women. She preferred me.'

'Did she ever mention a Gregory Villiers?' he asked, but Jean had gone back to her books. He was losing her.

'No,' she shook her head, 'I don't recall that name.'

'William Shakespeare?'

'Are you winding me up?' she frowned.

'No. Honestly.'

'No,' she shook her head again, 'I'd have remembered.'

'Of course. What about Carly Drinkwater? Georgianna Morris?'

'No. Look, Mr Maxwell, who are these people?'

Maxwell sighed and Maxwell shrugged. 'Ghosts,' he said, 'shadows of a life. The more I think about it, the less real they become.'

* * *

'Seen McKellan's *Richard III* yet, sir?' It was Alec Crossman, Leighford's resident eccentric, asking the questions.

'No, dear boy.' Maxwell swept past him on his way to an Assembly. 'Any good?'

'Brill. Encapsulating as it does the quintessence of Hitler's decadent Reich and Shakespeare's sense of evil.'

'How does he get away with the "My Kingdom for a horse" bit then?' Maxwell wanted to know.

'Jeep gets stuck on the battlefield,' Crossman told him.

'It's a bugger,' Maxwell agreed. 'By the by, oh-you-whose-excuses-for-missing-deadlines-are-legion, where's that little number you promised me on the rise and fall of the Chartists?'

'Ah, power-cut, sir.' There wasn't a glimmer of remorse in Crossman's eye.

'New York, Seventy-nine?'

'Probably,' Crossman nodded, 'But also Tottingleigh, last night. Nearly wiped my entire disc.'

'You know I shall be checking with the National Grid,' Maxwell said.

'Of course, sir,' Crossman smiled, 'I wouldn't have it any other way.'

'Where is this McKellan film being shown, then?' Maxwell asked as they reached the hall.

'That odd little place. The Leighford Film Club, Henshaw Street, back of the bus station. Surprised you aren't a member, sir. My revered papa is.'

And the denizens of Year Twelve fell silent as the Great Man hobbled in to throw more of this pearls before them.

'UCAS,' he said, 'another four letter word to add to your dismally limited vocabularies.'

* * *

Of all the names Peter Maxwell had rattled off to Jean Hagger, hoping for a response, a flicker, something, none burned into his own soul more than that of Georgianna Morris. But how do you find the victim of a madman? Answer — you talk to those whose job it is to deal with madmen. You talk to the law. To be precise, Peter Maxwell talked to Jacquie Carpenter.

'No,' she said, 'not this one, Max. Leave this one alone. She's been through enough.'

Maxwell rested the receiver against his chest. 'She's playing hard to get again, Count,' he told the cat, who liked to be kept informed of these things. 'I thought you wanted my help,' he spoke down the phone.

'Look, it takes training,' he heard her say, 'I told you — we have people who specialise in rape cases. That's all they do. The girl can't remember anything.'

'Does your boss still think there's no connection, between these abductions, I mean?'

'I haven't raised it with him again. I'm waiting for the right moment.'

'Then no one's talked to Miss Morris about it?'

'About Alice? No.'

'Then how do you know, Jacquie?' Maxwell caught himself waving his arms around, like some demented Italian, and stopped himself. 'You can't know, can you? Now, do we have an address?'

'Yes, but . . . my career's on the line as it is. I can't . . .'

'Jacquie. I came damn close to being steam-rollered the other day on behalf of Alice Goode. I hope that wasn't all for nothing. More importantly, if your theory's right, that chummie has killed twice and missed once, who's to say he won't do it again?'

'The last time we spoke you wanted to arrest a restaurateur.'

'That'll keep. Georgianna first.'

There was a silence. Or rather the sound of a policewoman in way over her head, wrestling with her conscience. 'I can't tell you,' she said. Maxwell poised himself to climb the walls, but what she said next dissuaded him. 'The Evening Standard,'' she said, 'June or July of last year. An indiscreet journalist, a careless editor, I don't know which. It gives you Georgianna's work place. As far as I know she's still there.'

* * *

But she wasn't. Maxwell played investigative journalist to the hilt. That Saturday, while millions went to Tesco's or mowed the lawn or watched the Grand Prix, he travelled to Colindale, to the National Newspaper Library there and signed the forms and filled in the requests and fiddled with the overhead whatsits.

Even through the blurred screen, his eyes still wobbling with the speed of the newsprint racing across it, the face of Georgianna Morris stood out. A pretty girl with short, bobbed hair. In that funny light, she could have passed for Alice Goode. And there it was: Marples Estate Agents, Streatham.

In John Major's England, Estate Agents worked seven days a week, desperate to prove to a disbelieving public that the recession was indeed over and all was becoming right with the world. The kid behind the desk, trained to sell snow to Eskimos, had pound signs in his eyes. Maxwell gave him the soft sell. Something in the £250K range, near a golf course if possible. Double garage *de rigeur*. That charming girl who was here last year, on his last homecoming from Juan les Pins — what was her name? Georgina? No, Georgianna. She'd been so helpful. Was she still with Marples? He shuffled the specifications of the property information the kid had placed before him and waited for the answer. He was about to try another tack when the lad blurted it all out. Georgianna had been attacked by a madman. It was like Suzie Lamplugh all over again. Another Mr Kipper. But the kid was at pains to point out that the whole tragic affair had nothing to do with Marples. Their employees were the soul of discretion and their clients carefully vetted. No, Georgianna had been lucky to survive, but it had changed her utterly. She'd severed all connection with the past. Worked in the public library now. Now, Mr Fortescue, when could Marples show him round the property on Sydenham Hill he rather liked the sound of?

* * *

Monday of course was a problem. However much it was John Major's England, public libraries didn't open on a Sunday. There was less call for books than for property. And for Maxwell, Monday was Sixth Form Assembly followed by Double Year Eight and after that his mind normally went blank. The solution, however, lay in the afternoon. Ben Horton, the long-suffering Head of Science, owed him one ever since Maxwell had covered up that appalling gaffe the man had made over the Year Twelve summer exams last year — and a gaffe like that could never be cancelled out by merely letting Mad Max pinch his Year 9 SAT day. So Ben Horton covered Maxwell's last class and the Head of Sixth Form was soon rattling north to Streatham, courtesy of the Southern Line.

He started in the History section. It came as no surprise to him that no one had taken out A. J. P. Taylor for at least five years. The only real surprise was that the old fogey had not been consigned to the stack ages ago. Nothing there he hadn't read, except something pretentious by an American. Deprived of any history of their own, the colonial buggers had come over here and pinched ours. He ducked into Romance, but the funny looks from the old ladies drove him out and he found himself wandering through Children's. Was there, he wondered, any escape from people under eighteen?

Suddenly, like a character in the Mills and Boons he'd just left, there she was, up to her elbows in newspaper clippings, at her desk in the Reference section. Or was it? The Colindale screen was blue. The Colindale screen was blurred. Perhaps, if he watched for a while. And waited. He placed his hat on the table and sat among the old gentlemen, the retired generals and winos who congregate in reference libraries to shuffle through *The Times* or the *Sun*, break wind and clear their throats with irritating regularity. It was ten to five, but Streatham was a civilised place. Its library stayed open until six thirty. In sleepy Leighford, it was different. At five o'clock, the town's librarian, Mrs Quinn, known, and with good reason, as 'Mighty', came along and chucked you out. Only Maxwell had been brave enough to dub her, to her face, Conan the Librarian.

'That's a very old joke,' Mrs Quinn had bellowed.

'I'm a very old comedian,' Maxwell had admitted with a twinkle.

There was a rumour that she'd once killed a man for coughing.

At closing time a bell sounded. Fighting down his Pavlovian urge to go and teach, Maxwell watched as Georgianna began to put away her clippings, switch off her computer and glance at the old men. One by one, they scattered the dailies so that the place looked like a bomb site, and shuffled out, Maxwell the last to go. How could he play this? A discreet word here in the library where she could summon help with a deft flick of an alarm switch? Or should he tackle her outside in an alleyway, where the reminiscent shock might kill her? He took his chance.

'Miss Morris?' He stood at her desk.

The dark eyes flickered up to his and then away. 'The library's closing,' she told him.

'Yes, I know. I just wanted a word.'

'You'll have to come back tomorrow' She was busy herself with something, anything, and the seconds crawled by like years.

'Tomorrow may be too late.'

'Who are you?'

'Peter Maxwell,' he said. 'I'm a teacher from Leighford on the South Coast.'

The dark eyes flickered. She took him in. Middle aged, well spoken. Eyes. He had kind eyes. But his face was battered, yellow. He'd been in an accident. 'Well,' she sat down, 'what do you want?'

'Alice Goode,' he said. 'The woman who was found murdered at the Devil's Punchbowl; she was a colleague.'

For a moment, her mouth hung slack, as though in a silent scream. 'I'm sorry,' she said.

'Miss Morris' — Maxwell had the good sense not to move. One wrong word in his body language now and he'd blow it — 'I have reason to believe that whoever attacked you also attacked Alice.'

That was it. The thunderbolt. The shattering. He waited for the scream, for the hysterics. At least the flexing of her shoulder as she pushed the panic button under her desk rim. Nothing. No sound. No movement. Georgianna Morris just sat there as if she was watching something, something in the middle distance.

'I don't remember,' she said, but it didn't sound like her voice. 'They asked me, all of them, the police, the psychiatrists. I don't remember.'

'Excuse me,' the voice was an intrusion on the moment. Maxwell swung around to face a pot-bellied man with unlikely side-whiskers, 'Excuse me, the library is closing now.'

'You are . . . ?'

'The Chief Librarian.' The little man extended his neck so that his eyes were level with Maxwell's bow tie. 'I'm afraid I must ask you to leave.' He looked like ET.

'I was just having a word with Miss Morris,' Maxwell explained, catching the heat that was thrown at him.

'In your own time, please.' The Chief Librarian's face began to change colour as he squared up to his man. That was the trouble with the Reference Library — all sorts of riff-raff drifted in. Half of them couldn't even read.

'Miss Morris . . .' Maxwell began, ignoring the pompous idiot under his nose.

'I don't really like popcorn,' she said, 'thanks all the same.'

And the nothingness behind those dark eyes told Peter Maxwell he was wasting his time.

* * *

'So, what have we got, Count?' Maxwell set aside the shabraque of the officer's charger to dry and leaned back in his hard camp stool. Before him lay the debris of another character of the Light Brigade, shattered pieces of white plastic as though man and horse had already ridden into the Jaws of Death and not come out of it too well. 'This,' he held up the Hussar officer's torso, legs and head to the light, 'is, or will be when he's finished, Colonel Shewell of the Eighth. His men called him "The Old Woman". A teetotaller and a fussy martinet. Say hello to Count Metternich, Colonel; Count, say miaow to the Colonel.'

The cat failed to oblige and Colonel Shewell was oddly reticent as well.

'His was one of only two horses unhurt in the entire Brigade. Poor bastard died on leave two years later — er, Shewell, that is, not the horse. Where was I?' He put the figure down. 'Oh, yes, I do wish you'd stop distracting me, Count. What have we got?' He reached for the Southern Comfort and freshened his glass, then leaned back again, staring up at his own reflection in the dark of the skylight where the rain bounced on the glass and put out the stars. 'We've got a dead woman, who may or may not be one in a series. Snatched at random by a madman? Or is there a pattern here? Georgianna Morris, abducted from a cinema by person unknown — I hope you're listening, Count, I shall be asking questions later. Carly Drinkwater likewise — except she, poor soul, didn't survive. So why did chummie change his pattern?

Why grab Alice Goode from the Museum of the Moving Image? Moving Image. Movie. Is that it, Count? The click-click of the film in the machine? The staccato of the sprockets. Celluloid. The ultimate fantasy. Then, of course, there's Alice's chequered past. I doubt our Mr Diamond would have been as quick to employ her had he seen the dark side of her CV "Immoral earnings" doesn't look too good, does it? "Deep throat a speciality". God!' He hauled his hands down his tired face, looking for a moment like Lon Chaney in the first *Phantom* before they killed it stone dead by making it into a musical. 'That's what I love about you, Count, your words of encouragement.'

* * *

Maxwell was in bed when the doorbell rang. He'd had a few minutes with Schama and with all due respect to a rattling good historian, had dropped back on his pillows like something out of the death of Chatterton. He fumbled for the clock. Half past twelve. Who the bloody Hell was this? Some stupid kid staggering home with his mates from a drunken revel, thinking it a great wheeze to get old Mad Max out of bed and then leg it? Or perhaps Deirdre Lessing's broomstick had run out of fuel and she'd come to use his phone.

His feet found his slippers unerringly and he grappled with his dressing gown as the bell rang again, 'All right,' Maxwell yawned, 'I'm doing my best. Keep your hair on.' And he was still muttering as he reached the front door.

He swung it wide. There was no one there. He peered out. If this was some herbert's idea of a laugh . . . Then he saw him, huddled in the driving rain, against the laurel hedge that was Maxwell's sole barrier between him and Mrs Troubridge, the Neighbour from Hell. And he looked ill. And he looked scared. But it was him all right. It was Ronnie. Ronnie Parsons. Back from the dead.

* * *

Maxwell had hung the boy's things in the kitchen. He'd offered him a bath or a shower, but the lad was already soaked. So Maxwell threw him a towel and the only spare bath robe he possessed and sat him down to a bacon sandwich and a cup of cocoa. Ronnie Parsons didn't like bacon. And he didn't like cocoa. But he'd been given these things by Mad Max. You just swallowed. That was it.

'Where've you been, Ronnie?' Maxwell held off the inevitable as long as he could. 'Your mum and dad have been frantic.'

'Have they?' the boy asked, his pale eyes blinking.

It suddenly reminded Maxwell of the Harrison Ford film of the same name, the one where Ford's wife disappears in Paris. He thought at the time the title should have read 'Mildly Worried'. Mr and Mrs Parsons had been a bit like that.

'Of course.' Maxwell was still part of the Establishment. Hell, he was the Establishment. There could be no breaking ranks now. He leaned towards the boy. 'Where have you been?'

'Brighton University.'

Maxwell smiled. 'When I suggested you should visit some higher ed. places, I didn't mean stay for a fortnight. There's what the American cops would call an APB out for you.' He gave Ronnie his best Kojak, except that Ronnie was too young to appreciate it.

'I know,' Ronnie nodded.

'How is she?' Maxwell was smiling again.

'Who?'

Maxwell raised an eyebrow; the same one he'd raised back in Year Nine when young Ronnie had tried his 'the dog ate my homework' routine. It hadn't worked then. It wasn't working now.

'Dannie's all right,' the lad grinned. He didn't feel he'd done that in a long time. 'She sends you hers.'

Maxwell laughed. 'Does she now? I'm not sure I want it.'

'Mr Maxwell . . .' Ronnie frowned.

His Head of Sixth Form held up his hand. 'Nothing personal against your light o' love,' he said, 'but the Dannie Roth you know and the one I remember are two vastly different people.'

'She's not.' Ronnie was staring at the carpet.

'Not what?' Maxwell was losing the thread.

'Not my "light o' love" as you put it. I found that out the hard way.'

'Ah, seduced by the hard men of Finals Year, eh?' Maxwell remembered his own days. Then a woman at Cambridge was as rare as anything that made sense by Rainer Fassbinder.

Ronnie shook his head. 'Some fuckin' poncy lecturer!' he snarled. 'Oh, sorry, Mr Maxwell.'

The Head of Sixth Form reached across to his drinks cabinet. 'That's all right, Ronnie. Some of the lecturers I've known, you couldn't have found better adjectives for them. Tell me, are you a Southern Comfort man?'

The boy frowned. 'Got any lager?'

Maxwell chuckled, his hopes for the youth of today shattered again. 'I think so.' He hauled out a can. 'It's not chilled, I'm afraid.'

After the bacon sandwich and the hot cocoa, Ronnie didn't give a damn about that.

'Ronnie, why have you come here? To me, I mean?'

The boy thought for a moment. 'Is it awkward, Mr Maxwell? Difficult for you, I mean? Look, I can go . . .'

Maxwell held his arm. 'You stay and finish your drink,' he said. 'Then we'll see about getting you home.'

Ronnie was sitting on the floor, his arms folded across his knees, shaking his head violently. 'No,' he said firmly. 'No, that's one place I'm never going back to.'

'Your mum and dad, Ronnie . . .'

'My dad . . .' the boy was staring at Maxwell now, his eyes wild and big with tears, '. . . my dad doesn't give a shit about me. He never has. You wouldn't remember this, Mr Maxwell; it was before I was in the Sixth Form, but I never wanted to do games. It wasn't that I was no good. I can run with the best and my ball skills ain't bad. You wanna know why I never did games?' He suddenly hauled the towelling robe over his head and showed Maxwell his ribs. There were parallel rows of white scars, wealed and jagged here and there. 'That's how frantic Dad is.' Ronnie was choking back the tears. 'If I was late for a meal, if I didn't make my bed right, if I stayed out after a certain time. He did that. Him and his studded belt. And Mum . . .' He lowered the bath robe, 'Well, Mum just stood there, saying nothing, doing nothing. I used to cry, to scream and run to her, trying to hide in her arms. Know what she'd say, Mr Maxwell? She'd say, "You know what your father's like, Ronnie. Don't upset him. You'll be all right." For the last three years my dad hasn't spoken a word to me. As long as he's got his smutty videos and me out of the way, he's as happy as a pig in shit. So, please, Mr Maxwell, spare me the trauma about what my mum and dad have gone through. If he's bothered at all, it's because of what I might tell Social Services or the police. Anyway,' the boy subsided a little. 'I can't go anywhere near the police now, can I?'

'Why not?' Maxwell asked him. 'Ronnie, why not?'

The lad looked bewildered. For all he was nearly eighteen, tall and spare, he was a child again, lost, confused. 'Ain't you seen the news? I thought when you said there was an APB out for me, you knew.'

'Knew what? For God's sake, Ronnie, what are you talking about?'

'There's a woman, right, Jean Hagger. Lived with Miss Goode.'

'That's right.'

'Well, she's dead, for Christ's sake. Didn't you know?'

'Dead?' Maxwell was on his feet. 'When?'

'I dunno. It said on the news at lunchtime. I caught it in Currys. I was on my way to the law. To tell them what I knew about Miss Goode. I was trying to get up the bottle, I suppose, killing time until I'd found the nerve. They showed it on the news, Mr Maxwell. They found a grey bag in her flat. It's my bag, Mr Maxwell. It's got my bloody name in it. They think I did it. They think I killed her.' His eyes widened as the cold light of it hit him. 'They think I killed them both. Her and Miss Goode.'

Peter Maxwell turned to the window where the last lights along the shore twinkled through the storm and the house lights flickered in sympathy.

'Help me, Mr Maxwell.' The boy was crying now, his nose red, his forehead creased in a frown. 'I don't know what to do.'

And Peter Maxwell, who had had so many sons, found himself hugging this one. 'Don't worry, Ronnie,' he whispered, 'we'll think of something.'

CHAPTER 10

Jean Hagger had been battered to death with a fossil she kept in the corner. 'A Jurassic ammonite, to be precise.' Jim Astley was weighing part of it in his hand. 'Funny to think a cephalopod from a hundred and thirty million years ago can kill people today, isn't it? Especially as it was harmless when it was alive.'

'That's unusually poetic of you, Jim,' DCI Henry Hall said, 'if I may make the observation.'

Astley looked at the copper over his rimless specs. They didn't exactly go back a long way, these two, yet there was something there, some spark of mutual respect. 'I'm a funny age,' the police surgeon muttered. 'Are these the photographs?'

Hall slid them across Astley's desk. In the harsh, unflattering flash of the police photographer, Astley saw again what he had seen the previous day. Jean Hagger lay on the hearth rug with one leg up on the artificial gas fire, the other sprawled on the carpet, its vicious blue now black with the appalling amount of blood from her head. Her sightless eyes stared out of their sockets through a mask of crimson, as though she was furious with the photographer for catching her at a bad moment, the worst moment of her life.

'She put up a helluva struggle,' he nodded, as if to confirm his findings of the day before.

'He'd be heavily bloodstained?'

'No,' Astley reached for his coffee cup over the shattered remnants of the murder weapon, 'because he washed it all off in the bathroom. Then he washed the bathroom. Clothes too.'

'You mean the cocky bastard used her washing machine?' Hall asked.

'Why not? She was in no position to object.'

'Even so, that's odd.'

'What is?'

Hall looked at the good doctor, sipping elegantly from the canteen crockery. 'Ever killed anybody, Jim?' he asked.

Astley chuckled. 'Are we talking on or off the operating table?' he asked.

'All right.' Hall never chuckled. It might crease his face. 'Let me put it another way. Ever stoved in the head of a divorced middle-aged teacher with an ammonite?'

'Don't tell me I'm a suspect!' Astley stared wide-eyed. 'What's your point, Henry?'

'Where's the panic?' Hall was asking himself the question. 'The fear? This is my eighth murder case, Jim, and in every single one of them, I've seen it somewhere. Whether it's premeditated, planned to the nth degree or the frantic fury of a split second, it hits them like a wall. Every murderer I've talked to, read about, it's always the same. You want to get away, run. You don't want to look at the mess you've made, the butcher's yard.'

'What about Ed Gein?' Astley asked, serious now. 'Didn't he wrap himself up in the skins of his victims? Became them, so to speak?'

'Is that what we've got here, Jim?' Hall still talking to himself. 'The South Coast's own Ed Gein? Jesus, it doesn't bear thinking about.'

'What about the Parsons boy?' Astley returned his cup to the saucer. 'The bag?'

'You saw it,' Hall reminded him, 'in the middle of the floor like a flashing neon sign. Tastefully filled with the clothes of the late Alice Goode.'

'Too pat,' Astley commented.

'You'd have made a reasonable detective,' Hall mumbled, 'given time.'

'So, what are you saying?' Astley leaned back in his swivel. 'The bag's too obvious. It isn't the Parsons boy.'

'Time of death you estimate at . . .' Hall leaned to his man, talking it through, worrying it, probing for a solution. Perhaps if he kicked the idea round for long enough . . .'

'Twelve, twelve thirty, not later than one.'

'The middle of the day,' Hall underlined it.

'Why wasn't she at school?' Astley asked.

'She was. She had a phone call,' Hall told him. 'A man's voice. There was a serious problem and she had to come home at once.'

'What problem?'

Hall shook his head, 'The school receptionist didn't know. It just sounded urgent. She fetched Mrs Hagger at once. And Mrs Hagger said she had to go. Her Headteacher covered her class and she was off.

'What time was this?'

'Half-eleven. It would have taken her twenty minutes, perhaps a little more, to reach her flat.'

'And chummie was waiting for her?'

'Nobody saw a damn thing. There was a sighting at the corner of Arundel Street half an hour earlier. But it's vague. Probably a window cleaner. At least he had a ladder and a bucket.'

'She let him in.'

Hall nodded. 'Like people let in the Boston Strangler. There was no sign of a break-in. The outside door was kept locked and can be operated only from the inside or with a key. Likewise, Jean Hagger's own flat door.'

'So she knew him?'

'Not necessarily,' Hall said. 'Perhaps whatever his message was overrode that.'

'In what way?'

Hall shrugged. 'I don't know,' he said. 'What if it had something to do with Alice? That would bring her running, wouldn't it? We know they were close.'

'So, once he's inside, he turns nasty.'

'She fought for her life, certainly. You thought four blows?'

'Possibly a fifth,' Astley acknowledged. 'The third killed her. But with a weapon like that,' he handled it again, the iron-hard ridges still dark with blood and matted hair, 'you can't be sure. In fact, Mrs Hagger had an unusually thick skull. The first blow would have done for most people.'

'How damaged is our man?' Hall asked.

'Difficult to say,' was the best Astley could do. 'There was no sign of debris under the fingernails, but the knuckles of her right hand were grazed.'

'She thumped him?'

'Possibly, but we don't know what she made contact with. It could have been the wall, the furniture, even the ammonite.'

Hall mused a little space, checking the photographs again. 'Nothing sexual here?' He wanted reassurance.

'Nothing obvious,' Astley confirmed it, 'no signs of rape. No bruising. No semen traces.'

'But not premeditated.' Hall was talking to himself again.

'You think not?'

'You don't go along for a murder and hope there's a convenient blunt instrument lying about. With different luck he might have had to have used a rolled-up newspaper, if that was all that came to hand.'

'What if . . . ? No.'

Hall collected up his photographs. 'You're an inscrutable sod, Dr Astley,' he said. 'Give me no ifs. What are you thinking?'

'Well, what if he did bring his own weapon? Knife, iron pipe, bazooka, in the bag he left behind? What if he saw the ammonite and saw his chance to reduce the risk of detection? If he used his own DIY gadget, he'd either have to lose it or sterilise it so that people like Forensic can't come along and find the odd telltale hair, the sliver of skin. By using something of hers, something that belonged in the flat anyway, he's shifting the probables, isn't he? Saving his arse.'

'Oh, yes,' Hall nodded, feeling worse now that Astley had confirmed what he already knew. 'There's little doubt our killer has done that. Not a print, or smudge. He's a calculating bastard, cool as a mountain stream.'

'And the Parsons boy?'

'The Parsons boy,' Hall dragged himself up from Astley's other chair, 'is alive and well and knows more than he's telling. And somebody's shielding him.'

'Did he do this? Smash the skull of Jean Hagger and rape and strangle Alice Goode?'

Hall turned in the doorway, 'We'll be in touch, Jim,' he said.

* * *

It was one of those curious lulls that soldiers say descend on battle-fields, when footweary grumblers lie in water-filled foxholes and light a lucifer before the flak starts again. Teachers call them free periods. There are never enough of them, they are always at the wrong time of day and, depending on the sickness record of your colleagues, you often lose them anyway to cover somebody else's classes.

Peter Maxwell was lucky that day. He hadn't lost his free so he was taking a rare moment to flick through *The Times Educational Supplement* in the staffroom. He was too old to get another job and besides, as usual, somebody had pinched the classified section. It was then that Anthea Edwards walked in.

'All hail!' Maxwell shuffled his paper at her.

'Sorry, Max,' she said. Whenever she saw Maxwell in the staffroom, it was like Boodles or the Garrick. She hated to disturb the old man in his club.

'Sit ye doon,' he was still in North British mode, 'an' stint not. I've been meaning to talk to you.'

She did as she was told. Mad Max scared Anthea Edwards. Come to think of it, nearly everybody scared Anthea Edwards. And the trip to MOMI hadn't helped. Deirdre Lessing had offered to arrange counselling. Almost daily the Head of Special Needs clutched the girl to her ample bosom and they talked knitting, and Delia Smith.

'About the trip.' Maxwell folded his paper and put it down.

'Yes?' It had been over four weeks now since she'd gone, but every night she sat on that phantom coach and wandered those dark and magic slide shows.

'Where exactly did you see Ronnie last?' he asked her. 'Do you remember?'

'Is it important?' She sorted her marking on the coffee table in front of her.

'It might be,' he told her.

'Well, I think . . .' and she screwed her face with the effort of remembering, shutting her eyes tight, '. . . I think it was at the Barry Norman interview bit, but I couldn't swear to it, Max. Why?'

'I know where he is.' Max muttered it out of the corner of his mouth.

She turned to face him, her eyes bright. 'You mean, he's alive?'

'Look,' the door had crashed back and Roger Garrett, the First Deputy, stood there. 'I've got a bit of a flap on,' he said. 'Angela Lord's gone home.'

'Well, fan my flies,' said Maxwell. 'And only the second time this week, today being Tuesday.'

'Have a heart, Max . . .' Garrett said.

'We are rather busy, Roger.' Maxwell stared his man down. 'You're free, I notice.'

A strange look came over Roger Garrett's face. It passed as a smile but Maxwell knew a sneer when he saw one. Ah, well, I'm time-tabling,' he explained.

'Oh, goody.' Maxwell clapped his hands together. 'Forward planning. I'm impressed.'

'It's only for half an hour,' Garrett wheedled. '10A4.'

'Now how did I guess that?' Maxwell smiled, wide-eyed. 'Funny how it's never 10A1, isn't it? Still,' he got up, sighing, 'it could be worse. I could be a supply teacher.' He looked down at Anthea, still open-mouthed on the chair next to him, 'Flies, dear,' he said and winked at her. 'Where away, oh, disturber of my dreams?' It took Garrett a while to realise that Maxwell was talking to him and he passed him the nasty little yellow lesson cover-slip that was Leighford High's equivalent of the Black Spot.

At the staffroom door, Maxwell stopped, tapping the side of his nose as Garrett scuttled off in search of a computer, 'Mum's the word now, Anthea. OK? I thought you'd feel better if you knew.'

She did. It was like a huge weight off her soul. She closed her eyes and found herself crying.

* * *

Peter Maxwell didn't usually go to the pictures with strange men. Not anyone quite as strange as Alec Crossman, the 1930s public schoolboy who'd got caught in a time warp and was in a '90s comprehensive by mistake. Alec had been insistent and it did kill two birds as far as Maxwell was concerned. The coach driver, Dave Freeman, had rung him a few days ago with the gypsy's warning about the new cinema club behind the bus station. In the helter-skelter days since then, he'd all but forgotten about it. Freeman was trying to be helpful, no doubt. The man felt guilty because Alice Goode and Ronnie had disappeared on his trip too. Not that anyone could hold anything against Hamilton's or their drivers, any more than anyone could hold anything against the Museum of the Moving Image. That was just how it was.

The green door was thrown back that Wednesday evening and a steady trickle of the faithful went through it.

Young Alec met Maxwell outside — young Alec dropped off by his dad, Jonathan, who was actually the Crossman family member and sometime club projectionist, old Maxwell parking his bike next to the riderless supermarket trolleys that the day's shoppers had abandoned, much as the French army did their horses in the dripping Belgian orchards after Waterloo.

Alec had a girl with him, a nonentity in a thin summer frock. She was introduced to Maxwell as Arabella which told him immediately that she went to the Grange Private School down the road. All she said all evening was 'Hello' with that upper-class twang that cuts like a knife through the water of the working class and that was guaranteed to turn Maxwell into an instant Marxist.

Ian McKellan hauled off his balaclava, having put a single bullet through the forehead of the Prince of Wales. HRH's HQ didn't look very much like the bloody meadow at Tewkesbury, but if you couldn't take liberties with the Bard, with whom could you take liberties? Maxwell enjoyed himself. The theatre was very intimate to the point of incestuousness. Room for what? Fifty bums, top whack? Only half the seats were taken, of course, in the manner of the great British cinema of these days. No ice cream, no popcorn, not even much by way of Pearl and Dean. As Sir Ian fell dying through the flames of his own destruction on the screen, Maxwell excused himself from his protégé and his piece and made his way to the exit. On the landing he ducked to his left through a black-painted door and found himself in a corridor, dark and narrow. He looked for the telltale flicker of the projector on the wall, listened for the whirr and click of what was probably a second-hand job lot. All he got was a solid, balding man who didn't take kindly to strangers wandering through his club.

'Can I help?' he asked.

'I don't know,' Maxwell said, 'I was hoping to find someone to talk to about the club.'

'Really?' The balding man placed a proprietorial arm across the corridor, 'Why?'

'I'm something of a film buff myself,' Maxwell told him, 'I'd like to join, Mr . . . er . . .'

'I'm sorry, membership by invitation only' The balding man was firm.

'Oh, but I've just seen tonight's show,' Maxwell explained.

'That's fine. Wednesdays are open to the public.'

'Ah, I see,' Maxwell nodded. 'Well, how do I go about attending on the other nights of the week? I can't usually do Wednesdays.'

'I told you . . .'

'Alec Crossman recommended you,' Maxwell intervened. A seventeen-year-old wasn't much of a name to drop in the scheme of things, but it opened the oddest of doors.

'Young Alec?' The balding man smiled. 'Jonathan's boy?'

'That's right,' Maxwell bluffed, not knowing the elder Crossman from Adam.

'Well, that's different, Mr . . . er . . . I didn't catch your name.'

That was because Maxwell hadn't yet thrown it in. 'Maxwell' — he extended a hand — 'Peter Maxwell.'

'Mr Maxwell,' the balding man gripped him fiercely with both hands as though he'd just found the lost tribe of Israel. 'I'm Douglas McSween. My friends call me Dee.'

'Do you know,' Maxwell was at his most affable, 'I had no idea you were here.'

'Ah, we're new' McSween took him by the arm and led him into a backroom stuffed full of metal film cases. 'Only been here a couple of months. Now, Peter, there are various formalities.'

'Of course, Douglas,' Maxwell smiled broadly.

'That's Dee, remember. Have a seat.'

'Thank you. That's Max.' Maxwell filled in a form, giving all but his inside leg measurement. When he'd finished, McSween popped out, taking the paperwork with him. Maxwell checked the corridor. Empty. He rummaged through the cans on the shelving around the room. Now Peter

Maxwell had been a film fan all his life. He was a Saturday matinee kid, along with Methusaleh, and if Peter Maxwell didn't know the title of a film, that was because no one had made it yet. But to his growing discomfort, he didn't know any of these. Many of them were in Dutch, some appeared to be in Urdu. There was no *Thirty-Nine Steps*, no *Maltese Falcon*, not even a decent editing of *Citizen Kane*. But before he could delve further, McSween was back.

'Sorry about that,' he beamed. 'Now, this shouldn't take too long. Three or four days at most. Oh . . .'

McSween's bland face had darkened, and his eyes flickered up to Maxwell's, then down to the form again. 'Is there a problem?' Maxwell asked.

'I see you're a teacher.' McSween had not read the small print.

'Don't tell me that's a bar to my eligibility?' Maxwell chuckled. 'Teacher blackballed! What a headline!'

McSween looked increasingly uncomfortable by the moment. 'I'm sure you understand, Max, that we do not deal in headlines here.'

'Oh, of course,' Maxwell frowned, nodding solemnly.

'It's just that, well,' — it was McSween's turn to chuckle — 'you're a lucky sod in some ways, aren't you?' and he elbowed him in the elbow.

'Well, there are the holidays, I suppose,' Maxwell acknowledged; 'the apples my pupils bring me every day, the joy of marking! Yes, come to think of it, you're right.'

For a split second, confusion crossed Douglas McSween's face, then he guffawed, nudging his man in the ribs this time, and said, 'I expect you're looking forward to the new Jeremy Irons, eh? I'll see you out.'

'Rather!' winked Maxwell in return. 'And thanks!'

* * *

'How are you on films, Ronnie?' Maxwell plonked an omelette down on the table in front of the boy.

'I like Quentin Tarantino,' the lad confessed.

'Yes,' Maxwell sighed, sliding his own chair back, 'I'm more of a *Quentin Durward* man myself. What about Jeremy Irons?'

'Who's he?'

'Well,' Maxwell reached for the salt as they both tucked in, 'that's the end of that little conversation.'

'Look, Mr Maxwell . . .' Ronnie was fidgeting with his fork.

'Not enough tarragon there for you, Ron?'

'What? Oh, no, that's fine. You're a great cook, Mr Maxwell, for a bloke, I mean. No, it's just . . . well . . .'

'Spit it out, Ronnie,' the Head of Sixth Form insisted, suddenly hoping the boy wouldn't take him seriously.

'Well, look, I've got to go. I mean, you could get into a lot of trouble with me here. It was on the local news again at lunchtime. Local youth sought in murder enquiry. They think somebody's shielding me, Mr Maxwell, and somebody is — you.'

Maxwell sighed and slid his plate away. 'You're right,' he nodded, 'not enough tarragon. If you leave here, Ronnie, will you go to the police?'

'No way.' Ronnie shook his head. 'No way.'

'Home, then?'

'No.' Ronnie was pale, on his feet suddenly, staring hard at Maxwell. 'I told you, I'm never going back there. Never!'

'All right, all right,' Maxwell said softly, raising both his hands to calm the boy down. 'If you won't do either of those things, then just sit tight here, just for a day or two. I need the time to think.'

Ronnie sat down again. 'You won't . . . you won't turn me in, Mr Maxwell?' he asked. 'Over to the law, I mean? I ain't done nothing, you know that.'

'Yes, Ronnie,' Maxwell nodded, looking the frightened boy in the face, 'I know that.'

* * *

Peter Maxwell was vaguely surprised that Ronald Parsons senior had an answerphone. When he rang the number that Thursday, he understood the reason. The man's monotone spoke of building jobs. He wasn't in at the moment, but the caller could leave a message after the tone. The caller didn't. He told Ronnie junior to stay away from the window, saddled White Surrey and pedalled into the gathering gloom.

All day he'd seen them — the photocopies of Ronnie's last school photo. Plastered all over town — 'Missing. Ronnie Parsons. If anyone has any information on this boy's whereabouts . . .' The eyes in the photo burned into his, like those of Carly Drinkwater and Georgianna Morris and Alice Goode and Jean Hagger. The eyes of the dead and the damned.

He rang the doorbell at Rondo. There were lights on in the living room and the kitchen at the side. There was a rattling of lock. A solid, swarthy face peered around the door. 'Yes?'

'Peter Maxwell, Mr Parsons. Can I come in?'

Parsons scanned the road. 'What do you want?' he asked.

'Just a word.'

'I've had bloody coppers here all day. Not to mention the fucking press. I'd like a bit of peace now, if it's all right with you.'

'Do the police know where Ronnie is?' Maxwell was prepared to slog it out on Parsons' front doorstep if he had to.

'If they did, they wouldn't be asking us, would they?' the man snarled.

'Is your wife in?' Maxwell tried another tack. Ronald Parsons was a brick wall, but Dorothy was the chink in it.

He watched Parsons' face darken. 'Piss off!' the builder growled and he started to close the door. Maxwell was faster, for all his aches and pains, and his foot stopped it. 'Why did you beat Ronnie up, Mr Parsons?' he asked loudly. 'Not just once, I mean, but systematically?'

Parsons opened the door again, straightening. 'Who says I did?' he wanted to know.

'Ronnie does.' Maxwell removed his foot from the builder's doormat. He stepped back and tipped his hat. 'It's been . . . an experience, Mr Parsons,' he said.

* * *

Ronnie was still asleep in Maxwell's spare room the next morning when the doorbell rang. The rain was drifting in from the west, as Suzanne Charlton had predicted it would, with the aid of several million pounds of sophisticated equipment and a bit of seaweed. The face under the rainhat was a picture of fear and grief. Dorothy Parsons.

'I can't stop, Mr Maxwell,' she said, 'I'm on my way to work. Ron doesn't know I'm here.'

Maxwell opened the door for her and she stood awkwardly, dripping onto his carpet. 'Let me take your coat,' he said.

'No, really. I'll be late. And . . . I don't want Ron to know I've been here. He'd . . . well, he wouldn't like it.'

'At least come up,' Maxwell offered, 'into the lounge.'

She climbed the stairs, but wouldn't take the seat he proffered.

'Last night,' she said, 'when you called, I was there. I wanted to talk to you, but . . . Is there any news, Mr Maxwell? Have you heard anything? Anything at all? Every night, I just sit by the phone and cry. Ron's sick of it. He just goes out. Goes to the yard. Or his club. Oh, the police are as kind as they can be. But . . . well, this other teacher, this Mrs Hagger. They think Ronnie's involved in that. But he can't be. I've told them he can't be.'

'Who have you been dealing with?' Maxwell asked her. 'In the police, I mean?'

'Urn . . . there's an Inspector Hall who's leading the case apparently, but we've had most to do with a Sergeant Hennessey and a policewoman.'

'Jacquie Carpenter?'

'Yes. Yes, that's her. She's ever so nice. Tells us not to worry and that. But that's easier said than done, isn't it?'

Maxwell heard a click upstairs. Damn. He knew all too well what that was.

'Would you excuse me, Mrs Parsons? Sounds like my cat's up to no good again. I shan't be a moment.'

Metternich hadn't heard the slander, because he was still asleep in the bathroom linen basket. But it wasn't the bathroom Maxwell was making for. It was Ronnie's room. But Ronnie wasn't there. The bedcovers were thrown back, the curtains flapping wide in the unseasonable weather. Maxwell grabbed the window catch so that the whole thing wouldn't crash back in the wind and shatter glass. There was no sign of Ronnie Parsons. The sprinter had gone, out onto the silver birch branch of Mrs Troubridge's tree, down over her hedge and snaking off down Columbine Avenue, through the still-waking estate, making for anywhere, nowhere.

'Shit!' Maxwell hissed, bolted the window and rejoined the boy's mother.

'Sorry about that.' He did his best to smile. Difficult when your heart's on the floor.

'I just wondered if you'd heard anything.'

For a moment he couldn't look the woman in the face. He'd never been, by grace of God, a mother. He'd only been a father briefly. What right had he to lie to Dorothy Parsons, whose only fault was that she loved her son? For a moment, he felt his nerve slip, his resolve buckle, then he tossed the moment aside. 'No,' he looked at her again. 'No, not a word.' And the lie hung between them like poison on the morning air.

* * *

'Mr Maxwell?'

The Head of Sixth Form didn't recognise the voice over the phone.

'Dave Freeman, here, Mr Maxwell. Hamilton's Coaches.'

'Mr Freeman. How are you?'

'Fine. Fine. How's yourself?'

'Been better actually.'

'Right. Yeah. I was just wondering if you'd taken in the cinema club in Henshaw Street yet?'

'Yes, I did, thanks. McKellan's *Richard III*. Excellent.'

There was a pause. 'Oh, you went on Wednesday. No, you want to join the club, if you can. Go on Thursday, Mr Maxwell. I think you'd learn something to your advantage.'

'Would I? Hello. Hello. Mr . . . ?' And Maxwell put the phone down. 'We can't go on meeting like this.'

* * *

There was usually a small queue outside Mad Max's door at Leighford High. Not the brave band of paparazzi who still waited in the drizzle beyond the school gates for any word. More of them besieged Bishop Billington Junior School where Jean Hagger had recently taught. Phone calls from there and from Leighford to County Hall in Winchester had elicited a measured and careful response from the Chief Education Officer, requesting respect, forbearance. Sadly, they were not words in the vocabulary of the media. And the paparazzi stayed.

But there was no one outside Mad Max's office on this Thursday morning. Only a man inside it, chain-smoking. He leapt up at the Great Man's arrival.

'Mr Maxwell?' he inhaled savagely before extending a hand. 'DS Hennessey,' and he flicked open his warrant card, 'I couldn't find an ashtray.'

'That's because I don't smoke.' Maxwell took the hand and invited the detective to resume his seat. He passed him a particularly revolting yucca, complete with plastic pot. 'Feel free to flick in there,' he said, edging himself into his chair. Peter Maxwell had invented body language and he loomed over the detective, across the safety barrier of his desk, across the vantage of the years.

'Er . . . the young lady on the desk showed me up. I hope you don't mind.'

'Of course not. What can I do for you, Mr Hennessey?'

'Well,' the copper reached into his back pocket for his notebook, 'I'm following up an incident in Soho earlier this month.'

'This is astonishing,' Maxwell smiled.

'What is?' Hennessey was smiling too.

'Your inter-force after-sales-care service. I thought you blokes were overworked.'

Hennessey chuckled, flicking the notebook shut. 'Oh, we are, sir. We are. It's just that . . . well, the officer who took your details thought you might have been a little . . . shall we say overwrought? Didn't get all the information at the time and when you discharged yourself . . . well, it was really down to us then.'

'I see.' Maxwell clasped his hands across his chest. 'What would you like to know?'

'Well,' Hennessey was still smiling, 'for a start what the fuck do you think you're doing with Jacquie Carpenter?'

'Tut, tut,' Maxwell shook his head slowly, 'and I thought that sort of language went out with the Sweeney.'

'You know she's under suspicion, don't you?' Hennessey asked.

Maxwell was more inscrutable than the corpse of Mao Tse Tung, when he wanted to be. Only his fingers tensed. Only his knuckles whitened. His heart and head were screaming. He just hoped Hennessey couldn't hear. 'Jacquie Carpenter?' he said. 'That's DC Carpenter?'

Hennessey leaned forward in the soft plastic chair, one of those salvaged from the sixth-form common room before the neurotic bastards had started pulling the stuffing out of it. He wasn't smiling now. 'Look, Maxwell, I know. All right? I've seen it happen before. I've got a lot of time for Jacquie. She's a sweet kid, but she can't take the flak. She lets things get to her. Now she's cracked, basically. Gone under. Another WPC found her crying in the ladies' at the nick. Not like you cry when you've caught your finger in the door or your budgie dies. The DCI sent her home. Then he sent me round to talk to her. And she told me. She told me all about you.'

'I see.' Maxwell unbuckled his fingers. 'So the follow-up from the Met was just a front, then?'

Hennessey leaned back. 'It's all bound up, isn't it? All part of the same story.'

'You tell me.' Maxwell could evade with the best of 'em.

'You know,' Hennessey said, 'Jacquie speaks highly of you. And that's the only reason we're doing this here rather than down the nick. At the very least you've been wasting police time. But I think there's more to it. I think you know something. Something about Alice Goode.'

'What do you know?' Maxwell asked the younger man.

Hennessey chuckled coldly. 'Uh-uh,' he shook his head. 'No doubt you'd say it's a cliché, but I'll ask the questions.'

All right,' Maxwell said, 'I went on a sleuthing spree at the end of last month. It was such basic detective work, that I expected you boys to have been there before me. I wanted to know something about Alice's past. Something that might have explained her disappearance and her murder.'

'And what did you find?'

'Porn. When she was a student, she did modelling for a company in Soho. That's where I got my beating.'

'Why didn't you tell the Met that?'

'I didn't think it was any of their business. How is Jacquie?'

Hennessey shook his head, reaching for another cigarette. 'I don't know. The police doctor's given her something to make her sleep. There'll have to be an enquiry.'

'Into what?'

'Into what she told you.'

Maxwell saw a loophole yawning before him, a light at the end of the tunnel. 'What did she tell me?'

'Don't muck me about, Mr Maxwell. I need to know.'

'What if I told you she didn't tell me anything?'

Hennessey blinked. 'We know she came to see you,' he said. 'We know you rang her up at home.'

'Aren't policewomen allowed to have a social life?' Maxwell asked.

Hennessey felt the tables turning, ever so slightly. 'You mean . . .'

'I mean that Jacquie Carpenter is a very attractive girl. Unattached, I believe. I may not be in her league in the attractiveness stakes — it's hardly for me to say — but they don't come any more unattached, believe me.'

'So . . . Carly Drinkwater? Georgianna Morris?'

Maxwell frowned, a smile playing over his lips. 'Who?' he asked.

It was Hennessey's turn to smile, 'You've never heard of them, I suppose.'

Maxwell shrugged. 'You hear a lot of names in my profession, sergeant. I shudder to think how many have passed through my hands at one stage or another.'

Hennessey stood up, 'If what you're telling me is true . . .' he began.

'Then Jacquie Carpenter's in the clear, isn't she? Not very well, perhaps, in need of a rest, certainly, but her job's not in jeopardy, is it?' Maxwell stood up too.

'No,' Hennessey smiled. 'No, I wouldn't think it was.'

There was a jarring electronic clanging in the corridor outside. 'Ah, la damn bell sans merci,' he said, 'Now, unless you want to hear Thomas Jefferson lying through his teeth in the Declaration of Independence with Year 12, I'm going to have to love you and leave you. Well,' he smiled broadly, 'leave you, anyway.'

CHAPTER 11

Maxwell's confirmation came through the next day. The Travellers, the Conservative, the Cavalry, Boodles — one by one they'd blackballed him, but the Leighford Film Club's doors were open wide. For a mere £200 p.a. he could attend their monthly meetings on Thursday evenings in that pokey little place in Henshaw Street behind the bus station.

'There's an old piano,' he found himself crooning to Metternich, 'and they play it hot behind the green door. Frankie Vaughan, Count, a singing star of my youth, when you weren't even a twinkle in your great-grandfather's eye.'

'Wass all this, then?' Mrs B. had a devastating line in originality italicised all the more by the thud of her size nines on Maxwell's stairs. She was holding up a fairly revolting T-shirt with the words 'Pearl Jam' scrawled all over it. A boy's T-shirt. Ronnie Parsons'.

'Where did you find that, Mrs B?' Maxwell's grin was frozen as a Tesco chicken.

'Stuffed down behind the bed in your spare room,' she told him, waving it about.

'What the devil was it doing there?' Maxwell wondered aloud.

'Is it yours, Mr Maxwell?' The cleaning-lady had her doubts.

'Please, Mrs B.,' the Head of Sixth Form frowned, 'if it were mine it would have "Perry Como" on the front. No, I found it at school the other day and, without thinking, popped it in my briefcase. I keep meaning to take it to Lost Property.'

'But there's blood all over it.'

'Blood?' Maxwell crossed the living room to her. The old girl was right. On the left sleeve and in short, sharp dashes across the chest, brown stains. 'Are you sure?'

'I've seen enough in my time,' she said. 'Mr B. used to play for Leighford Rovers. ''E was always comin' 'ome with blood on 'isself. Looked just like that. What are these kids doing up at the school, Mr Maxwell? Killin' each other?'

* * *

Detective Chief Inspector Henry Hall didn't like working Saturdays. Perhaps it was only rabbis who did. He didn't like it even more when things didn't add up. And that particular Saturday in the middle of May, he was like a man with no batteries in his calculator, no beads on his abacus. And the sour face of Dick Hennessey didn't help.

'Will this take long?' he asked.

'Hope not, guv,' Hennessey said. 'I was just wondering about Jacquie.'

Hall looked at his man. 'No comment, Dick,' he said.

'The boys . . . well, no, I was wondering what the score was.'

'The score is that she discussed confidential matters with a member of the public. That's the subject of an internal enquiry. Until that takes place, she's under suspension.'

'Can I go and see her?'

'I wouldn't, Dick,' Hall advised. He'd seen men go this way before. The contamination of corruption. It was like a computer virus, but more deadly and more difficult to stamp out. 'Keep your nose clean. Let internal affairs handle it.'

'But she's not well, guv . . .'

Henry Hall wasn't given to outbursts of any kind. He hadn't shown an emotion since he was six and he was damned if he was going to start now. But he took off his rimless glasses and threw them down on his desk, the desk cluttered with the paperwork of two murders. 'Off the record,' he said, 'I know perfectly well she isn't well. But which came first, Dick? The chicken or the egg? Did she blab to Joe Public and is she shamming to cover her tracks? Or is she genuine and did she blab out of confusion or whatever private Hell she may be in? Am I qualified to judge that? Are you?'

Hennessey took a chance. 'What about Peter Maxwell?' he asked.

'Who?' Hall took up his glasses again.

'It's common knowledge, guv,' Hennessey said. 'Everybody in the nick knows it was him she talked to.'

'Do they now?' Hall doubted it. He had talked to Jacquie Carpenter, on her own. It was his distinct impression that she'd told no one else. 'Well, we know Mr Maxwell of old, don't we? The Sherlock Holmes of Leighford High. He can't help himself.'

'What if he says Jacquie didn't talk to him?' Hennessey was looking for a way out, the same one that Maxwell had taken. A lifebelt to throw to Jacquie, floundering in life's seas as she was.

'If Mr Maxwell says the Queen of England is Elizabeth II, I'd like to check it first,' Hall said. 'I'm afraid our Mr Maxwell has the right end in sight, but his ways and means bother me.'

'He's a liar?' Hennessey didn't know the man as well as Hall did.

'Let's say he's capable of bending the truth,' Hall nodded.

The phone rang for the umpteenth time that morning.

'Hall. What? Where? Good. No. Incident Room. Number Two. Do his parents know? Good. Keep it that way for now' He hung up. 'The missing link, Dick.' The sergeant thought he saw his DCI smile, but it was obviously a trick of the light. 'We've found Ronnie Parsons.' And he grabbed his jacket and made for the door.

The missing link. Dick Hennessey knew that story. If DCI Hall was talking about the Piltdown skull, the missing link between ape and man, then that was a hoax. This missing link was a lie.

* * *

The sea crashed along the groynes out beyond the bay. Hysterical children dared each other to rush headlong into the surf and delirious dogs barked and gambolled in the foam. Jacquie Carpenter was trailing along the water's edge, watching her toes disappear under the EU-approved froth that heralded each rippling wave. The wind blew her hair from her face and she looked at the man beside her.

'Thank you for agreeing to see me,' Maxwell said. 'It can't have been easy.'

He looked an unlikely tourist did Mad Max, his trousers rolled up like a pair of plus fours, his jacket slung over his shoulder, his hat for once gone and the breeze playing havoc with his hair. He dropped a Hush Puppy and quickly stooped to pick it up before the tide got it.

'Did you think I'd be chained to a wall?' she asked him.

'After what your Sergeant Hennessey told me. I didn't know what to think.'

'He's not my sergeant,' she said.

'He seems to care for you,' he told her. 'We all do.'

She looked at him, this latter-day Crusader, this bow-tie knight errant. 'That's nice,' she said, barely audible above the roar of the surf. 'You're a strange man, Peter Maxwell.'

He laughed suddenly, turning to her, 'Now that's something I've never heard before.'

'They've found Ronnie,' she said and winced as he gripped her arm.

'Where?'

She turned to walk on. 'I don't know the details. Since my suspension, I'm rather incommunicado. I gather he was found sleeping rough in Brighton.'

'Couldn't leave it alone, eh?'

'What?'

Maxwell sighed, scanning the tufted dunes ahead and the knots of children building their little silicon Kraks des Chevaliers in the wetter sand by the sea. 'If your boys found him this time, I found him first. Or rather he found me.'

She stopped in her tracks, her mouth hanging open, her head shaking in disbelief. 'What are you talking about?' Her hands were fluttering in the breeze.

'He came to my home' — Maxwell kept walking, the girl trying to keep pace with his larger strides — 'he didn't know where else to go—'

'Why? Why didn't you tell us?' She was screaming at him now, above the screams of the children and the blare of the ghetto blasters behind the windbreaks.

'Why didn't you tell me about the letter?' He rounded on her and saw her furious gaze fall away. 'What it said.'

'I couldn't,' she said.

'Quite,' and he trudged on along the line of the bay. 'The boy was terrified, Jacquie, and exhausted. He'd last seen Alice Goode in the Museum of the Moving Image. That had nothing to do with his disappearance.'

* * *

'Oh, didn't it?' DCI Hall was staring coldly into the nervous, pale face of Ronnie Parsons. The boy looked at the brief the law had called in, a pompous old arsehole in a pinstriped suit. He looked at the men across the desk from him in the Incident Room interview room. The blank expressionlessness of DCI Hall, the almost unremitting smirk of DS Hennessey. He looked at the silently turning tape in the corner, the one 'they' couldn't doctor anymore, the one that would record every nuance, register every jangled nerve end.

'I told you' — Ronnie was tired — 'I'd planned to go anyway. The Museum trip seemed the perfect opportunity. Slip away in London and you blokes'd never find me. Kids go missing all the time, round the 'Dilly and that. You never find 'em.'

'Sometimes we do,' Hall told him. 'Fished out of the Thames and swollen and black. Others times they've got dirty needles sticking out of their arms. Or their underpants are tied tight round their necks. Not a pretty picture, is it, Ronnie? That's because it's not a pretty world.' He leaned back, giving the boy some air, some space. 'How well did you know Jean Hagger?'

* * *

'The letter,' Jacquie told Maxwell, 'was a silly, adolescent thing. But it might have hanged him in the good old days.'

'Leave those to me,' Maxwell smiled, 'I was there then, remember? What did it say?'

She threw up her arms in exasperation. 'I'm under suspension because I talked to you,' she said.

'In for a penny,' he told her.

'Were you followed?'

He turned to look back at the happy grockles cavorting in the sun. 'Any of those look like Mr Plod?'

'What does it matter now?' she asked the wind. 'It's the end of my career anyway.'

She felt him grip her shoulders, shaking her gently, 'Not if I have anything to do with it. But for now, Jacquie, you're out of it. Who's going to carry on?'

She blinked back the tears. 'I don't know,' she said. 'You?'

'Me,' he nodded and held her close for a moment. 'But,' he held her at arm's length again, 'I need the answers. All of them you've got. Now, what did the letter say?'

* * *

'"My Darling Alice",' Henry Hall was reading the letter in his hand, '"It was wonderful last night. You were wonderful. When I got home I couldn't stop thinking about you. I think you needed it as much as I did. I can't wait for tomorrow night. Usual time and I'll bring the bottle of wine. Will the old bag be out? We don't want her snooping around, do we? I love you, Ronnie." Did you write that, Ronnie?'

The boy shifted in his chair, looking instinctively at the brief, who seemed as intent on hearing his answer as Hall was.

'We can check, you know,' Hennessey prompted him. 'Hand-writing samples. I'm sure the school would oblige. And then of course, your prints'd be all over that, wouldn't they?' He nodded in the direction of the letter.

'Yeah, I wrote it,' the boy said.

The policeman leaned back. 'But it wasn't true.'

'You didn't fancy Miss Goode?' Hall asked. Ronnie shrugged. 'I may have done. But I didn't do nothing about it. Christ. She wouldn't have looked at me twice.'

'That's not what the driver says,' Hennessey told him.

'What driver?' Ronnie was lost.

'The driver of the coach that took you to the Museum of the Moving Image. When we interviewed him he said you two seemed very close.'

'What does he know?' Ronnie blurted, becoming more annoyed and defiant by the minute.

* * *

'Are you seriously telling me that Alice Goode was having an affair with one of my sixth form?' Maxwell asked.

'This is 1997, Max,' Jacquie shrugged. 'It wouldn't be the first time.'

'It'd be the first time for Ronnie Parsons,' he said. 'Although . . .' 'Although . . .'

'He had the hots when he was younger for an older girl — a sixth former. That's where he was when he absconded from the Museum. Playing the Wild Rover at Brighton University. Unfortunately for him, she'd graduated to higher things.'

'Nuclear Physics?'

'University lecturers. Always rather big time was Dannie Roth. No, I'm sorry. I just don't buy it. As you say, a piece of adolescent silliness. Still . . .'

'Still, it gives him a motive for killing Jean Hagger.' She kicked the seaweed swirling around her feet. 'How close were they, her and Alice?'

'Lovers, she told me,' he said, wandering up from the water's edge to crash into the dry sand on the slope of the dunes. 'Wonder why there are always washing-up-liquid bottles on beaches?'

'What if the letter was true?' Jacquie sat next to him, letting the pale sand drift through her fingers. 'What if Ronnie and Alice were at it like knives? Jean found out — worse, walked in on them. There was a row. He panicked and hit her.'

'It doesn't make sense,' Maxwell said. 'Alice was dead before Jean was murdered. At least five days had elapsed.'

'I'm sorry' — she buried her face in her knees for a moment — 'I'm not thinking straight. Doc Astley's given me some tablets.'

'Jean had a message,' Maxwell said, 'at school, remember? A man's voice telling her to go home quickly. A man's voice. Her murderer's voice.'

'Ronnie is eighteen,' Jacquie said. 'His voice would pass muster over the phone.'

'Yes,' Maxwell nodded. 'Yes, it would.'

* * *

'So you didn't ring Mrs Hagger at Bishop Billington?' Hall asked the boy. 'On the morning she was killed?'

'No,' Ronnie shouted. 'Look, I've told you all this once.'

'He is right, Chief Inspector,' the brief broke his silence for the first time that afternoon. 'And he's given you his answers.'

'Tell me,' Hall lifted up the grey holdall onto the interviewing table, 'about this.'

* * *

'It was a grey sports bag,' Jacquie remembered, 'Nike, if my memory serves.'

'Empty?'

'No. It had Alice Goode's clothes in it. The ones she was wearing when she disappeared.'

'Jesus! Where was it found?'

'In Jean Hagger's living room.'

'That's odd.'

'What is?'

'If Ronnie had lured Jean Hagger back to her flat, he'd have had to have waited somewhere nearby until she arrived.'

'Presumably.'

Maxwell was in full cry now, chewing his lip, squinting at the sun on the waves. 'With a grey holdall, which was full of clothes of his last victim. Why would he bring those with him? Did anybody see him there, carrying the bag?'

'I don't know,' she said. 'There are just so many unanswered questions.'

* * *

'So you left the holdall in the middle of the lounge after you'd battered Mrs Hagger to death?' Hall leaned back, waiting for the answer.

'No,' Ronnie said. 'The last time I saw that bag was at the Museum. I left it in the cloakroom. And it didn't have Miss Goode's clothes in. Just my own stuff. Look, can I go now?'

Hennessey chuckled.

Hall leaned over the microphone. 'Interview terminated by DCI Hall at three thirty-one,' and he clicked off the machine.

'I'll let you see your parents,' he said. 'But as for you going, son . . . Not till hell freezes over.'

* * *

But Ronnie Parsons didn't see his parents. He didn't want to see his parents. Instead, he asked to see Peter Maxwell and that night a large white patrol car purred to a halt outside Number 38 Columbine and the boys in blue asked Peter Maxwell to accompany them to the police station.

This was not the first time that Leighford and Tottingleigh had seen an Incident Room set-up. The enquiry was into the death of Jean Hagger, coupled with that of her flatmate, Alice Goode. The press, both national and local, were camped outside it in one of those media explosions that surrounds any untoward death these days. The world looked hungrily in on the Meridian bulletins and picked up South Coast Radio. That boy, the one who'd gone missing, they'd found him. The police weren't saying anything. That meant he did it. You could always tell. Typical, wasn't it, of kids today? Look at poor Jamie Bulger and that girl they found under the slide in the playground. It wasn't safe to go out on the streets. And the group most afraid to go out, the elderly, the least likely group to be targeted, locked themselves in and muttered about collapsing society. And the group least afraid, the group most likely to end up on the pavement with a face full of broken glass, the young men, continued to go out. All, that is, except one.

Ronnie Parsons looked very small and very isolated in the cell where they'd put him. Peter Maxwell was allowed a quick look through the eye-level grille before he was bustled away down the corridor, through the Incident Room with its clutter of VDUs flickering in green and blue, its incessantly clattering keyboards and its clanging telephones. Policemen and women, in shirts and blouses sat at rakish angles, following up this lead, chasing that. They all looked tired. And to Peter Maxwell, they all looked so young.

Only Henry Hall looked his age — and more. He sat in his office, the phone off the hook, a cup of cold coffee at his elbow. His family smiled at him from a school photograph — just to remind him he still had a family.

'You'll get my eldest next year,' he told Maxwell, 'He likes History. And dancing, but that's from his mother.'

'Excellent,' said Maxwell. 'I've always said all you need in life is brains and feet. The rest'll take care of itself.'

'Coffee, Mr Maxwell?' Hall asked.

'I'd rather see Ronnie.'

Hall patted the air with both hands. 'In time,' he promised, 'but first, I'd like a little word.'

'Ah. I wondered why the guided tour.'

'I'm sorry?' Hall could be as inscrutable as Maxwell when the chips were down.

'First, I'm taken in by the front door. Very dramatic. Very unnecessary. Right in the glare of the television cameras. I'll be all over the Leighford Advertiser come Friday, I shouldn't wonder. "Teacher helps police with their enquiries".'

'Do you, Mr Maxwell?' Hall asked. 'I wonder.'

'Ah, but the magical mystery tour continued, didn't it? Your affable PC apologised for not knowing the layout of the station. Just drafted in, he said. Odd that I've seen him directing traffic by the Town Hall roadworks for the last two months, then, isn't it? So we went to the cells, had a quick shufty at the condemned man, then through the centre of the hive, where there are nasty photos of dead women all over the place.'

'Welcome to the real world,' Hall shrugged.

'I understood that Ronnie asked to see me.'

'So he did,' the Chief Inspector nodded. 'What I'd like to know is why.'

'I'm his Year Head,' Maxwell said.

Hall leaned back, the flicker of what might have been a smile hovering around his lips. 'You're not going to give me all that pastoral guff, are you?' he asked.

'It may be guff to you, Chief Inspector,' the Head of Sixth Form told him levelly, 'but to some of us, it matters. What about Ronnie's parents?'

Hall shrugged, 'They've been here for the past four hours. He won't see them. They weren't, you'll notice, part of the guided tour.'

'Clearly,' Maxwell said.

'What's the boy got against his mum and dad,' Hall asked. 'Can you tell me?'

'Common enough, isn't it, among teenaged boys? Sense of resentment, arrogance. It's all to do with male domination, deep down. A challenge to the leader of the herd.'

'And in Ronnie's case?'

'I don't suppose you've seen his back?'

Hall shook his head.

'Beatings. His father took his strap to him on more occasions than he cared to remember.'

'You knew about this? At Leighford High, I mean?'

'No,' Maxwell said. 'I only found out recently.'

'How?' the Chief Inspector was a terrier when it came to pinning men in tight corners.

'Look, Chief Inspector, let's just say I know. Is that OK?'

When a man like Peter Maxwell was driven to saying 'OK?', he was rattled, off his guard. Hall sensed it, not in the man's words, but in the tension round his eyes. He'd seen it before.

'Tell me about Jacquie Carpenter,' Hall said.

'What do you want to know?' Maxwell asked.

The Chief Inspector sighed. 'Mr Maxwell, I have two women dead, one on my patch, the other from it. I honestly don't have the time to fence with you all day. There are more pressing matters.'

'All right,' Maxwell conceded. 'But first, you must tell me something. How much hot water is Jacquie in?'

Hall hesitated for a moment. This might be the only lifeline Peter Maxwell was prepared to throw him. 'She is under suspension currently pending internal enquiries. We would have had to interview you sooner or later anyway. Ronnie asking for you has saved us the bother.'

'Why me?' Maxwell was at his most obtuse.

'Because DC Carpenter confided information to you that she ought not to have done.'

'Has she?'

'Mr Maxwell!' It was the closest Henry Hall had ever come to hitting a member of the public — or the roof, but Maxwell was nearer.

'I won't be responsible for getting her into trouble,' Maxwell said flatly.

'She's already in trouble,' Hall assured him. 'You can help get her out of it.'

'How?'

'By telling the truth.'

Maxwell sat back, taking in his man and his moment. 'If I tell you the truth, then you'll drop charges against her?'

'There aren't any charges against her — not yet.'

'Now who's fencing?' Maxwell asked.

'Very well,' Hall nodded, 'let's say if I'm satisfied with your answers, I'll do my level best with internal affairs. The weight of a DCI goes a long way.'

'Does it?' Maxwell had watched Prime Suspect. He wasn't so sure. 'All right. I'll have to believe you.'

'Thank you.'

'Jacquie came to me five weeks ago — a bit longer than that, in fact. She was looking into the disappearance — that's all it was then — of Alice Goode.'

'Why you?'

'We'd met before, remember? The murder of Jenny Hyde?' Hall nodded. He remembered.

'I was a colleague of Alice's and it was my trip. If I'd been well, she'd never have gone to London in the first place.'

'So you felt guilty?'

'I felt . . . involved, shall we say?' Maxwell hadn't even convinced himself. 'Oh, all right. Guilty. Yes. Guilty as sin. I should have been there. It's that simple.'

'And what did Jacquie bring you?'

'A theory. A theory that linked up one murder and one attempted murder.'

'Carly Drinkwater and Georgianna Morris.'

'That's right. She said she'd told you about them and you didn't want to know.'

'I didn't see an obvious connection — then. But then, as far as we knew, Alice Goode was still alive.'

'And now do you see a connection?'

'I'm open to any suggestions,' Hall said.

'Then you'll follow up on them and lay off the girl?' Maxwell was on the edge of his seat.

'I told you I'd do what I could. What did you do with the information Jacquie had given you?'

'I found Georgianna Morris.'

'How?'

'I'm an historian, Chief Inspector, I looked up primary source material, as any good historian should. The *Evening Standard* gave me an old job address. The rest was something your boys specialise in, foot-slogging.'

'And?'

'The poor kid's mind's gone. Or at least her memory. Whoever the bastard was who did that to her made a pretty thorough job of it.'

'Not as thorough as the job he made of Carly Drinkwater.'

'And Alice Goode,' Maxwell said. 'What about Alice?'

'You tell me, Mr Maxwell,' Hall murmured. 'Carly Drinkwater and Georgianna Morris were snatched from cinemas. Alice Goode from a cinema museum. Was Jacquie right after all? Was I just too busy and too blind to see it?'

Maxwell looked at Henry Hall, his heart on his sleeve, his conscience naked to the neon light. 'I've got a lead,' the Head of Sixth Form said. 'Are you going to let me follow it up?'

'Are you going to tell me what it is?'

'No,' Maxwell shook his head.

'I could do you for obstructing the police,' Hall warned.

'There's nothing you could do to me I haven't done to myself already,' Maxwell told him. 'It was my trip, remember. This is my movie, Mr Hall, and if you'll stay out of my way, I'll load the last reel.'

'You know you can't see Ronnie alone,' Hall said.

Maxwell nodded. 'What about Jacquie?'

'I'll do what I can. You've got my word on that.'

'And my last reel?' Maxwell was on his feet.

Hall hesitated. 'You're the projectionist, Mr Maxwell.' He shrugged. 'It looks like the rest of us are just the audience. Roll 'em.'

CHAPTER 12

They let Ronnie Parsons go the next day. First, because they couldn't legally hold him any longer and second because of the miracles of modern science. They'd taken a blood sample from him and it didn't match the semen traces found in the body of Alice Goode. That wasn't in itself, of course, conclusive. He could still have kidnapped and strangled her; and as for the murder of Jean Hagger, that was still wide open. Henry Hall was keeping a very open mind on that one.

And Ronnie? Well, Ronnie still had to check in with the police every Thursday — 'for a good smacking' as they put it jovially down at Leighford nick. But the boy was a known runner. You couldn't be too careful with a boy like that. He wouldn't go home. Couldn't bear the atmosphere at Rondo again. It was because of that that he'd vanished in the first place, just taken off, doubling out of the side doors in the Museum of the Moving Image, nipping over the barrier, out of the fire exit. He'd half expected an alarm to be triggered, but he heard nothing. It wasn't until he was across the river, losing himself in the roaring maze of the Underground just to put everybody off his scent that he realised he'd left his bag, the grey holdall with his spare underpants, socks and sandwiches, in the Museum cloakroom. Too bad. He wasn't going back for it.

'Did they give you a hard time?' Maxwell's office was the safest haven a lad like Ronnie had just at that moment, cosier than the council flatlets in Monterey Street, with their elegant view of the Tottingleigh gasworks.

Ronnie shrugged. 'Not as bad as French GCSE oral,' he remembered.

'I haven't had a chance to thank you,' Maxwell said.

'What for?'

'Not mentioning that you shacked up with me for that couple of days.'

'That's all right,' Ronnie said. 'I shouldn't have done it anyway. Shouldn't have landed you in it.'

'No,' Maxwell had put on his stern face, 'what you shouldn't have done was a runner when your mum called round.'

'You'd have shopped me,' Ronnie said.

'You're right,' Maxwell nodded. 'That's how I discovered you'd gone. A couple of minutes and there'd have been a reconciliation. How did your parents take it when they saw you at the cop-shop?'

Ronnie hung his head. 'Well, Mum was Mum, you know. All tears and hugs. Dad, well, he just stood there, like the shit he is. It's what I expected.'

'Tell me about the blood, Ronnie,' Maxwell said softly.

The hum of Mrs B's polisher started up in the corridor outside. It was the butt-end of another day. In the common room, the politicos of the Sixth Form Council were arguing the toss about the washing-up rota and the Leavers' Ball, the meeting chaired, in Maxwell's absence, by his Number Two, Helen Maitland, The Fridge.

'What blood?'

Maxwell rummaged in the battered portmanteau he called a briefcase, the scraps of leather and brass that he'd carried his soul in since the heady days by the Cam when he lay under Grantchester skies with Rupert Brooke and played with Lord Byron's bear on his staircase at St John's. It was the Pearl Jam T-shirt, its sleeve still stiff and brown.

'Where'd you get that?' Ronnie seemed to have turned paler so that his face matched Maxwell's wall.

'Mrs B. found it in my spare room,' the Head of Sixth Form told him. 'First the bag at Jean Hagger's, now this. You seem hell bent on leaving telltale evidence of scenes of crime behind you, Ronnie.'

'Look, it's not what it seems.'

Maxwell knew panic when he saw it. Ronnie was licking his lips because they were dry as a brick, waving his arms around because he wanted to lash out at his tormentor, bracing his legs with both feet on the ground because he wanted to run. The door was shut and older as he was, slower as he was, Maxwell knew he could get to it before Ronnie. Ronnie knew it too.

'Read my thoughts, Ronnie.' Maxwell's George Bush was lost on the boy. 'What does it seem? You're an historian, dammit. This is primary evidence.' He shook the rag in his hand. 'Whose blood is it?'

'His name's Justin somebody,' he was shouting and Maxwell's quiet, calm delivery made him sound all the louder.

'Who's Justin?'

'Some bloke, some lecturer. I told you. Dannie Roth was going out with him. I didn't like that. He got funny and I hit him. It was daft, really.'

'Daft, indeed,' Maxwell nodded. 'So this isn't Jean Hagger's blood?'

Ronnie's eyes said it all. He forgot the rising terror inside him. 'No,' and his voice had dropped to a whisper.

Maxwell looked at the gangly lad in front of him. Then he slid back his desk drawer, slipped the T-shirt inside to join the confiscated bits and pieces he'd collected over the term — the fags, the chewing gum, the lighter, the dog-eared copy of *Fiesta* — and he turned the key in the lock.

'Did the police accuse you of murdering Jean Hagger?' he asked.

Ronnie was blinking back the tears. Why was Maxwell doing this? He had been the only one he could trust when he came back to Leighford. There had been no one else. But now he was like a Rottweiler with attitude. 'More or less,' he managed.

Maxwell threw down his drawer key. 'You look after that for me, Ronnie,' he said, 'for the time being. If I have a sudden hankering for a fag, a piece of chewing gum or a quick shufty through *Fiesta,* I'll get it back from you. Fair enough?'

'Fair enough,' the boy nodded and he felt the warm metal burn into the palm of his hand.

* * *

Old cases. Dead cases. They'd long ago closed down the Incident Rooms on Carly Drinkwater and on Georgianna Morris. They'd happened out of Henry Hall's manor, out of present time. But a murder was a capital offence. If there was a referendum today, Joe Public would bring back hanging. In his darker moments, Chief Inspector Hall often mused on that. They still tested, he knew, the apparatus of death at Wandsworth Jail, still placed the sack of sand on the doors, still hooked up the hemp and drew the bolts to eternity. But there was no Jack Ketch now, no Albert Pierrepoint. Another Old English craft had gone. And if Joe Public got his way, who'd train the hangman?

So the cases of Carly Drinkwater and Georgianna Morris lay open, like gaping wounds; untended, festering, but never quite forgotten. Hall looked at the paperwork obligingly passed to him by the Met. He was still looking at it that night when his wife finally dropped her Patricia Cornwell over the edge of the bed and muttered something he didn't catch. And he was somewhere in the forensic reports on Carly Drinkwater when the kids kissed him and dashed off for the bus, leaving him in the kitchen on his rest day, with the clock ticking and the rumble of the tumble drier for company.

Carly Drinkwater was twenty when she died. A student at the LSE, she was, as they always said on *Crimewatch*, a likeable girl with a bubbly personality who hadn't an enemy in the world. She lived at home. Mum. Dad. No siblings. In the holidays she worked in a travel agent's in Raines Park. She had a steady boyfriend, Kenneth Cassidy, who'd been interviewed by the police on four occasions. He was a likeable boy too — Carly's parents spoke warmly of him. But the likeable boy and the likeable girl had had a row on the night she died. He said it was about a party she wanted to go to and he didn't. Carly had no comment at all on that. But her body told tales out of school when the Council stray-dog catcher found it on the waste ground where the old Devonshire Hotel used to stand years before.

Hall had the scene-of-crime photographs in front of him now, the sort he'd vowed never to let his wife and kids see. When he brought this stuff home and it wasn't in his hands it was in his study, under lock and key. She was a pretty girl, with short, bobbed hair. Or she had been, before some maniac took her off the street. Except it wasn't the street, it was the Studio 3 Cinema in Leopold Road. The usherette remembered her going in to see *The Unforgiven*. She'd remembered because the girl had mascara running down her face and she'd asked what the matter was. The girl had shaken her head. Nothing.

Now, the camera didn't lie. The dog catcher had found her under an old sheet of corrugated iron. She was lying on her back, her head inclined to her left, her pale purple tongue contrasting oddly with the pallor of her skin. A more poetic man than Henry Hall would have remembered G. K. Chesterton's 'Lepanto' — her face is as a fungus of a leprous white and grey, like plants in the high houses that are shuttered from the day.

But there was nothing poetic about this death. Nothing quick about the kill. There was a livid crimson line around her neck where something, perhaps a clothes line, had cut deep as the bastard strangled her.

The forensic report told the rest. Bruising on the thighs and vagina spelt out forcible intercourse — rape. Abrasions on the face, knuckles and ribs meant that she'd put up a struggle. In the closing minutes and seconds of her life, she'd fought back, against the worthless piece of shit who was not killing her softly. And it hadn't happened on the scattered bricks and debris of the Devonshire. She'd been killed somewhere indoors, wrapped in a blanket with pale blue fibres and dumped. It would have had to have been at night. The area was too open for a daylight drop, too well frequented. The waste ground was surrounded by a wire-mesh fence, ten feet high, but the wire had broken in places and kids played their games there, as their grannies and granddads had when London was ringed with bomb craters and lives and houses were smashed to pieces.

And Carly Drinkwater's life had been smashed to pieces too. And those of her parents. And Kenneth Cassidy, her boyfriend.

And Henry Hall found himself musing once again, that there were no winners in the game of murder. Only losers. And the loss was real and the loss was for ever.

Georgianna Morris had gone to the cinema too. That was in Notting Hill, a year after the murder of Carly Drinkwater. She'd been luckier — or had she? Hall looked at the broad, smiling face, the holiday snapshot taken three months before. The girl had survived, but who knew in what private hell? Her priest had spoken to her, good Catholic girl that she was, hour after hour in the kindly quiet of the confessional. He'd taken down the mesh partition, slid aside the screen, sat with his hands on hers. Father Conlon was out of his depth and he told her so. How could he know her pain? Her terror? He couldn't. But God could. And God was there, listening. And he'd seen the disbelief on Georgianna's face. Where was God when she'd needed Him most? When some madman was hacking at her body with a breadknife as though she was a crusty cob?

The rape-crisis counsellor fared no better. She didn't have Father Conlon's kindly eyes, but she was professional, she was experienced and she was female. No good.

Georgianna couldn't remember even the name of the film she'd been to see. The Met had established that it must have been *Four Weddings and a Funeral*, but all the girl could remember was leaving home that night. She'd crossed London from Streatham, where she worked in an estate agent's, and had gone to the cinema, the Star in the High Street, to meet a friend. Except that the friend never turned up. The Met had checked her out. She'd gone down with flu that day and had forgotten all about her date with Georgianna. They'd checked the estate agent's too — Marples of Streatham — Georgianna's colleagues, Georgianna's clients. Not that she had clients in the accepted sense. She was too young for business of her own and ever since Suzy Lamplugh, no estate agent in the country sent out young women on their own. Too many weirdoes buying property these days.

Georgianna had been found in the driving rain, in Holland Park. Her shoes had gone, so had her dress and tights. There was no sign of her coat and she was cowering in some bushes in only her bra and panties when an elderly couple walking their dog had found her. She had bruising to her face and thighs and six separate cuts, one deep, the others superficial, to her forearms.

Hall could see all that. What he couldn't see were the scars on her mind. That coloured canvas where our memory is etched, where sights and sounds and smells take us back to our childhood. And Mad Max could have told Hall that Georgianna was a child again — 'I don't really like popcorn'.

* * *

Mad Max sat in the cinema that night. He'd always avoided *Jurassic Park*. Not because it was a bad film, but just because it was hyped to death. Now, on its umpteenth tour of duty, he succumbed. He was glad he did, smiling with delight as that dishonest fat bloke got his, being impressed as always by Jeff Goldblum, wondering what women saw in Sam Neill and which parts of Scotland Lord Dickie Attenborough was supposed to hail from. But that wasn't really why Maxwell had come. He'd come to watch the audience.

The four Years Tens in the front behaved themselves as soon as they saw him. Shit! No sliding on the seats and lobbing ice cream at each other now. And Tommy Hollis, the Don Juan of Year Eleven, felt he couldn't shove his hand quite so far up Tracey Eccleston's skirt as he'd planned to do before he caught sight of Mad Max. But Maxwell wasn't interested in them. There were two unattached women in the theatre. One was knocking sixty and Maxwell was mildly astonished to find she'd brought her crocheting along — she'd obviously seen the film before.

The other was in her late twenties, early thirties, attractive in a boyish sort of way with a long trench coat over a loose and shapeless jumper. Maxwell waited for the Pearl and Dean to finish, then trotted down the shallow, plush-carpeted steps and bought a carton of popcorn from the raddled old floozy who sold it. So different, Maxwell thought, from the radiant popsy of yesterday, whose fish-net stockings and tray of Kia-Ora filled the silver screens of his youth.

At the stair nearest the single girl, he tripped and the popcorn went everywhere. The Year Ten kids stifled their giggles and Don Juan missed the whole thing because he was too busy eating Tracey Eccleston at the time.

'I'm terribly sorry,' Maxwell flustered, raising his hat.

'That's all right.' The girl was brushing popcorn off her lap. Before she knew it, Maxwell was on the seat beside her, flicking the sticky bits in all directions. He felt her stiffen, edge away.

'Trust me!' he said, smiling. 'I really am very embarrassed about all this.'

'No, no,' she said, smiling back. 'It was an accident.'

'I'm just glad it wasn't a lolly' Maxwell said. 'They stain so, don't they? Enjoying the film?'

'Er . . . yes.'

'Seen it before?'

'No, no, I haven't. Look, would you excuse me?'

'Of course,' and gentleman that he was, he got out of his seat and watched her go. She didn't run. Didn't look back. He knew she wouldn't. She turned left at the top of the stairs, making for the loo. Was that, Maxwell wondered, how it was done? How Carly Drinkwater and Georgianna Morris had been picked up? He sat back down, extricating the last of the popcorn from under his bum. Of course, he didn't know if the victims had known their assailant or not. But if they hadn't — or even if they had in a passing sort of way — wouldn't that have been their instinctive reaction? It was all about body language really. In the dark of a cinema, countless millions had lost themselves to the magic, the make-believe. What woman's heart had not leapt when Clark Gable had told Vivien Leigh where to stick it? Who had not gulped back a tear when Dirk Bogarde stood on his tumbril in the shadow of Madame Guillotine and told a frightened peasant girl it was a far, far better thing than he'd ever done before? And somewhere in a South Wales cinema, Maxwell had good reason to believe, still lay, in the dust and sweet wrappers under the seats, the dentures of an aged great aunt of his, so terrified by Lon Chaney's *Phantom of the Opera*, that her scream had sent her false teeth hurtling through the air.

But Maxwell had done the unthinkable. Whoever the girl was over whom he had tipped his popcorn, she'd had her evening ruined. She'd felt threatened, vulnerable. He, an old pervert in a bow tie and ridiculous hat, had invaded her space, engaged her in conversation. And she'd retreated. She'd run. There were those who'd have brazened it out. The little hussy who showed Maxwell into the Girlie Peep Show in Soho would have sat there, legs open and breasts uptilted, and would have fetched him a nasty one in the nuts if he'd got fresh. But this girl had taken refuge in an inner sanctum, that last of sanctuaries now that the medieval church was no more. She'd gone to the Ladies'. She'd gambled that Maxwell would not follow her there. For Maxwell, like the men who killed Caesar, was an honourable man.

But the man who killed Carly Drinkwater and did his damnedest to kill Georgianna Morris wasn't an honourable man. That's how he got her out of the cinema. There were always fire exits in those places and they were invariably near the loos. Maxwell wandered to the back to check. Sure enough, there it was, feet rather than yards from the door marked 'Ladies'. There'd be . . . what? Three, four cubicles inside? It would take Carly two or three minutes to reckon she'd shaken Lover Boy off and then she'd nip out. Except that she hadn't shaken him off. He was there, by the loo door. He'd have grabbed her wrist, quietly, quickly, pulling her to him. She'd have felt the knife rip through her coat and he'd have rasped some cliché like 'Scream and you're dead.' Except that Carly Drinkwater couldn't have been thinking about clichés at a time like that, even assuming she knew what a cliché was. She'd have been in a blind panic, the normal, everyday safe world hurtling by her in a blur as he waited until the coast was clear and smuggled her out of the back way, down the fire exit stairs and beyond into the Raines Park night.

Then what? A car? A van? Somewhere where he could throw her and she'd stay thrown. He couldn't have risked a struggle in the street. It would have been dark, but not invisibly dark. For Maxwell's money, it was a van. He probably knocked her out, a single powerful fist in the face, and threw her in, perhaps sampling the goods as he did so, sliding his hands over her breasts, under the skirt. Then he slammed and locked the doors and no one saw Carly Drinkwater again.

It must have been similar with Georgianna Morris, except she screamed or struggled or both. She was in her underwear, so he must have got her into the van, if van it was. Perhaps he couldn't wait this time. Perhaps she came to as he was stripping her. He panicked, there in the cramped space in the lights of the High Street, and thumped her again to shut her up. Perhaps he used his knife there. Perhaps later. Perhaps he locked her in, drove like a madman for the Park intending to rape her, strangle her and dump her, like a used condom, like a broken doll, like Carly Drinkwater. But when he opened the van doors, she lashed out at him, caught him off balance with both feet. Now he had to kill her quickly. They were in the Park and it was night time. But the Park was still open and there were people here and there, shadows under the dripping trees. He slashed her again — or was it for the first time? Hacking at her, trying to stop her from screaming, from crying out. But her arms were in the way. There was blood, flying in the rain, trickling the length of his blade, over his knuckles, but he couldn't reach her throat. He couldn't cut her head off. That would stop her. That would shut her up. Just the gargle of her death rattle. That was what he wanted to hear. But he slipped on the wet tarmac, lost his balance and she was gone, rain plastering her hair to her head, her arms dripping blood. He'd slammed the van into gear and was away, his heart racing with the engine revs.

Perhaps. It was all perhaps. Maxwell turned to the couple necking in the back row now that the lights were dimming again. 'I'll be asking you questions about this film tomorrow,' he said. 'So keep your eyes on the screen and your hands where I can see them. Oh and by the way, Casanova, Nazi Germany GCSE coursework. My office. Nine ack emma. Or I'll nail your nuts to the wall.'

* * *

'You want to do what, Max?' Jim Diamond, Headteacher of this parish, couldn't believe his ears.

Maxwell sat in the not very great man's office that Wednesday morning, the window in his day between 8A1 and the Double Coma the timetable laughing called Year Ten History. 'It's quite simple, Headmaster,' Maxwell was talking slowly, 'I want to take another trip to the Museum of the Moving Image. Using exactly the same people as before. Except of course for poor Alice. I shall play her.'

'It's out of the question, Max. The parents.'

Maxwell leaned to his man, 'I'm not inviting the parents, Headmaster,' he said.

'I mean they'll never wear it.'

'What harm can it do?'

'What good?'

'Good?' Maxwell smiled at the Head's unintentional pun. 'Quite. It's a long shot, but I think it'll help catch Alice Goode's killer.'

'You can't use children like that, Max,' Diamond said, his by-the-bookishness displayed for all to see.

'As far as they're concerned,' his Head of Sixth Form told him, 'it's just another "jolly". And as you know, Headmaster, on my trips, nobody disappears.'

'How does Anthea Edwards feel about all this?' Diamond set great store by embracing democracy, casting his safety net as wide as he could.

'She's ready to help catch Alice's murderer, of course,' Maxwell smiled. 'As you'd expect.'

'I don't follow any of this, Max,' the Headmaster confessed. 'You'll have to be more explicit?'

'All right,' Maxwell said, 'M-O-M-I. A little testette for you, Headmaster. What does it stand for?'

'Urn . . . the Museum of the Moving Image?' Diamond guessed, never liking to look a complete prat.

'Close,' Maxwell winked. 'And on one level, you're right. But in fact,' and he stood up, longing to meet the intellectual challenge of 10C3, 'I got to thinking in the wee, small hours, like we bachelors do, and I came up with what it really stands for. The magic ingredients of murder. M is for Motive, O is Opportunity, M is Means.'

'And I?' Diamond frowned.

Maxwell half turned at the Head's door. 'Ah, yes,' he chuckled. 'I is for Incompetence. Mine.'

CHAPTER 13

What are you doing on the eighteenth?' Jacquie Carpenter heard the voice say at the other end of the phone. 'If you're asking me out on a date, Max,' she answered, 'I shall have to disappoint you.'

'Gee Gosh A'mighty.' Maxwell's Doris Day as Calamity Jane needed a little work, it had to be said. He just didn't have the freckles. 'How about a trip to MOMI?'

'MOMI?'

'The Museum.'

'Yes. Yes. I know. Why?'

'A little action replay. It might refresh a few memories, Anthea's, in particular. Ronnie's too. I need to pinpoint precisely how Alice left the Museum.'

'I can't,' she muttered.

'Can't?' he challenged her. 'Or won't?'

There was a pause during which he could have kicked himself. 'Can't,' she said. 'It's the day of my internal enquiry. Besides, you'll never walk alone,' and she hung up.

'Well, who'd have thought it, Count,' Maxwell turned to the cat, the receiver still in his hand, 'Woman Policeman Carpenter is a football fanatic. She's not old enough to remember Gerry and the Pacemakers, let alone *Carousel*.' He put the phone down, frowning, 'Unless . . .' and he crossed the living room to the window. He flicked aside the blinds, glancing down at the twilit street where Mrs Troubridge, his neighbour of the Abyss, was just out on her way to her Thursday Bingo and the ecstasy of instant riches beyond the dreams of avarice. Across the road, well away from the orange glow of the oncoming streetlight, a parked car crouched in the shadows. Dark. Unmarked. Police.

'Well, well,' whispered Maxwell, 'Hello, hello, hello.' He turned to the cat, stretched in feline abandon on the settee, 'It looks like the Force is still with me, Count,' but his Alec Guinness was wasted on Metternich, who merely yawned, having heard it all before.

* * *

Now this cinema was vastly different from the one in Leighford High Street. And it seemed oddly different from its Wednesday night atmosphere too. There was no bill on the wall by the green door, no 'open to the public'. This was by invitation only and it was Maxwell's inaugural visit.

If he'd been expecting some ceremony, some baring of the right nipple or locking of buffalo horns and aprons, he was singularly disappointed. The clientele he'd never seen before. He'd lived in Leighford half his life, teacher and boy and he didn't recognise any of them. One of them, in unseasonal mac, might have been Alec Crossman's dad. But then one of them might have been Lord Lucan, for all Maxwell knew. They had a certain out-of-townness about them. They looked furtive, hunted, watching each other's faces until the eye contact was made, then turning away.

The only friendly face in the place appeared alongside his now as the muttered conversations grew less and the whispers even more hushed. 'Mr Maxwell. Max, isn't it?'

'Indeed . . . er . . . Dee?'

'That's right,' Douglas McSween shook his hand. 'Thanks for coming.'

'Thanks for inviting me. I came a little on spec. Is there a programme?'

McSween chuckled. 'Well, yes and no. Sorry to sound cryptic, but you can't be too careful. We used to have printed programmes, but you can't always get the films and to be honest, one or two of the wives got a little curious.'

'Did they?' Maxwell bluffed. All sorts of pennies were just beginning to drop in the minefield he called a brain. The audience were all men. The only girl appeared on the screen ahead of them both now. And the audience fell silent. Dave Freeman's gypsy warning echoed in Maxwell's ears.

'Jonathan's on the projector tonight,' McSween whispered, 'I'm taking the month off. You'll like this one. *Sweet Seventeen*,'' and he was gone into the rustling darkness.

Maxwell had seen films like this before. They had been sold over the counter in the good old days of the '80s when the world was agonising over whether to buy VHS or Betamax and before the Mary Whitehouse Parliament realised what was happening. In the days of his youth, Maxwell had snuck into the bioscope theatres of the Lumiere brothers to watch the odd skin flick. Plotless stories, lots of ripe lips and heavy breathing, ever-so-slightly-out-of-sync with the action.

But what he saw now was different. In the years of under-the-counterness since the exhilarating eighties, the subject matter had got nastier, the writhing more explicit. But it wasn't that that bothered Maxwell. It wasn't the girls peeling off their fol-de-rols in the dry ice and flashing lights of the Vegas flip-joint. It wasn't the stiffness of their ice-cubed nipples or the urgent thrusting of their hips against the lubricated poles. It wasn't even the furtive jerking of arms to his left and right in the cinema. It was the second girl from the end, with the long black wig and the carefully trimmed pubic hair. The camera lovingly followed her bouncing breasts, the curve of her hips and belly to focus brazenly on her groin and what her fingers were doing there. Then the lens flashed upwards to her face, trickling with perspiration to the unrelenting beat of the music and the look of pain and ecstasy that distorted it.

Maxwell's colleague. Alice Goode.

He coughed loudly, painfully. And went on coughing until his fellow punters began to turn round and give him annoyed looks. He apologised a few times, then got up and made his exit, in search of a drink of water. His eyes hadn't acclimatised to the light on the stairs before he collided with someone on his way up as he was on his way down.

'Sorry,' they both said simultaneously and recoiled. The newcomer spun on a sixpence and bolted down the stairs, but Maxwell was faster. He caught up with him at the bottom and pushed him against the wall, gripping his collar with one hand and pointing a finger at his nose with the other. Fisticuffs weren't really Mad Max's strong suit. His heart was firmly in his mouth and he couldn't feel his legs at all. But Piers Stewart didn't know that.

'Well, well,' Maxwell said, 'I'm glad I bumped into you. Felt badly about not leaving a tip when I last visited your establishment.'

'Now, look . . .'

'Uh-huh.' Maxwell wagged a finger under the restaurateur's nose, 'You see that car over there,' and he pointed to the solitary vehicle in the car park that abutted the bus station, 'that's driven by a Detective Sergeant Hennessey. Nice man. Sticks very close to me at the moment. If I nip out now and flag him down, he'll take about . . . oh . . . ten seconds to feel your collar.'

'Piers?' a voice broke the moment.

Both men turned to see Douglas McSween at the top of the stairs, peering at them in confusion, 'Is anything the matter?'

'I just had a bit of a coughing fit,' Maxwell beamed. And who should I bump into but my old friend Piers. Dee, you dark horse, you didn't tell me Piers was a member.'

'Er . . . confidentiality, old boy, that sort of thing.' McSween didn't like the look on Piers Stewart's face. 'Piers, are you all right?'

Piers Stewart didn't like the look on Peter Maxwell's face either, even though it was smiling. 'Fine,' he sounded a little strangled.

'Look, Dee,' Maxwell was bonhomie itself, 'I'd love to rejoin the film, but . . .' and he burst out coughing again, 'I'd only spoil it for the others. Lovely bits of tottie, by the way.'

'We like to please,' McSween said, still searching both men's faces for an explanation.

'You haven't got a room somewhere, have you? There's a little business venture Piers and I would like to discuss and it's rather private. Could you oblige?'

'Er . . . well . . .'

'That one at the back,' Stewart remembered, 'where you keep your archives.'

'Well, all right, but isn't there a pub or somewhere?'

'Rather private, old boy.' Maxwell tapped the side of his nose.

'Ah,' McSween tried to share Maxwell's private joke, 'of course. This way,' and he showed them upstairs and along the corridor to a poky little room he unlocked.

'Thank you, Dee,' Maxwell beamed, 'we won't be long. Be in for the film later. Tell me, have you seen it before?'

'Oh, yes,' McSween enthused, 'I vet all our stuff.'

'Excellent. That bit of skirt, the one with black hair . . .'

'Hmm?' McSween's eyes were bright at the memory of her.

'See her again, do we?'

'Rather,' he smirked like a naughty schoolboy, 'shags like a rabbit in the second half'.

'Great,' said Maxwell through gritted teeth, resisting the climbing urge to break the man's nose. 'We'll be in presently, then,' and he ushered McSween out of the door before whirling to haul Stewart down onto a chair across the table from his own. A naked light bulb swung in the dusty office space overhead, throwing lurid shadows across the sweating forehead of the restaurateur.

'You told me you weren't police,' Stewart hissed, pulling away.

'You told me I was a pimp,' Maxwell retaliated. 'But then, Richard Nixon said there'd be no whitewash at the White House, didn't he? Life's all lies and videotape, isn't it? You see, I didn't twig at first, amateur as I am at the sleuthing game. You said when I dined at your rather dubious caff that you'd had the law swarming all over your place after they'd found Alice Goode's body and that she was some sort of tart. Now, having only a Cambridge MA and an IQ in a mere four figures, I naturally assumed that those two facts were related. In other words, that in the course of their conversations with you, the Surrey Plod had let something slip, intentionally or otherwise, about Alice's erstwhile career. And that didn't square with what I knew about that, that the police hadn't cottoned on to that at all. I got there before they did. So how did you know about Alice? Answer, you were a member of the Leighford Low-life Filth Club, Douglas McSween, prop. You'd seen her as you saw her in your car park, hadn't you? Naked as the day she was born.'

Maxwell was shaking. It was all he could do not to snake out his right hand and knock Piers Stewart through the wall.

'Yes!' the restaurateur hissed. 'Some bastard stitched me up. As soon as I saw the face I recognised her. Christ, I'd seen her dozens of times. She made films with Pryce Garrison about three or four years ago, when the club was in Guildford.'

Maxwell leaned back. 'So the club moves around?'

'Of course,' Stewart said. 'It has to. You can only keep up the front of respectability — the odd Wednesday showing — for so long. Then tongues begin to wag.' Piers frowned. 'Are you kosher? As a member, I mean?'

Maxwell smiled. 'I'm an agent provocateur,' he said, 'And they don't come much more provocative than me, I can tell you.'

Stewart was on his feet before Maxwell gripped him by the sleeve. 'Look,' the man was sweating, 'I can't afford to get involved. Wendy, my wife . . .'

'Doesn't she understand you?' Maxwell mocked. 'I thought you'd turn out to be the awfully wedded husband.'

'She owns the business. If she had an inkling of all this . . . I'd be out on my ear, for Christ's sake. Look, can't we do a deal? Er . . . if it's money. What are you, an Inspector or something?'

'Or something,' Maxwell nodded.

'Look,' Stewart fumbled in his pocket, his fingers trembling on his wallet, 'I'm not a rich man. I mean, it's all tied up in the business, but, well, I can manage . . . five grand.'

Maxwell chuckled.

'All right, all right. Ten. Ten thousand pounds. It'll take me a day or two.'

'Answers,' Maxwell said.

'What?'

'Just give me some answers. And we'll call it quits.'

Stewart all but collapsed into the chair, his nerve gone. 'You don't understand,' he whispered, 'I can't get my name in the papers. The police . . .'

Maxwell leaned back, bluffing for all he was worth. 'Contrary to popular belief,' he said, 'we're reasonable men.' He threw his head in the direction of the theatre where Alice Goode was moaning her head off as though her life depended on it, 'Men of the world.'

Stewart visibly relaxed. 'What do you want to know?' he asked.

* * *

Piers Stewart had got involved in the film club before its Guildford days. The main distributor then was a man called Gregory Villiers and Dee — Douglas McSween — fronted the club and found the members. The list was impressive — businessmen like himself, academics like Maxwell, even the odd copper when the whole thing ran from Greek Street. It was an addiction really, like the lottery or the arcade games. You got hooked on the skin game. It was too risky to get your hands on the totty themselves, although some punters were up for it. Invariably it led to broken noses, blackmail and a lot of awkward questions. The more technocratically minded had veered away into surfing the net for likely talent, but Stewart had never been into kids like that. He knew damn well that Alice Goode wasn't really 'sweet seventeen', but that hardly mattered.

Imagine his horror then when a girlie he'd been drooling over for nearly two years in celluloid turned up dead by his back door. The irony was that that was why he'd come down to Leighford tonight, not to watch, but to have it out with Dee. Some bastard had deliberately dumped that poor girl's body where he could be implicated. And it had to be someone at the club. Stewart had wrestled with it, chewed it over, whatever analogy you like, but it wouldn't go away. Who? Maxwell had asked. Stewart had shrugged. He didn't know anyone capable of murder. People at the club just before he'd stopped going regularly had talked about snuff movies — you know, where they actually killed people. Stewart didn't want to know about any of that.

To Peter Maxwell, that was an urban myth, like choking Dobermen. To Piers Stewart, it seemed highly real. But then, presumably, to Piers Stewart, Alice Goode was grinding her crotch against him.

Maxwell maintained the policeman myth to the very end. It was very much on a need-to-know basis and Piers Stewart, a rather sad and frightened man for all his green Mercedes and his righteousness, didn't need to know the truth about Peter Maxwell. The Head of Sixth Form made his excuses and left.

In the car park, he took his time adjusting his cycle clips under the stars. It would be June tomorrow and Alice Goode had been dead for six weeks. Time to cross a few t's and dot a few i's. At least put in a few full stops. He'd start with the club. He saddled White Surrey and wobbled past Dick Hennessey, who slithered down in his seat in an attempt to stay out of sight. It didn't really convince anybody.

* * *

The Great Man stepped silently over Metternich the cat a little before two thirty. Not that the Count let him get away with it. The man laughingly known as his master was dressed in a black track suit he'd worn on Mufti Day at school last year, when he'd gone as a Ninja. It didn't fit him anywhere and the balaclava itched like buggery. Metternich turned away. Maxwell didn't take White Surrey, resting in the back alley. Instead he padded out of the house and across the lawn, careful not to collide with the rotary clothesline. Damn. That pair of Y-fronts still dangled there like a battle standard. They'd been dangling there since last Monday.

All the back gates along Columbine opened onto a path they used to call a gully in working-class areas when Maxwell was a lad and David Lloyd George was Prime Minister. He felt like a burglar, with his striped vest and bag of swag. 'Ho-ho for the robbers,' he heard himself muttering, 'the cops and the robbers, ho-ho.' Shit! Why did there have to be a full moon? He kept to the hedge for as long as he could, but it was nearly a mile to the centre of town and there wouldn't be cover all the way.

About twenty times in the steady stride to the bus station Maxwell nearly changed his mind. To say he had cold feet was an under-statement — they were blocks of ice. It was the glorious first of June, the day that Admiral Howe had trounced the French over two hundred years ago. That only served to remind Maxwell, not only how ridiculous he must have looked, but of the daunting task ahead. He'd never broken into anywhere in his life. Wasn't the wrong side of fifty-two a little late to start? But he needed the information he suspected lay behind that green door. And the face of Alice Goode spurred him on.

Bus stations by night aren't the most enticing places. A cat was rummaging in the dustbins at the back of the Asda store as he got there — some ginger oppo of Metternich's he supposed, although to be fair he was guessing the animal's sexual orientation. The deckers, double and single of the Leighford and District Bus Company were safely under lock and key in vandal-proof compounds, where the more dissolute members of Leighford High School couldn't get at them. A dog was barking sporadically somewhere behind the High Street where the shop signs creaked in the summer breeze.

This was ridiculous. He hauled off the balaclava and stuffed it into his pocket. Shit! A car's headlights circling the tarmac. Maxwell ducked back into the shadows, his back to the wall. He heard the braying from the passenger seats. Pissheads out on the tiles. The car lurched off in the direction of Tottingleigh and the sea. Maxwell reached the green door. It rose above him like the Tower of Babel. He'd seen a kid do this at school. Some herbert in Year Nine whose dad was an old lag. The kid had slipped his way into the examination cupboard, where they kept all the GCSE and A-level papers, just by using his library ticket. It had made Maxwell's blood run cold at the time, but mercifully the herbert wasn't the type to want to cheat in exams. He didn't turn up for them anyway. He was, however, the first name on the police's list when a couple of computers went walkabout from the school the following term.

Maxwell dropped his credit card at first — damn slippy those Lloyds Bank Gold jobbies. He picked it up in gloved fingers and pressed it into the door jamb. He leaned against it, sliding it up and down, listening for the telltale click. Bugger! Nothing. He wiped the beads of sweat from his forehead — it would all add to the realism if he was stopped and claimed to be a jogger on a midnight run. This was useless. He toyed for a moment with shoulder-barging the door, taking a flying kick at it, smashing through the flimsy woodwork with his trusty torch. Each of those approaches was flawed. He'd probably break his shoulder, for all that the wood was flimsy, in which case he'd been in no fit state to drop-kick anything. And as for the torch, well it came free with something so there was no telling how much punishment that would take.

At least he hadn't been followed. No dark car had begun to crawl behind him, at a nonchalant distance, no echoing feet on the tarmac behind. He looked up at the windows above. Hopeless. He couldn't even get up there. The drain-pipe was yards away, and anyway he'd then have to smash the glass and all these *modes d'emploi* would bring the entire West Sussex constabulary down on his neck.

He kicked the club's brickwork for good measure and jogged back home.

* * *

Wednesdays were not red-letter days for Peter Maxwell. He'd been up half the night on a wild goose chase and was still feeling murderous at those pompous old hypocrites dribbling over the celluloid writhings of Alice Goode. He vowed that if a kid looked at him funny that morning, he'd kill him.

'Penny for your thoughts, Max.' Sylvia Matthews was snatching a rare respite in the safety of the staffroom, well away from the PMT and classroomphobia that filled her day.

'Ha, Nursie,' he smiled, emerging from behind his coffee cup, 'I'm thinking of changing my career.'

'Oh?' For a moment, she half believed him and a sudden emptiness yawned before her.

'Burglary,' he said. 'Pays better than teaching.'

'Ah,' she smiled, relieved it was just more of Mad Max's nonsense. 'But the penalties.'

'Well, it's not so much that as the basics. There's probably a GNVQ course somewhere in sheer wall climbing and jemmying. It's just that I'm too old to enrol.'

'Don't do yourself down,' she scolded him. 'Where do you want to break into?'

He flashed her one of his smiles. Perceptive cattle, women, he pondered, but he knew it was more than his life was worth to say so. 'Nowhere in particular,' he lied, 'anywhere.'

'Can you get into this place legally?' she asked.

'Yes,' he frowned, 'but I can't steal what I want in broad daylight.'

'No, of course not,' she flicked open her copy of the Nursing Times, 'but you'd wait, wouldn't you?'

'I would?'

'Really, Max, I thought you were a Cambridge graduate.'

'So I am,' he bridled mischievously, 'but I didn't read Quantum Deviousness.'

'Take the Tower of London,' she said. 'You queue along with everyone else and in you go. You ogle all the armour and stuff and then pop to the loo. At closing time they lock you in, you help yourself to the Crown Jewels and when they open up the next morning, you walk out with everybody else. Simple.'

'You clearly haven't seen *Topkapi*, Sylv,' he sighed, but he was beaming broadly, 'but I love you anyway.' He bent to plant a smacking kiss on her forehead. 'You've made a middle-aged man very happy.'

And he didn't see the look on her face as he left. It was a look of pure joy.

* * *

Maxwell couldn't help chuckling as he queued along with everybody else outside the cinema club that night. Wednesday. Open-to-the-public night. He was chuckling because they were showing *Mission Impossible*. Now, he'd find out how to break into places. All you really needed was a genius for disguise, several hundred thousand dollars' worth of sophisticated computer equipment and the backing of the American government and it was simple. He enjoyed the film, but it had to be said he missed the comfortable, craggy face of dear old Peter Graves marshalling his troops. There was a new realism about the Tom Cruise version, a sense of the Establishment cracking, the work coming unglued, which fitted the '90s — and Peter Maxwell — well. Somehow, in the days of the Cold War, when everybody's finger was poised on the button, you felt safer. It was just Us and Them. Now it was Us and Everybody Else.

There was no sign of Douglas McSween, nor, naturally, of Piers Stewart. The restaurateur had told Maxwell, just before he threw up in the litter bin, that he had no intention of returning to the club, ever. He wanted his name off the membership list. And it was precisely the membership list that Maxwell was here for. He blessed dear old Sylvia Matthews again, but her scam was flawed. All right, so there'd be no electronic devices to worry about in this building, but the next time it was open to anybody was in a week from now, next Wednesday, ready for the next Open-to-the-Public showing. Maxwell would have died of starvation by then, his passing made all the more painful by the smells wafting from the Leighford bakery next door.

He slipped out in that nail-biting bit when Tom Cruise and Jon Voight are fighting it out in the Channel Tunnel, and ducked onto the landing. The projection room he knew was to his left, at the end of the corridor. Ahead of him was a second landing, up three stairs, and it contained the office where he and Stewart had had their little tête-à-tête the night before, the room where Dee McSween 'kept his archives'; that door he knew was locked so in a sense he was back to square one. But in a sense he wasn't. Interior doors were weaker than exterior ones. He wouldn't bother with credit cards and hair grips and effete nonsense like that. This time he'd take it head on — well, shoulder on.

This time he reeled back, clutching the great throbbing pain he used to call a shoulder. He didn't remember loose rucks being that hard in the rugger days of his youth. He rested against the wall, ready to try again, checking that the thud hadn't been heard in the projection room. Then something, and he never knew what, made him reach gingerly forward and try the knob. It turned under his hand and the door swung wide.

A number of expletives tripped whisperingly off his tongue. Then he was inside and rummaging in Douglas McSween's drawers. Thank God. No safe. If the list was here at all, it was in an unlocked drawer. Bills. Letters. Copies of porn magazines you couldn't buy over the counter anywhere except Holland. Nothing. He tried the second drawer and the third. More of the same. The fourth was empty, but the fifth contained nuggets of gold — a printed list, on long, tatty computer paper, perforated at intervals with those annoying holes at each side. Names. Addresses. Telephone and fax numbers. If Peter Maxwell had been of a certain persuasion, the scope for blackmail was immense. He ran his finger down the list, anxious not to miss anybody. Stewart had been right — businessmen, professionals, the odd copper or two. McSween had carefully listed their occupations, presumably because you never knew when a club member, grateful for continuing titillation — and continuing anonymity — wouldn't be useful. There could be no other reason for a list like this. The News of the World would go ape.

But Maxwell threw it back in disgust. The one name he wanted wasn't there. The one person who had to have killed Alice Goode and Jean Hagger didn't show on the printouts at all. Unless he'd used an alias. But if he had, he'd also have had to lie about his address and his job. And if he'd done that, there'd be no chance of Maxwell tracking him down. He switched off the light and got back into the theatre just as Lalo Schifrin's thumping score was belting out under the credits.

He tried to make it out innocuously, as Sylv had suggested he should, along with everybody else, but he was hailed at the top of the stairs by Douglas McSween.

'Max,' he motioned, 'can I have a word?'

'Er . . . well, it is a little late, Dee,' Maxwell hedged, 'lots and lots of marking.'

'It won't take long.' McSween was more insistent than Maxwell remembered, his face set, his voice hard.

He extricated himself from an old lady already unfurling her umbrella, just in case the flaming June night was less than clement, and slipped into the office he'd just burgled. His prints were on the doorknob, the light switch, all over the desk, not to mention the paper in the fifth drawer down.

'Max,' McSween had closed the door, 'I think I'm going to have to ask you to revoke your membership of the club.'

'Dee.' Maxwell looked mortified. 'Why, for Heaven's sake? I've only just joined.'

'It's about Piers, really' McSween told him. 'He was very upset last night. I don't know what you said to him, but he barely spoke to me before he left. I can't have you upsetting an old and valued friend like that. The whole point of the club is the calm and confidentiality it engenders. We don't let just anybody in, you know. I was only admitting you in the first place to oblige a friend.'

'Really?' Maxwell could play the ingénue with the best of them and launched into his Ardal O'Hanlon, 'Who's that then, Ted?'

McSween's face darkened, 'That doesn't matter.' He realised he'd said too much. 'The point is, you're out. I must admit I had my reservations about you in the first place.'

'Too normal?' Maxwell beamed. 'Sorry about that. And anyway, I'm afraid it wasn't I who upset poor old Piers. It was you. Showing him porn films of Alice Goode one day and dumping her body on his tarmac the next. Not a very friendly gesture, was it?'

McSween stood there, open-mouthed. 'I haven't got the faintest idea what you're talking about,' he said.

Maxwell sighed, shaking his head. 'That's an appalling cliché, Dee,' he said. 'And yes you do. The girl in *Sweet Seventeen* with the black hair. "Shags like a rabbit in the second half." A colleague of mine. Alice Goode. She was found murdered in the car park of Piers Stewart's restaurant a few weeks ago. Are you seriously telling me you didn't know about that?'

McSween blustered, 'I knew about the body, yes,' he said. 'In fact I rang Piers the next day to commiserate. But he didn't say . . . You mean, she's the girl with Pryce Garrison? *Temp Girl, Legends of Bondage*, all those?'

'I don't know,' Maxwell said, 'I haven't seen all those. Some of us consider cinema to be fine art, not filth. Alice Goode may have been sex on a stick to you, but to me she was a sweet kid embarking on a career in teaching. I'm prepared to bet she was trying to put her past behind her. Living a normal life . . .'

'Normal? With that old dyke Jean Hagger?'

Maxwell paused. McSween had gone too far, his neck mottling crimson, beads of perspiration forming on his lip, trickling from his ever-receding hairline.

'Would you like to reconsider what you just told me?' Maxwell asked.

'All right!' McSween shouted, throwing himself down in the chair. 'All right. Of course I knew who Alice Goode was. It's not the name she used of course in the flicks, but as soon as I saw her photograph in the papers, I recognised her. But I didn't know she lived here in Leighford until . . .'

'Yes?' Maxwell's patience was fast running out.

'Until that frightful cow Jean Hagger came to the club.'

'When was this?'

'I don't know. It was the day I turned down the membership of . . . well, never mind. Come to think of it, this Hagger woman was funny about him. Here we were, in this very office and I was having to tell him no — for all sorts of reasons — and she came storming in, ranting about my showing disgusting material of her Alice and how all men are beasts. Well, I ask you. Contrary to her view — and clearly, yours — the films Alice starred in are art; things of beauty.'

'What about Jean Hagger? How did she find out about the club?' Maxwell asked.

'She said someone had told her. Tipped her off. She'd had a phone call.'

'And what about your would-be member? Why did she react to him?'

'I really haven't the faintest idea,' McSween said. 'All I know is that she screamed we were both perverts, that we'd kidnapped the girl and were doing unspeakable things to her. She said she was going to the police.'

'And did she?'

'How the hell should I know? I assume not, in that the club is still here and there've been no boys in blue sniffing around so far.'

Maxwell smiled. 'It's early days, Mr McSween,' he winked at him.

'Look, Maxwell,' the club's proprietor's gloves were off, his defences down, 'all I can say for sure is that I didn't kill Alice Goode or dump her body in Piers Stewart's backyard. And I didn't kill Jean Hagger either.'

'Haha,' Maxwell wagged a finger at him, 'but you know a man who did.'

CHAPTER 14

Wouldn't you know it would be raining? Rory had gone down with appendicitis two days before, but other than that, and Mr Maxwell substituting for Miss Goode, it was the same team. Maxwell had haggled with Hamilton's Coaches. No, Dave Warwick wouldn't do. Nor Bert Fentiman. Nor John Harold. And were they seriously suggesting that Sandra Wickham could handle a fifty-three seater? Even allowing for the fact that Maxwell was letting his male chauvinist piggery show, they'd let him have Dave Freeman after all.

He sat by Anthea Edwards, who wanted to relive this day like she wanted a frontal lobotomy. The rain bounced on Freeman's wind-screen and the traffic roared past in a blur of lights and toxic waste. Maxwell smiled at Anthea. He turned to smile at Ronnie Parsons and Leila Roberts, sitting across the aisle behind the driver. Then he changed places.

'This is how it was, then, Ronnie, right?' he asked above the snarl of the engine and whatever cacophony the kids' tape was belting out. 'Alice was sitting where I am now?'

'That's right,' Ronnie said. 'Oh, by the way,' and he fumbled in his coat pocket, 'guess what?'

'Today's object,' said Maxwell in his BBC voice, looking at the grey thing in the boy's hand, 'is a flexicurve. A flexi-curve. Yours?'

'Mine,' Ronnie beamed. 'I went back home last night. Got a call from my mum. Dad was out so I went round, you know, just to get a few things. I was cleaning out my room and there it was I half hidden under the carpet. The law told me Miss Goode was strangled with something like this and when they searched my place while I was away, they couldn't find mine. Don't know why I kept it really. I just do graphs on computers these days.'

Ronnie was disappointed. He'd expected Mad Max to jump about and sing. All he got was a faint smile.

'Well, aren't you pleased, Mr Maxwell?' the boy asked. 'It's evidence, isn't it? Proof I didn't kill Miss Goode. If I had, it would have her fingerprints or something on it . . .'

'Ronnie, Ronnie,' Maxwell said as softly as the engine's roar and kids' chatter would let him, 'I'm afraid it doesn't prove a damn thing. Who's to say you didn't go out and buy that yesterday?' He saw the crestfallen look in the boy's face and thumped his shoulder. 'But you went home. That's good. I'm pleased about that.'

'Yeah,' said Ronnie, turning his face to the misted window.

Maxwell leaned forward over the driver's shoulder, 'Did you make a loo stop, Mr Freeman,' he asked, 'the last time?'

'Yes,' Freeman shouted back, 'Guildford Cathedral. Do you want me to do the same again?'

Maxwell surveyed the gum-chewing hordes behind him, delirious to be out of uniform and destroying their eardrums with their Walkmans. 'We'd better,' he said, 'my money's on Tamsin Gregory, ninth row back, the one who pinched her mum's makeup this morning.'

The fifty-three seater snarled around the curve and up the rise to the monstrosity that was Guildford Cathedral. The sky was as dark and threatening over its black tower as it had been when they'd filmed it for *The Omen*, although Maxwell suspected they'd cheated there with filters and wind machines.

'Got a touch of PMT this morning, Anthea,' he told her as he helped her down off the coach. 'Always the same before a storm — pre-Maelstrom tension.'

'And don't drop any litter!' Leila was practising her school-ma'am routine.

'I don't know what she does to the enemy,' he gave Anthea his best Arthur Wellesley, 'but she terrifies me.' And a gaggle of giggling girls ran past him, bound for the loo. Sure enough, Tamsin Gregory was at their head.

* * *

'Coming with us, Mr Freeman,' Maxwell asked as the coach coughed to a halt in that labyrinthine, road-worked entrance to the Museum of the Moving Image, 'when you've parked this monster?'

'No, thanks,' Freeman said. 'Not this time.'

'Go on,' Maxwell urged, 'it'll be like old times. *Picnic at Hanging Rock* is bound to be shown in the Odeon inside. Go on, give it a whirl.'

'Well, OK, then,' Freeman grinned, 'I'll be about ten minutes.'

'That's fine,' Maxwell said, 'I want a word with the kids anyway.' And he waited while Leila clapped her hands for quiet. Nothing. The kids were on the pavement, jostling, restless now that the rain had stopped and the sun was threatening to burst through the leaden cloud banks.

'Right!' Maxwell roared and half London came to a halt. Leila looked astonished, making a mental note to pay for some voice training so that she too could roar like the MGM lion. He had the full attention of fifty-two people and most of the others on their way in and out of MOMI. Even the bloke with the road drill had switched off and hauled off his ear-muffs.

'Now then,' Maxwell's voice was steady and calm, 'you all know that you haven't paid for this visit. And some of you might think it odd. The reason that Mr Diamond has been so generous is that he wants — and I want — you all to help us in an experiment.'

'Like in science, sir?' one of the braver lads piped up.

'Sort of,' Maxwell nodded, 'but nothing like so boring. Now you all know that when you were here last, Miss Goode was with you.' He watched their faces as he spoke, their eyes fixed to his. No one was jostling now. The Walkmans were away. Those with chewing gum in their mouths swallowed hard. 'You also know that Miss Goode disappeared inside this Museum,' he waved to the glass front and the blue lights behind him. 'Now I want you to help me find out what happened to her. In there.'

He saw some mouths open, silently. He saw eyes widen, heads turn. 'And remember,' he said, 'Miss Goode didn't just vanish. Whatever you see in there is make-believe. What I think happened to her is that she was taken out of the Museum, not by a monster, not by an alien, not by a ghost, but by a man. Now, this time, keep together. Miss Edwards and Leila will lead us in. Ronnie and I will bring up the rear. And no one,' and his bass voice burned into their souls, 'no one is to wander off alone. Do I make myself clear?'

Maxwell did. And to those fifty kids, he was God Himself. Maxwell's word was law.

* * *

Anthea got the group ticket, the one with the strange wording that said you weren't allowed to stand up inside MOMI. The prospect of getting the entire party to crawl was too daunting, however. Napoleon may have said that an army marches on its stomach, but fifty kids? Never. Dave Freeman joined the slowly moving column as it clicked and creaked its way past the turnstiles of yesterday. The lights went down and they were in the land of lost content again, each of them with his or her own dreams and memories. Maxwell watched their reflections on the first stairway, saw their anoraked shapes scatter and fan out on the black and white check of the floor. Here the zogroscope whirled and the shadow puppets danced on sticks. A massive human eye looked down on them, watching as it had watched Alice Goode making her last journey. There was no readmission.

Maxwell paid particular attention to the exits. They all seemed to be alarm activated and there were cameras everywhere. Tamsin's heart sank anew at the signs which told her that these were the last toilets for two thousand years. The Leighford party did as it was told happily enough and followed the yellow brick road into the gloom. In the Phantasmagorie the silent eighteenth-century crowd in their grey plaster Macaronis watched, along with the camera-clicking Japanese tourists, the face on the screen turn into the face of Satan. The Satan who had stalked Alice Goode that day, the last time. Slithery-tailed rats emerged from the spinning hole of the Phenakistoscope before the fresh-faced Edwardian toff hailed Maxwell.

'Sir,' he boomed, doffing his wideawake and sweeping open his fur-collared coat, 'do I understand you have the misfortune to be *in loco parentis* today?'

'And everyday, sir,' Maxwell doffed his tifter in return.

'My condolences,' the toff beamed, 'but come, children of tomorrow, and let me tell you all about Mr Mack Sennett and his Keystone Cops . . .' and he held the braver ones enthralled with his well-rehearsed patter.

The cinema went to war in the next section of the Museum, with sepia photographs of mud and khaki. The kids looked up the periscopes at the barbed wire and bodies hanging out on No Man's Land. At this point, Maxwell calculated, it was about fifteen minutes to the last positive sighting of Alice Goode.

'Uniform's good,' Maxwell commented to Dave Freeman, both of them looking at the huge poster of Pola Negri in a dashing white pelisse.

'I didn't know you were *that* old sir.' Leila Roberts swept past her esteemed Head of Sixth Form and the poster that read 'Max et les Crêpes' circa 1918. He merely beamed beatifically. As the ragged column marched past the glitter of

Gloria Swanson's dress and the mirrored walls and giant caryatids of the stars, a dismembered voice blared over the intercom about a child who had gone missing. Maxwell caught Anthea's gaze and they both shook their heads. Not one of theirs.

The Chaplin memorabilia window stood at the top of the cinema staircase and the neon sign flashed to herald in the Talkies — 'OK for sound'. Maxwell let the kids onto the Agit-prop train again, not because they enjoyed Russian history or understood Communism in the slightest, but because they were determined not to miss out on anything.

'Daddy,' a little girl asked her father in the forbidden films section, 'why are they cutting that lady's eye open with a razor blade?'

'That's Continental cinema for you,' her well-informed dad said. Maxwell wandered away, checking that his own eyeballs were intact. Some of those creepy thirties numbers made Quentin Tarantino look like a choirboy. Through opaque glass, the sinister, jerking image of Max Schreck's Nosferatu stared coldly at him. There was no sunlight down here to dissolve his cadaverous body. No shining Christian cross to thwart his evil ends. Just shadows.

'How technical are you, Mr Freeman?' Maxwell asked as they reached the window that looked in on the Museum's Control Centre. The kids had gone surging ahead into the Paramount set, anxious to replay the end of Ricco. This was boring. They were even bored by the *Outlaw* censorship story and brooding, heaving, pouting Jane Russell. 'Just some woman wiv big tits,' as young Jamie put it later.

'I can fix a fan belt,' the driver said. 'Why?'

'I was just wondering,' Maxwell pointed at the myriad television screens beyond the glass, 'whether all exits are covered in there. And whether they record the video footage. If they do . . .'

Freeman saw the point. 'If they do,' he clicked his fingers, 'they'd have your teacher's disappearance on film. If somebody snatched her, I mean.'

'Yes,' said Maxwell, shaking his head, 'but that's the first thing the police would have checked, once they'd discovered Alice s body. And by then I'd be prepared to bet it'd be too late. My guess is they keep the loop intact for twenty-four hours, perhaps forty-eight, then change it. Ironic really. They probably filmed Alice's abduction and it ended up on the cutting-room floor.'

'But that bloke,' Freeman was clutching at straws, 'he — or whoever was on duty — must've seen it happen.'

'Indeed,' Maxwell nodded, 'if it happened in the angle of a camera. But how many screens has he got to watch? Twenty? Thirty? If Alice went quietly, he'd have no reason to notice it, would he?'

The two men drifted into the kiddies' corner where talentless little oiks were scribbling on pieces of paper in an effort to prove they were the Walt Disneys of the Millennium. Their proud mums looked on. Tired teachers wandered away.

'A duel then, Mr Freeman.' Maxwell was looking up at the rapidly changing clips outside the Odeon cinema, where a liveried commissionaire, all burgundy and gold lace, waited to admit them.

Freeman chuckled, 'Oh, I doubt I'm in your league, Mr Maxwell.'

'Don't do yourself down,' Maxwell said. 'Yul Brynner, *Magnificent Seven*.' The scenes flashed thick and fast, as the black-shirted gunfighter flicked to the thatch-haired Greek.

'Tom Conti, *Shirley Valentine*,' Freeman said.

'Ingrid Bergman, *For Whom the Bell Tolls*,' Maxwell gabbled, 'I particularly liked Katina Paxinou in that.'

'Laurence Olivier, *Henry V*. I liked Felix Aylmer in that.'

'Right,' chuckled Maxwell, 'they say he's not dead yet, you know. Oh, bugger,' it was on the tip of his tongue, 'Charles Boyer, *Arch of Triumph*. Christ knows who else was in that.'

'Ah,' Freeman was home and dry, 'William Holden, *Sunset Boulevard*. Crap musical.'

'Tragic waste,' Maxwell agreed. 'Rod Steiger, *The Pawnbroker*.'

'Blimey you're good,' Freeman gulped, blinking at the rapidity of the clips. 'Jamie Lee Curtis, *A Fish Called Wanda*.'

'Robin Williams, *Mrs Doubtfire*.'

'Kurt Russell, *Tombstone*.'

'Ah, not a patch on Burt Lancaster.'

'No, no,' Maxwell laughed. 'No one's a patch on Burt Lancaster.'

And it was with sheer physical relief that the two of them collapsed into the Odeon to feel the fuzzy flock of the seats and let the gentle Plasticine creatures of Nick Park lull them into quietude.

Beyond the Odeon, where all the kids were now, was the television section, where Hughie Green was wowing audiences by doubling their money and a dusty fifties family sat enthralled around their nine-inch screen. It had happened. The goggle-box, the one-eyed monster, had found its way into people's living rooms. And consigned the cinema to a long and lingering death. Longer and more lingering, Maxwell hoped, than the death of Alice Goode.

He felt a tug on his sleeve. 'They're everywhere, Tamsin,' he told the girl who looked up at him with anxiety all over her face. 'The loos. Lots of them.'

'No, Mr Maxwell, it's not that,' she said. 'This was the placc. This is where I saw Miss Goode last.'

Maxwell looked at the pale face and beyond it the mad staring yellow eyes of Dr Mabuse. He half turned and Mohawk the Gremlin stood there, hideous arms trailing the ground, ears spread and teeth like razors, laughing at him.

'Naughty, naughty boy' He heard the harsh, expressionless tones of Maggie Thatcher boom from the window of Number Ten as she soundly smacked the bottom of John Major, sitting sheepishly on her lap.

'Here,' Tamsin shouted, her memory of it vivid now in that rush of sound and colour and light. She was pointing upward. Up at the huge Brain that crackled and spat electrically overhead. 'There was a man,' she screamed, 'I saw him. I saw him. He was in there.' Maxwell put his career on the line again. He grabbed the girl, held her to him, cradling the shaking head, feeling the tears splash onto his hands as he hugged her. He looked up. The giant Brain showed their reflection, distorted, swaying together. The crowds moved away from them, like the slithering rats in the Phenakistoscope, embarrassed at the silly, hysterical girl and her over-protective dad.

For a moment, Maxwell and his little girl saw the same thing. They saw Alice Goode in the reflection of the Brain, for all the world as if she was really there. And they saw a man gripping her arm, pulling her backwards to an exit. An exit with no alarm. An exit with a door already ajar. Maxwell tried to focus on the blurred face of Alice's abductor, on the flashing silver of the knife. Then he turned to find Dave Freeman. But Dave Freeman had gone.

* * *

He calmed Tamsin Gregory down. He took her to Anthea and the others in the gift shop, which was all T-shirts and pencil sharpeners and kaleidoscopes. 'Stay here,' he told them all. 'Nobody goes home.'

'Mr Maxwell . . .' Ronnie was at his elbow, fists clenched. Ready.

'No, Ronnie,' Mad Max said, 'you stay here. This time, huh? This time you stay.'

And the boy nodded. And the man in him understood.

* * *

Maxwell leapt the steel turnstile back into the Museum. He hurtled along the passage and down the stairs, his reflection looming and vanishing again in the fish-eye reflection of the Brain, as Alice Goode's had loomed and vanished all those weeks before. He was out of the side entrance where the sunlight hurt his eyes. The street lay empty to right and left. He ran forward, past the parked cars, the meandering knots of tourists, the posed Japanese group, one camera taking a photograph of half a dozen others. He rounded the corner and was there. In the new coach park. Face to face with the sleek red and white luxury vehicle, the fifty-three-seater ten-tonner that had carried Alice Goode to her death.

Dave Freeman was sitting on the steps, the door slid back, the keys in his hand. Maxwell walked towards him, carefully, slowly.

'How did you know?' the driver asked.

'I didn't,' Maxwell said, 'not until you ran.'

'That kid,' he was staring at the ground. 'She couldn't have seen me.'

'She did, Mr Freeman,' Maxwell assured him. 'It's a funny thing, the mind. And in there, of all places, it takes over. The mind is a blank wall, a screen. Life throws images at it, shadows like the Zeotrope and it blends and blurs and twists. Then somebody puts the lights on and the image is gone for ever. That's what happened to Tamsin. She got lost in the magic in there. All those images. All those shadows. You threatening Alice with a knife and taking her out, all of it seen in the fish-eye lens of the Brain — it was just one more image. One more piece of make-believe. It wasn't real. None of it. But it was, Mr Freeman, wasn't it?'

The driver buried his face in his hands. When he looked up at Maxwell, his cheeks were wet with tears. 'I didn't want to do it,' he said, softly. 'She was so . . . I'd seen her on the films. I knew what she was like under the clothes. Under that front. Pretending to be a teacher!' He spat contemptuously. 'I knew better. On the way into the Museum I asked her. Told her what I'd seen. Asked her if she was up for it. What she charged. You should have heard her language. I've got girls myself, Mr Maxwell. I wasn't having that. Nobody talks to me like that. So I stayed with her, only behind, of course, so nobody from the school knew I was there, watching, waiting. I knew the Museum, of course. I knew my way around. But there were too many people. Always too many people. The Brain was my last chance. She'd have been in the gift shop next and I'd have no chance then. So I grabbed her, told her

I'd cut her if she struggled or made a fuss and brought her out here.'

'You killed her here?' Maxwell frowned. 'In broad daylight?'

Freeman stood up slowly. 'I'll show you,' he said, and climbed to the aisle of the coach. Maxwell followed carefully, keeping his distance. 'See, you're higher than the ground by a long way,' the driver said. 'Can't be seen from the road. I closed the door and strangled her.'

'With what?' Maxwell had to know.

'A fan belt,' Freeman said. 'I was carrying a spare in my pocket. It didn't take long.'

'So,' Maxwell was trying to stay calm, trying to stay rational in talking to this madman, 'her body was here. On one of those seats. But you were due to pick up the party shortly. What did you do with her?'

Freeman smiled, tapping the side of his nose, suddenly proud of his prowess, smug in his skill. 'Black bags,' he said, 'all coach drivers carry them for the tons of rubbish your little out-of-control bastards leave on our coaches. I wrapped her up in them. It only took three, curled up as she was. She was still soft of course at that stage. I popped her in the boot. There's a lot of storage capacity under these seats.'

Maxwell gripped one of those now. 'Are you telling me that Alice was under here when you drove my kids back?'

'Yeah,' Freeman shrugged, 'what of it? The rest of it was easy. I doubled round to the front entrance and found the party again. I felt sorry for that other teacher, mind. Chasing her own arse, she was.'

'Why did you dump Alice's body at the Devil's Ladle?'

'I got my own lock-up, see.' Freeman was smirking now, enjoying the memory. 'I kept Alice for a while. You know, loving her, stroking her . . . but she'd start to smell soon. I had to lose her. Then I had a brainwave. Those smug, self-satisfied wankers at the film club. You know, they'd got the nerve to turn me down. And why? 'Cos I ain't a bleedin' banker or doctor or ty-fucking-coon, that's why. That toffee-nosed git

McSween told me 'cos I was just a coach driver, he couldn't allow it. I told him straight . . . him and that arsehole friend of his, that Piers Stewart. I told him I wasn't having any of that. Nobody talks to me like that. That I'd sort 'em.'

'But you sorted yourself, Mr Freeman, didn't you?' Maxwell said. 'So anxious were you to finger the film club, you pointed the finger squarely at yourself.'

'No other way.' Freeman shook his head. 'I had to nobble Stewart and I had to get you onto him.'

'So you left Alice on Stewart's doorstep?'

'That's right.'

'Because they wouldn't let you play with them?' The contempt was thick in Maxwell's throat as he watched Freeman turn self-righteous.

'Then it dawned on me. When I realised that Parsons kid had gone missing. What a perfect opportunity. Just before we left the Museum, I half-inched his bag from the cloakroom, pretending to be looking for Alice. In the fullness of time I stashed Alice's clothes in it. 'Cos the problem was that old bag Jean Hagger. That lesbian.'

'You knew her?' Maxwell asked.

'Oh yeah,' Freeman was walking back towards the door now, edging Maxwell in front of him. 'Yeah, I knew her. She'd run a trip to Chessington last year, said I was interfering with her kids. I mean, the cheek of the cow! I've got girls myself. Happily married man, me. She put in a complaint to Hamilton's, trying to get me the bleeding sack. Then, when I was having it out with that ponce McSween, who would walk in, effing and blinding, but her. She was whingeing on about her Alice this and her Alice that. Well, I wasn't having any of that. I rang her at the school, told her I had news of Alice. She came like a shot, of course, tongue hanging out. I took my knife. I took my belt, but when I'd got her in the living room I see this lump of stone on the hearth.'

'A Jurassic ammonite.' Maxwell couldn't help correcting him.

'Yeah, whatever.' Freeman waved his hands. 'So I stove in her head. Christ, it was messy. Had to clean myself up good and proper before I left. Then I left the kid's bag there, just to point the filth in the wrong direction, you know?'

'Yes,' Maxwell nodded, 'I know.'

'Now, Mr Maxwell,' Freeman sighed, 'it's been fun having this little chat, but I really have to go now.'

'Go?' Maxwell looked at the man, astonished. 'I'm afraid I can't let you do that, Mr Freeman. Especially now we've had this little chat.'

Freeman gurgled with laughter. Though Maxwell didn't know it, it was the man's death rattle. He should have been ready for the boot in the pit of his stomach as he heard the hydraulic whoosh of the opening door. He should have half expected the coach to spin in his vision and to feel the fan belt hook under his chin and slice into his throat. And he certainly should have anticipated the sickening thud against his back as he toppled forward down the steps to roll clear of the coach.

'Thank you for travelling Hamilton's,' he heard Freeman shout above the throaty rattle of the engine. Then, with lights flashing, Dave Freeman drove through the coach park, bouncing off other vehicles as he went, his wipers lashing non-existent rain.

And Mad Max should certainly have been prepared for the thud and crash as the fifty-three-seater ten-tonner ploughed into the wall of the Museum of the Moving Image, leaving its driver's shattered body twisted like a broken doll in the red of the brick dust and the silver of the crystal glass.

* * *

Peter Maxwell sat that night in front of the blank television screen. He'd given his story to the police. He'd refused to give it, or any part of it, to the media and eventually, past midnight, even the most tenacious paparazzi had gone home.

There was a ring at his doorbell. He put down the glass of Southern Comfort. He padded down the stairs. In the frosted glass of his front door he saw the face of Jacquie Carpenter, Woman Policeman.

'Do you believe in happy endings?' she asked him.

'Is the Pope Polish?' Maxwell countered, and motioned her inside.

'Do you feel like talking?' she asked when he'd closed the door.

'I'm Mad Max,' he told her softly, 'I always feel like talking.' And he followed her upstairs.

'Dorothy Parsons came to see us today' she said, 'or rather, to see the DCI.'

He waved her to his sofa. 'Drink?'

She shook her head and spread her coat as she flopped.

'She told us a rather interesting story.'

'Oh?' He was trying to stay awake, trying to come to terms with his day. Just another routine 'jolly' for Leighford High.

'Her husband, Ron. He's a jobbing builder.'

'Well, I never . . .' Maxwell rescued his drink.

'In March, two years ago, he was working on a travel agent's in Raines Park. One of their part-time operatives was a student called . . .'

'Carly Drinkwater!' Maxwell was on the edge of his seat now, the exhaustion gone in an instant from his face.

'Correct.' Jacquie was smiling. 'In July of last year, he was doing some repairs to an estate agent's in Streatham . . .'

'. . . where Georgianna Morris worked,' Maxwell was smiling at her.

'One of the witnesses who saw Georgianna running in the park remembers seeing a light-coloured van, possibly grey, possibly beige. Ron Parsons drives a beige van.'

'Can you prove any of this?' Maxwell asked.

'He's confessed,' Jacquie said. 'Forensics will be able to tie him in with Carly at least. DNA's a bitch to buck. We've got him bang to rights.'

'And I thought it was Dave Freeman,' Maxwell said, 'I was just about to broach the subject when he kicked me off his coach.'

'Happy endings,' smiled Jacquie.

'Indeed,' Maxwell said. 'Now, how about that drink?'

'Better not,' she said, 'not when I'm on duty.'

Realisation dawned on Peter Maxwell. This was the day. The day of Jacquie's internal enquiry. He saw the tears in her eyes, the quiver of her lips and he hugged her and he kissed her.

'Jacquie,' he said, 'I'm so pleased. Pleased for you, I mean.'

She nodded through the tears. 'Well,' she sighed, 'if we aren't going to have that steamy sex scene, I'd better go.'

He nodded and saw her out.

'Will we meet again, do you think?' he called after her, trying not to sound too much like Vera Lynn.

She turned at the end of his garden path, 'I'd be prepared to bet on it,' she said.

And Peter Maxwell ran back up his stairs three at a time.

'Count,' he said, snatching the miffed animal up in his hands. 'It's not often I'm sufficiently overcome to clasp you to my bosom, so, be grateful. Tell you what, let's have a spot of telly, shall we?'

He fumbled for the remote, Metternich sliding out from under his arm as he hit the settee, grateful to assert his independence again. BBC1 flashed into focus and the logo twirled. 'And now,' said a disembodied voice, 'in a change to our advertised programme, BBC1 presents Alfred Hitchcock's classic, *Psycho*.'

Cut to blackness.

THE END

THE JOFFE BOOKS STORY

We began in 2014 when Jasper agreed to publish his mum's much-rejected romance novel and it became a bestseller.

Since then we've grown into the largest independent publisher in the UK. We're extremely proud to publish some of the very best writers in the world, including Joy Ellis, Faith Martin, Caro Ramsay, Helen Forrester, Simon Brett and Robert Goddard. Everyone at Joffe Books loves reading and we never forget that it all begins with the magic of an author telling a story.

We are proud to publish talented first-time authors, as well as established writers whose books we love introducing to a new generation of readers.

We won Trade Publisher of the Year at the Independent Publishing Awards in 2023. We have been shortlisted for Independent Publisher of the Year at the British Book Awards for the last four years, and were shortlisted for the Diversity and Inclusivity Award at the 2022 Independent Publishing Awards. In 2023 we were shortlisted for Publisher of the Year at the RNA Industry Awards.

We built this company with your help, and we love to hear from you, so please email us about absolutely anything bookish at feedback@joffebooks.com

If you want to receive free books every Friday and hear about all our new releases, join our mailing list: www.joffebooks.com/contact

And when you tell your friends about us, just remember: it's pronounced Joffe as in coffee or toffee!

ALSO BY M.J. TROW

SCHOOLMASTER MYSTERIES
Book 1: MAXWELL'S HOUSE
Book 2: MAXWELL'S FLAME
Book 3: MAXWELL'S MOVIE

Printed in Great Britain
by Amazon

43441888R00128